Som.

The Interfacers

A Novel By
David C. Swenson

First Edition 1997

BEST WISHES FOR A HAPPY HOLIDAY SEASON.

David C. Swenson

12/18/04

Eastern Dakota Publishers
www.edpublish.com
E-mail: edpublish@edpublish.com

www.rrv.net/interfacers

Edited by Eileen Zygarlicke
Cover Photography by Gaylor E. Offerdahl

ISBN 1-890939-03-X

First Edition, First Printing 1997
First Edition, Second Printing 1998

All quotations listed in this book are taken from *The International Thesaurus of Quotations* (New York: Harper & Row, 1970) and the page numbers are given after each quote. The one exception to this is found at the top of Chapter X. This quote was taken from *The Book of the Dead: The Hieroglyphic Transcript and English Translation of the Papyrus of Ani* (New York: Grammercy Books, 1995), p. 483.

Published by:
Eastern Dakota Publishers
P.O. Box 334
Fishers, IN 46038
Ronald G. Gallagher, Publisher

E-mail: edpublish@edpublish.com
on the Internet at:
www.edpublish.com

Foreword

This book is pure fiction. With the exception of the quotations, any similarities to real people, places, and events are purely coincidental. Were they not, we would be forced to completely rethink our relationships with mankind and the universe.

Acknowledgements

I wish to thank the following people for their help and encouragement:

Robert Kuchar, for your technical assistance and invaluable help with the medical and rescue scenes.

Ronald Gallagher, for seeing the potential in co-publishing this novel before I rewrote it.

Eileen Zygarlicke, for your patience as you helped me edit and rewrite the manuscript.

Nancy Swenson, wife, editor, paramedic, and coach, for helping me through the many rewrites with your encouragement, technical advice, and editorial help.

Bob, Skip, Don and Merle, Dan, Kimber, Linda, Dick and Holly, Diana, Julie and Kimber, Mary, Pastor Karen, Ken, Yvonne, and Brenda, for reading the early manuscripts and offering your advice and support. I value your opinions, and your friendships sustain me.

About the Author

David C. Swenson has been interested in spiritual and religious matters since his teen years. A retired bank president, David currently lives in Baudette, MN, where he serves his community as a county commissioner in Lake of the Woods County. A 1970 graduate of the University of North Dakota, he spent 24 years in industry and banking. He also enjoys playing classical violin. His wife, Nancy, also a graduate of the University of North Dakota, is a nationally registered paramedic and teaches emergency medicine in Northern Minnesota. They have three children. To contact David, email: dswenson@means.net.

This novel is dedicated to the over five million people who have returned from their own near-death experiences and to the countless millions who have encountered loved ones from the other side of death.

I

"If thy whole body therefore be full of light, having
no part dark, the whole shall be full of light..."
—*Bible* (KJV) *St. Luke* 11:36

Date: Monday, November 24, 1997
Time: 2:00 A.M.
Place: Duluth Skyline, Duluth, MN

A shimmering orb of pure energy passed effortlessly through the outside brick wall into the luxury condominium, camouflaged by the glare of street lights from downtown Duluth, Minnesota. Two feet in diameter, the opaque ball radiated softly from within. It proceeded from the living room to the den and hovered over a large walnut desk, casting a soft glow over piles of not-so-neatly stacked scientific and medical journals, work papers, and letters. A black and white photo of two boys and a black dog and snapshots of a classic red Corvette convertible lay flat under the glass top near the telephone. A faded newspaper article was pressed neatly beneath the glass on the left side of the desktop under several dulled yellow pencils.

The light pulsed. The pencils rolled off the desk, clattering softly as they hit the carpet. Exposed to the energy, the old newspaper article faded slightly as if it were in sunlight. A droplet of water kissed the glass as the light moved down the hallway into the master bedroom and positioned itself near the man sleeping alone in his king-sized bed.

II

Date: November 17, 1963
Time: 3:00 P.M.
Place: Edina, MN

The neighborhood was upper middle-class suburbia. Recently built homes were nestled into the heavily wooded hills surrounding a small lake and park area. Still rich with wildlife, the fight for the supremacy of man over wild beasts and birds was not so evident here on the edge of man's developing settlements as it would become after thirty years of traffic, pesticides, and habitat destruction.

For now, it was a beautiful new suburb of the Twin Cities metropolitan area, far removed from the growing scenes of urban blight, dereliction, and social unrest that many core areas of the Twin Cities had to offer. There was room here to stretch out and raise a family. There was privacy. Living at the end of a street or on a cul-de-sac, days could go by before a single car drove by that didn't belong in one of the neighborhood garages.

After the first major snowfall of 1963, a fresh seven-inch coat of snow lay on the ground from the previous day and night. Temperatures were in the low twenties. Snow and hoarfrost clung to every branch of every tree. Two ten-year-old boys were perched in readiness on a toboggan atop a hill, waiting for an imaginary launch clearance.

They cared little about the traffic, their parents' flight to suburbia, or man's fight with nature. Ben and Jim were interested in snow removal—the kind they could form into snowballs or make into a snowman, and the wake they could move with their toboggan.

Jim reviewed the checklist as Ben answered in pilot fashion. "Flaps down?"

Ben fiddled with an imaginary control panel. "Check."

"Engine?"

"Check."

"Ready for countdown?"

"Check."

"Cleared for takeoff. Start the countdown."

"Five, four, three, two, one. Go!" Jim pushed the toboggan, then jumped on the back. A barking black Labrador ran beside them, providing a noisy

3

escort down thirty feet of drop over the hundred-and-fifty-foot run to the shoreline of a small lake. The boys dashed down the hill, bobbing and weaving to avoid hitting any trees.

It was a glorious day! They'd been to a snowball fight, built a small fort, and made angels in the snow. All day long, Missy, Ben Bradley's four-year-old black Labrador, had been their third companion and compatriot. She'd taken her share of snowballs, probably thinking they were tennis balls as they smacked her in the face. She tried to catch every one that was thrown her way. Sometimes she rode the toboggan with the boys, barking furiously as they careened down the slope.

The youths were slowing down after some twenty runs down the hill and the reciprocal walk back up. Once in a while, even ten-year olds get tired. After narrowly avoiding a disastrous collision with a stout oak tree, they rolled off the toboggan and laughed heartily.

"I thought we were gonna crash, Jim," said Ben, whose given name was Benjamin. His mother persisted with the cutened version of Benjie. Soon, he'd have to set her straight on the matter. "Jimmie's" mother had the same idea about nicknames; the boys didn't use them.

Jim lay on his back in the snow. "I thought we were goners, Ben. That last swerve saved our butts."

"Yeah! We lucked out," Ben declared as he looked around the area. "I gotta pee."

"Me, too." Jim stood. "Let's go over there," he said as he pointed to a small clump of trees. Boys under pressure will be boys. They walked along the shoreline. "This'll do." The trees would help obstruct the view of their private parts, just in case anyone else in the world might try to peek.

When they finished, Jim noted, "This is better than having to put the seat up and down."

"Yeah, I think girls could do one or the other. They're just so bossy."

Jim agreed, "You said it, man." He looked around. The sun was dropping in the western sky. "My mom says I gotta be home before dark."

"Mine, too," Ben confirmed. They were both wet from their boots to their caps, so they kept moving to stay warm.

"I don't want to go home. I'm having too much fun," Jim protested.

"Maybe you can come an' stay overnight at my place."

"Hey, that's a great idea."

"What are buddies for?"

They had been best friends since Ben's family moved into the neighborhood a year ago. They vowed to be friends forever.

They stood together and admired the small lake. Jim offered, "This place sure is cool."

"Yeah. I like it lots more than my last house. The only time I could go sliding there was when my mom and dad took me and my sister. It's no fun sliding with your little sister. Girls scream too much when you aim for the trees." Ben meant it as a compliment to Jim.

Jim said, "Let's check out the ice."

"Mom says I'm supposed to…"

Jim completed the sentence, "…stay off the ice. I know! My mom says the same thing. But I don't see any water, do you? Looks to me like it's froze solid all the way across."

Ben surveyed the lakeshore until he spotted some reassuring evidence that the ice was safe. "Hey, look. Those guys are fishin' over there. It must be okay. Do you think they'd go out if it wasn't safe?"

Sure enough, two men were ice fishing in a small bay area near the park, about a hundred yards beyond the outlet of the creekbed that flowed into the lake.

"Sometimes I think mothers are just a bunch of worrywarts," Jim responded. "It looks okay to me."

"Besides," Ben said, "we can't be their little boys forever, can we?"

"Heck, no!"

"We could be all grown up and they'd still call us Benjie and Jimmie."

"If we do this, we can't tell anyone. We have to keep it a total secret."

"Deal." The desire for things forbidden and the delicious aftertaste of a secret well kept were nearly overwhelming.

"Cross your heart and hope to die."

"Cross my heart. My lips are sealed." Ben made an X across his chest and gestured, pretending to zip his lips. "If I say anything, you can have first blood." Ben completed the contract by spitting into his mittened hand and offering a handshake to his friend.

As they shook hands, Jim continued, "Besides, there's two of us. If one has trouble, the other is here to help. After all, that's what buddies are for."

"Yeah!" They stepped out a few yards from shore. Ben kicked the snow away, clearing a small area of ice. "Hey, neato mosquito, Jim! Look at this!" He could see through the thin ice down four feet to the bottom of the lake.

"Wow, that's really cool, Ben." Jim enlarged the clearing with his mittens.

Ben continued, "I bet if we go out farther and stand really still, we can even see the fish swimmin' under us."

"We would have to be vewy, vewy quiet, wike we were hunting wascawy wabbits."

Ben laughed at Jim's imitation of a cartoon character. "You crack me up." A lightbulb came on in Ben's head. "Hey! I got an idea!" Ben said. "Let's throw a stick out for Missy. If the ice holds her up, it's prob'ly safe."

"Good idea. I'll get a stick." Jim ran to the shoreline and picked up a short fat stick and two four-foot-long branches which had fallen from an old willow tree and were sticking up through the fresh snow. He returned to Ben.

Missy got the idea and started barking as she circled Jim. "Here's one for Missy—and look at these babies I found for us. We can poke holes in the ice with them."

Ben praised Jim for thinking ahead. "Great idea, Jim." He thought great explorers armed with mighty staffs and their faithful dog would surely be invincible!

Missy circled the boys, barking impatiently. Ben knew they were driving her nuts.

"Throw it over there," Ben said as he pointed away from the shore. Jim wound up a couple times with the stick, pretending to throw it just to get the dog more riled up. Each time he faked a throw, the dog ran a few steps in the direction of the aborted throw. Realizing she'd been faked out, she would skid to a stop and turn back toward the boys, barking furiously as if she were saying, "Hurry up! Throw the damn stick! Let's go!" The boys walked a few more steps out onto the lake.

"Okay, Missy, okay! Here you go." Jim launched the stick. It was a nearly perfect throw. The dog and the stick moved in unison across the lake. The stick followed a high-arching trajectory, allowing the dog a precious second or two to catch up with it. After nearly a fifty-foot run, the dog leaped into the air to catch the stick. She did it! She caught it in mid-air! She was poetry in motion.

Missy's landing area was covered with a heavy coat of snow, insulating the top of the ice and allowing the warm current of runoff water from the nearby creek to melt it from the underside. Ben gasped as Missy broke through the thin ice and disappeared under the water's surface. Watching the tragedy unfold, Ben yelled to her, "Missy! Missy! Oh, God." Her head appeared above the surface as she found the hole. Ben desperately called her. "Here, girl. C'mon, Missy. Come on, girl."

"Oh God, Missy," Jim moaned. He turned to his friend, "Ben, I'm so sorry."

The dog pawed furiously at the edge of the ice, trying to get a secure footing so she could climb out. Each time, another chunk of ice broke off and floated in the water surrounding her. Where the ice was more solid, her paws slipped back into the water. Missy started yelping, as if realizing how serious her situation was.

Ben watched her struggle. "We gotta save her, Jim. We can't let her die out there."

"What are we gonna do?"

"We gotta get her out." Ben's determination was building. "Maybe we can reach her with our sticks. I'll hold one end of your stick and you hang on to me. If I go through the ice, you can pull me out."

"Ben! Don't even say that."

6

"I'll try to reach her with my stick. Maybe she can grab on with her teeth or climb up on it, or somethin'."

Cautiously, they edged toward the hole where the dog continued to struggle. It only took a few seconds to close the distance between them. From ten feet away, Ben stretched out on his belly and reached for her. "Here, Missy. Grab the stick." Ben turned to Jim, "We gotta get closer. I can't reach her."

Jim fretted, "It's too dangerous. We gotta get help."

"We can't just leave her here," Ben pleaded. "It's just a couple more steps." He pulled at his end of the stick that joined them together. Ben was four feet from the hole when the ice gave way under him. Down he went into the cold water, still hanging onto the stick, his lifeline to Jim. Jim held on with all his strength, but the weight of Ben falling into the water tugged at him. There was nothing he could do to stop as he, too, slid into the hole.

Ben thrashed at the edge of the ice with the dog, desperately trying to get an arm up on the ice. Jim gurgled out a scream, "Help! Ben, help me. I'm sinking!" Their clothing and boots filled with frigid water, weighing them down and making it difficult to move.

Ben turned and reached out to his friend. "Grab my arm." Jim obeyed, frantically pulling himself to Ben, jerking Ben off the edge of the ice. "Not so hard, Jim." Ben struggled to get his arms free.

"Help me get out, Ben! I can't..." Instead of words, Jim could only cough up water. Their heads bobbed under the surface. Ben kicked and thrashed until his head reached the surface. He coughed and spit the water that filled his mouth and nose. Jim pulled himself tightly to Ben.

"No, Jim! You gotta let me grab the ice!" Jim's tight embrace allowed neither boy to move.

"Jim!" Ben fought to get loose from Jim. He could feel himself sinking.

As they struggled, Ben shouted, "You gotta let go! You gotta let me..." Their two heads submerged together.

Ben choked as his lungs filled with frigid water, but then, he had a sort of peaceful feeling. He heard a buzzing sound in his ears, but pretty soon that went away. The panic left him. There was no more choking, no more struggling. Ben felt strangely calm. He couldn't even feel Jim hanging onto him. He knew that he and Jim were now on the lake bottom, but it just didn't matter.

Ben looked up. Missy's feet were still thrashing at the edge of the ice a few feet above him. He thought to himself, *So this is what the fish see.* He was so close to the hole.

Ben felt a new sensation, like he was floating. Up he moved, above the ice, above the dog. He looked down and saw two bodies intertwined on the muddy bottom. *That's weird*, he thought. *How can I be looking at myself?* He heard Jim's voice.

"Ben, don't forget me."

Ben cried out to him from the very core of his being, "Jim! Jim! Where are you?"

"I'm right next to you. Can't you see me?" Ben looked down at their bodies.

"No, silly. Look at me. I'm right next to you." Ben turned to see Jim hovering nearby, bathed in a white light. Ben felt as though he could reach out and touch him. A woman floated next to Jim. Her beautiful long hair gently flowed in the breeze.

"Who is that?"

"She's my grandma, Ben. She says I gotta go with her."

"Go where?"

"She says we're goin' home."

"Jim, don't leave me here alone."

"Don't forget me, Ben."

"You're my best friend in the whole world, Jim. Don't go." The image of Jim and his grandmother faded into the white light. "Please, don't leave me. Jim!" Ben pleaded, "Take me with you!"

"Do you see the men?"

Ben turned and looked. The two fishermen were running along the shoreline toward them and the hole in the ice.

"Yes, I see them."

"They'll help you and Missy. I gotta go. See ya."

Ben turned back to his friend, but he was gone. The light had disappeared.

"Jim! Don't leave me here!... Jim!" There was no answer. In his confusion, Ben heard a different voice. It was warm and comforting.

"Benjamin, do not be afraid. You must go back to your body. The men are here to save you."

There was only darkness and silence until another voice called out to him, "Come on, little buddy, breathe! I know you can do it. Breathe!"

III

Solitude isn't all it's cracked up to be.
—Author, 1996

Date: Monday, November 24, 1997
Time: 5:30 A.M.
Place: Duluth Skyline, Duluth, MN

Ben Bradley awakened ten minutes before his alarm clock/radio had a chance to earn its keep. Half awake, he found himself still in a partial dream state. Was he calling for his old friend, Jim, or had he been with him? The dream faded away, finding a safe hiding place in his subconscious where it would wait for another night.

Groggily, he groped for his wife, then remembered she wasn't there. He was so tired. She'd been gone nearly two years. He forced his eyes open. He was drenched in sweat and tangled up in his bedcovers.

Ben reached for the clock/radio and turned the button to Radio. The morning local talk show was playing. The two disc jockeys, Marty and Jones, bantered with each other in their typical style, satirizing the news and playing games with words and each other as they awakened their market share of the Duluth broadcast area.

Ben sat up in his bed. He stretched and looked out the window. It was still dark. Only the glow of street lights shone through the undraped window. He vaguely recalled sensing that something was in the room with him, but he wasn't afraid. It had happened before.

Ben untangled his six-foot frame from the covers that held him captive and stumbled into the bathroom, keeping an ear out for the weather as he took care of his necessaries. He hated looking into the mirror to shave. What used to be fit and trim was beginning to sag. Through the day-old stubble of whiskers, he could see traces of a second chin forming. What was left of his dark brown hair was graying around the temples. His steely blue eyes were surrounded by reddened blood vessels and punctuated by blackened half circles hanging under them. The mirror image of his trim body showed a few wrinkles and signs of age as he stood before it in his blue boxer shorts.

He'd had the dream again. God, he hated it. It kept coming back to him, over and over. It was always the same, always in order, always in color, correct in every detail, as clear as the day it had happened. Thirty-four years had passed since he had nearly drowned with Jim in the small lake, since he and Missy had survived and his best friend had died. Ben wished he could forget that awful day, but he still carried the feelings of loneliness and guilt for not heeding Jim's plea to get help, for struggling to get away from him, and for surviving when his best friend did not. Yet, at times, it seemed like Jim was still with him.

For years, Ben had tried to push most of his conscious memories out of his mind, but he couldn't prevent them from coming back in his dreams. When the dreams came, he would force himself to wake up. Then, lying in bed, he would remember, afraid to go back to sleep and dream it all over.

Finished in the bathroom, he walked out to the half-empty living area. His ex-wife had taken the dining room set, the drapes, and half the French Provincial furniture with her. Ben had not made the effort to replace the missing pieces. He walked into the den to peer out the sliding glass doors from his fourth-floor luxury condo overlooking the city. Even in the morning darkness, the view of the city and harbor area was fantastic. He paid dearly for it, nearly twenty-five hundred dollars a month, but that included parking for his 4x4 and the 'Vette, now mothballed and covered with a silk dropcloth for the duration of the winter.

This morning, the view seemed hazy, like a light snow or fog was in the air. Ben stepped to his executive-style walnut desk and turned on the lamp. He noticed the pencils on the floor. "Hmm," he thought out loud, as he picked them up and set them back on the desk. He noticed the newspaper article under the glass on the desk top. That and a faded black and white photo were his only momentos of a time gone by. He just didn't have the heart to throw them out.

Ben touched his finger to the glass over the picture of the boys and his dog, Missy, as if he could again touch his friend, to feel some connection with what might have been had Jim lived. His finger felt wet. He wrinkled his brow as he examined it, rubbing the tip of his index finger against his thumb. "I wonder where that came from," he muttered. Through the glass top, he reread the short article that was carried in a Minneapolis paper thirty-four years ago:

Local Boy Drowns

What started as a day of fun in the fresh snow ended in tragedy yesterday afternoon when two boys fell through the thin ice while trying to rescue a dog.

Jim Simonson, Jr., son of James and Margaret Simonson of Edina, Minnesota, was pronounced dead on arrival at Fairview Hospital after being pulled from the frigid water.

Ben had tried to tell the doctors, nurses, and his parents about what had happened that day after he and Jim had slipped under the water. He tried to tell them how he'd seen Jim and Jim's grandmother and how the voices had called out to him. They didn't believe him. Nobody believed him. They told him all about hypoxia, hallucinations, and some other fancy words that he didn't understand. When he went to medical school, he discovered there was no room for superstition and ghosts in science and medicine. That was when he started to suppress his conscious memories. Reason told him it was just a dream, but still it gnawed at him.

Ben missed a lot of things about Jim, but what he missed the most was his sense of humor. Without it, Ben never really found his own. After the accident, very little seemed funny. Missy had died when she was only seven. The veterinarian said it was from congestive heart failure, but Ben knew it was from a broken heart. He had ignored her after Jim's death. Even at age ten, he knew the accident was not her fault, but it hurt to play with her. It reminded him of the day he'd lost his best friend.

Looking at the picture, Ben recalled how the accident had helped shape his career. His interest in medicine, particularly trauma medicine, was largely sparked by his desire to save people's lives, to compensate somehow for the loss of his friend. He came to Duluth to participate in the hypothermia studies, to learn and practice medicine on the cutting edge of cold weather emergencies. He always wondered if both boys might have been saved if today's more modern techniques had been available thirty-four years ago.

His thoughts were mercifully interrupted by one of the DJ's voices saying, "And now for the local news...." Ben listened intently as he walked back to the bedroom and dressed. A twenty-year-old man had been murdered. There were a couple of fires and several automobile accidents. The patients were all taken to St. Mary's Hospital. The two DJ's started joking with each other.

Damn! Ben thought. It wasn't that he liked to see patients die at Mercy Hospital any more than he wished for them to die at St. Mary's. It was just that the Mercy Hospital Board of Ethics had agreed to install in the trauma unit some new pieces of experimental equipment that he and a small team of coworkers had recently developed. They were anxious to see the equipment in action. That was the only exciting thing that Ben had scheduled for what would otherwise be just another week of work, just like the last week, just like the last thousand.

"And now for the weather...."

Finally, Ben thought.

"Well, folks, we don't have much better news for you on the weather scene. The snow is on the way. It looks like winter is going to hit us hard with the first major blizzard of the season. It's coming directly out of the west and is just now blasting its way into central and eastern Minnesota." The DJ continued, "It's going to get rough outside. We're looking for accumulations of ten to twenty inches of the white stuff and falling temperatures. So, put on your long johns and tune up the snowblower. This storm's gonna last for three or more days."

Jones finished the weather segment with a serious warning to his listeners, "Folks, this storm is no joke. If you can stay home, I'd advise you to do it. And while you're sitting there, you should start calling family and friends to cancel your Thanksgiving travel plans. There is absolutely *no* travel advised until road crews are able to get the mess cleaned up. If you want to get out of town, you should leave now before it gets any worse."

That was all Ben wanted to hear from those two. Some days they were good. Today was not one of their better days. He walked over to the clock/radio and shut it off. At least he wouldn't have to worry about his family and friends risking life and limb traveling to see him. Dad had died when Ben was in medical school. The cigarettes had killed him. He just keeled over one day at the office. Mom was living in San Diego with his sister's family. Ben hadn't seen them for five years.

He looked out the curtainless bedroom window. The morning was turning from black to dark gray. The DJ's were right—it was starting to snow and blow.

Mesmerized by the images before him, he thought, *This view is too nice to cover with drapes.* Besides, there were no neighbors to peek in. The next building was twenty feet lower down the hill and was only three stories high, offering Ben an unobstructed panoramic view of the port area from two sides of his condo.

Nothing exciting ever happened in his condominium anyway. Ben had no need for privacy. He lived alone. No wife. No kids. No dog. No girlfriend. No personal time. He had practically driven his beautiful young wife out two years ago with his obsessive behavior. Ben was a strong type-A personality, a workaholic. A serious man, he had little time for the lighter side of life. Those attributes helped make him a good trauma surgeon and director of the Shock/Trauma Unit of Mercy Hospital, but they had served him poorly in the role of husband.

Ben didn't know when he'd married his medical school sweetheart that he wouldn't have time for a wife. He didn't understand how difficult it would be to live with someone who wanted to be really close and intimate. He just couldn't open up to her the way she wanted him to, the way she needed him to, the way he couldn't… or wouldn't. It took a year before Ben understood why she had started seeing someone else and why she had, in the end, left him.

Ben's life was lonely. He missed his wife, but he filled the void by spending more time at work. All the activity, all the people with their crises, their needs, problems, emergencies, and traumas helped keep his mind off the fact that he was alone in his luxurious nest.

Ben hadn't even dated another woman in… how long had it been? It seemed like it had been years. Not that he wasn't interested—he was just too busy. A nurse on his trauma team aroused some interest, but he didn't know if it was a good idea to mix business with pleasure.

Other doctors and nurses burned out from all the stresses they faced year after year in the trauma unit. Some lasted longer by using avoidance methods like liberal time off and a macabre sense of humor. Some leaned on the perilous crutches of drinking, drugs, or sex. Ben lasted because he was disciplined, because he stayed fit. He neither smoked nor drank. He ate moderately and worked out as often as the demands of his career allowed. Ben endured because he used his work as an escape from his loneliness. It was his personal life that he had burned out on, not his career.

He decided to go to the athletic club for a workout and breakfast before going in to the hospital. Exercise usually helped to shake off the veil of dreams that clung to him. He could still get to work early. Besides, he justified to himself, it might be all the exercise he'd get this week. Ben had volunteered to be on call for the holiday weekend so his colleagues with families could have the time off. He'd be busy taking extra shifts. If the weather got as bad as was forecasted, he might just stay right at the hospital.

For the hundredth time, Ben thought about giving up his lease and changing his address to Mercy Hospital. That's where he really lived. He wouldn't even have to cook for himself. Then he reminded himself how little he enjoyed eating at the hospital cafeteria. The typical choices usually seemed to be either patient-type food which was low in salt, cholesterol, and taste, or food which was high in sugar, fat, and cholesterol—convenience food like burgers, fries, and desserts.

It was tough to eat well when you couldn't graze over a nice fresh selection of pastas, fruits, and vegetables. He always suspected that was why there were so many fat people on the medical staff. Ben couldn't understand how so many health care professionals could let themselves go like that. They knew better. It seemed like a quarter of the staff looked like regulars at the lutefisk and meatball suppers in church basements.

There! he smiled. That felt better! At least he'd talked himself out of moving into the hospital and into a good workout at the gym, all in one short vision. Besides, they'd never give him an extra parking space for the 'Vette!

Ben fished through his dressing room closet as he threw on some dirty clothes, fussing to find some fresh clothes to stuff into his gym bag to change into after his workout. A plain white shirt with a button-down collar and fresh khaki slacks would have to do. He'd already worn most of his favorites in the last two weeks.

At least he didn't have to worry about cleaning and doing his own laundry. The "maid" would be coming today. She was a very dependable woman who did a good job. She even kept the fridge stocked with basics for him. The only time he saw her was when she stopped by to get paid. He could send the checks by mail, but he really didn't mind visiting with her. Ben paid her well for her efforts—she needed the money to help support her family. He could have her come more often, but he never made much of a mess.

He slipped into a pair of loafers, grabbed his gym bag, and shut off the lights in his closet. Walking quickly to the front door, he pulled his down-filled parka out of the front closet and stepped out into the hall. He pulled the door shut and checked to make sure it was locked. Instead of the elevator, he took the stairway down to the parking garage. It was 5:56 A.M.

IV

Man finds his highest dignity by lowering himself to his work.
—Author, 1996

Date: November 24, 1997
Time: 7:30 A.M.
Place: Gary New Duluth, MN

Jarod Martin quietly left the house, hoping not to disturb his sleeping wife. Dawn was breaking above the cloud-filled sky as the aging compact car backed down the driveway and headed toward Commonwealth Avenue. Like millions of Americans who headed for work in the early hours, Jarod Martin would drive his early morning commute in the near darkness for almost three more months. The proprietor of a modestly successful neighborhood hardware store located near the cloverleaf at Grand and I-35, Jarod owned the privilege of being the first to arrive at work and the last to leave. He'd kept this routine ever since he had started working full time for his father. Since then, his father had retired and sold the business to him on favorable terms. Now that his own two children were at college, the routine was even more necessary. Except for his college years and two years in the U.S. Army, Jarod had lived in Duluth all of his life. He always said he didn't know any better.

Overnight, the road before him had accumulated a fresh coat of snow. *It shouldn't be a problem by the time I turn onto Commonwealth Avenue,* he thought. *There should be enough traffic to keep the road passable.* Jarod wondered how busy the store would be today, especially since he had lunch plans with his good friend Matthew Lockner, the pastor of his church. The forecast for bad weather often chased retail customers away, but in his business, it made people think more about certain hardware items such as flashlights, batteries, cords, shovels, and snowblowers.

The store didn't open until eight-thirty, but there was always much to do before then. His wife, Betty, came in later each morning and helped with the bookkeeping and the computer. He still had to unpack freight, stock shelves, make sure the place was clean, shovel the front sidewalk, and get the cash registers ready for business.

Jarod was proud of his business. The store survived and even prospered despite the invasion of the mall-type hardware stores and discounters. His business philosophy included being ready for the customers when they walked in the door. He believed that his customers did not want to see a clerk's backside as he or she was kept busy stocking shelves during store hours. They wanted undivided attention. Jarod believed that philosophy and his knowledge of the business were the keys to his modest success. It didn't help to get the best prices if the clerk couldn't understand what you needed. Jarod knew what his customers meant when they asked for a "doo-dah on the widget" that goes in the sink drain. He stocked the items his customers needed such as plumbing and heating parts to repair the old fixtures and heating systems still plentiful in the aging neighborhood.

Now in their late forties, he and Betty had raised two children. Their daughter, Julie, would graduate from the University of Minnesota next spring, and their son, Michael, was a sophomore at a private college in southern Minnesota. Jarod occasionally thought of slowing down, but for now, there were bills to pay, lots of them. Julie had plans to marry after she finished college. Michael would be in college for two more years. Boy, private tuition was expensive! He was a good kid, and Jarod was willing to help pay the bills for him to get a good education as long as his son worked hard.

Mike might want to take over the business from his father, just as Jarod had done. It was too early to tell how that would turn out. Sometimes kids had a different idea of how they wanted to invest their lives. So many of them resented the time their fathers spent working, even though they grew to expect the benefits their fathers' successes could buy.

Jarod shivered as he turned north on Commonwealth. Inside the cold car, the windshield fogged from his breath and the snow that had gotten sucked into the defroster. The road was worse than he had expected. Jarod thought about putting his seatbelt on, but he hadn't done that for years. Why break a perfect record? He thought if he could survive Vietnam, he could survive a little snow in Duluth. Besides, he would probably have to pull over and stop so he could dig the belt out from under the seat.

The radio was tuned into the Marty and Jones Morning Show. The two crazy radio announcers predicted that by early evening driving would become even more treacherous than the usual take-your-life-in-your-hands approach that winter brought to the hilly roads in the Duluth area. Jarod enjoyed their joking about why people lived in Duluth. He loved the city, but days like this were a test of that love.

Jarod met a city truck with its blue and amber lights flashing as it plowed and sanded its way south toward Highway 105. As he drove to the northeast, the road turned into Grand Avenue. Soon he would be at the cloverleaf intersection with the freeway. The road was four lanes wide with no barrier between opposing sides. Traffic was very light. It looked like a lot of people were waiting to hear of closings and cancellations before going to work.

The frost that was forming on the inside of his windshield was obscuring his view. Jarod reached down under the seat and felt for an ice scraper.

Finding it, he sat full upright and started to scrape the frost off the windshield when he saw the glare of headlights from a large sedan as it came over the center line directly toward him. He peered through the small area he'd scraped. The oncoming vehicle appeared to be driverless!

Alarms went off inside Jarod's brain. *Hit the brakes! Turn out of the way!*

It took but a split second for the view of the oncoming car to be perceived as a threat, to mentally calculate a solution, and to send the commands to his hands and feet. His right foot hit the brake pedal and his hands jerked the steering wheel to the right to avoid the impact. The tires broke traction, and his car skidded straight ahead over the packed snow—not the evasive action he had anticipated! Jarod thought... *Pump the brakes*. He gasped as the two vehicles collided head on.

Jarod watched as his front bumper was forced down under the front end of the larger vehicle coming toward him. The other sedan passed through the grill and radiator and into the engine compartment of Jarod's car. He heard the shrieking sounds of metal grinding and crushing as radiators hit fan blades, belts, and pulleys. The engine and gears ground to a halt as the larger car continued to push the engine and steering rod of the smaller car into the fire wall, then into the passenger compartment, where the inertia of Jarod's body was traveling in the opposite direction at thirty miles per hour.

Time nearly stood still for Jarod as he slid forward unrestrained over the seat. His chest impacted the steering wheel and post which were moving backward and upward into the cab area to greet him. He heard several of his ribs snap and then felt his left lung pop like a paper bag filled with air. *Ouch*! Jarod's face caught the top of the steering wheel. *Crack*! *Pop*! He felt his nose and jaw break. He continued to move forward, hitting his head on the windshield and his knees on the dashboard. Jarod blinked as blood spattered on the broken glass. He felt the intense pressure of the steering wheel as it continued to inflict damage to his chest and abdomen, pushing inward to within three inches of his spine. His upper spine whipped forward, impacting and bruising his heart from behind. As Jarod's body came to a complete stop, his internal organs finished hurtling themselves toward the dashboard of the car, tearing tissue and blood vessels loose.

Once the impact stopped, Jarod's head snapped back in a secondary whiplash until it reached the seatback and the wholly inadequate headrest on the seat of the aging and now-wrecked compact sedan. Jarod screamed from the intense pain until he heard a buzzing noise and experienced a huge rushing sensation that penetrated down to his toes. Then, he stepped out of his car... right through the door!

A Duluth Transit Authority, or DTA, bus was the first vehicle to come upon the crash. The driver stopped the bus, hit the button to start the emergency flashers, picked up the handset for his radiophone and keyed in a call to the DTA dispatcher. Several passengers started grumbling about being late for work. Complaining wouldn't help. A good Samaritan, the driver would not leave until help arrived. They would be delayed for several minutes until the police routed the large bus around the accident scene and the traffic that would be stopped. The driver stepped off the bus with another man close behind.

Contrary to what he might have expected, Jarod Martin no longer felt any pain from his crushed bones and tissue. He turned his attention to the accident scene next to him. He was upset and talking to himself, "Pump the brakes, dummy! Geez, I can't believe I didn't pump the brakes." He looked at the two wrecked vehicles and wondered how he'd stepped through the door. Snow was blowing and swirling around him, but he didn't feel cold!

He watched a DTA bus pull to a stop and turn on its flashers. The driver and a second man stepped out of the bus and started walking toward him with difficulty. Jarod waved at them and called out, "I'm over here! I'm all right! Hey, you guys! Look at me!"

The men took no notice of his summons. Jarod decided to head them off before they got to his car. "Hey, look at me when I'm talking to you," he confronted them. "Hey! Don't you understand? I'm right here talking to you!"

One of them walked right through Jarod as he approached the cars—as though Jarod wasn't even there! *What the...?* Jarod stopped abruptly and looked down at himself. *How did that guy do that?*

The men approached the scrap heap and looked into the larger sedan. Jarod heard one of them ask, "Is he alive?"

"I can't tell. He's not moving."

"Do you think we can get him out of there?"

The second man pulled on the door. "Hell, no. It's jammed like an accordion. Looks like the poor SOB is going to have to wait for the rescue squad."

Curious, Jarod moved in closer for a peek while the two men slithered on the slippery road over to Jarod's vehicle. Inside the large sedan, Jarod saw a gray-haired man, still belted into his seat, slumped over the steering wheel. He thought to himself, *Maybe the old guy had a heart attack.* Then he heard the men talking next to his own car.

"This one doesn't look any better," the DTA driver said.

"Can you tell if he's breathing?"

"Nope."

Jarod moved over to the two men next to his crumpled car and scolded them, "Of course I'm breathing. I'm right here, you idiots. I'm not in the...." Jarod stopped. If he wasn't in the car, who was? He took a careful look through the broken glass. A bloodied and motionless body behind the crumpled steering wheel was wearing his clothes, the ones he remembered putting on this morning. *What the...? It sure looked like him... like me....*

Was it possible to be in two places at the same time? Jarod lost his sense of balance, as though he had an extreme case of vertigo, as he stared at his own body inside the car.

"Can we get this door open?" the man asked.

"It doesn't look good. Maybe if we both pull on it." They tried unsuccessfully.

Jarod was mesmerized by the vision of his own body trapped in a compartment that was now crushed to half its normal size. There were glass and blood everywhere. He could see his face was smashed in. Blood ran down onto his jacket and pants. "This can't be!" he shouted. "Come on, you guys, you gotta help me!" Either no one heard his cry or they were being very rude.

The two men continued to tug at the driver's door of Jarod's car when the DTA driver looked down at a puddle of fluids forming under them. "We better get out of here."

"What's the problem, man?"

He pointed at their feet. "I'm not interested in burning up in a gasoline fire while dinking around an accident scene."

"Hey, you're right," the other said as they backed away.

The DTA driver continued, "I had the dispatcher call 911. There's a fire and rescue station less than a mile from here. They'll be here soon."

Jarod could hear the faint sounds of sirens in the distance. Once again, he heard that whooshing sound. He felt a strange sensation as he was sucked back into his body. In a microsecond, Jarod experienced the most agonizing pain he'd ever known. He turned his bloodied head and looked directly at the two men who were now standing ten feet away from the car. He gurgled from the blood in his mouth and airway and called out softly, "Help me. Please!"

It was like seeing a ghost! The driver was the first to respond, "Jesus, man, hang on! We have to wait for the rescue squad."

"Please!" Jarod entreated.

The other man spoke, "Hang on, mister! We got people comin' who can help."

"I'm trying." The world went black as Jarod slipped into unconsciousness.

V

"They also serve who only stand and wait."
—Milton, *Sonnet 19* (1655) (p. 681)

Date: November 24, 1997
Time: 7:30 A.M.
Place: Duluth, Fire Station 8

The station crew was coming to life. They had slept or, at least, rested for a couple of hours since cleaning up after their last run. Several were gathered in the kitchen area for hot coffee and breakfast. After a casual inspection of the rigs in the fire hall, the captain was the last to enter for breakfast. Fire Captain Steven "Sparks" Johnston sorted through the conglomeration of fresh and leftover food in the refrigerator.

"All right, which one of you low-lifes ate my fresh strawberries?"

Several smirks erupted as the crew members looked around the table at each other. The one they called Fearless was the first to respond. "What did they look like, Cap'n?" Johnston thought he saw Fearless winking at the others.

"Sure, like you don't know what strawberries look like. You all look guilty as hell."

Each of the crew members lifted a small handful of plump, juicy strawberries from under the table and placed them in their cereal bowls. Fearless pointed at his bowl, "Hey, Cap'n, did they look like these?"

Johnston surveyed the table. "Dammit, those are my berries." His face turned red as the crew broke into laughter.

"You want us to eat healthy, don't you?"

"Not if I can't eat my own food."

One of the paramedics from the medic unit also housed in Station 8, Sawbones Taggart, corrected Fearless, "It's not healthy, it's healthfully."

Fearless pointed at Sawbones and retorted, "We'll have our health officer, or our healthful officer, Sawbones here, make a full inspection of the joint and file a report in the proper King's English."

Sawbones, a registered nurse/paramedic, along with a female paramedic nicknamed Smitty were assigned to the ambulance designated as Medic 803. The designation 803 defined the ambulance as being Unit 3 at Station 8. The crew had nicknamed him Sawbones because of his recent acceptance to the medical school in Duluth. He'd only worked part time since starting classes in the fall. Prior to that he'd been a respected squad member for four years. Medical school classes were dismissed for quarter break, and the group enjoyed having him back around the fire hall, though they wouldn't admit it to his face. The only way Sawbones knew he was really liked by the crew was by the modest scholarship account at the credit union that department members had anonymously donated to him.

"I'm not the health officer, you idiot. I'm just trying to save you from being so uncouth," Sawbones scolded.

Fearless continued his prodding in a poorly faked British accent, "Ahh, yes. The barbarians are banging on the castle door. How quickly they forget when they're in medical school."

"Shit!" Captain Johnston declared. "I hope you're all happy eating my breakfast." The grins at the table were ear to ear. "You got any idea how hard it is to find fresh strawberries in November?"

"Come on, Captain. Sit down. We saved lots for you," Smitty said as she raised a huge bowl of the berries and set them on the table.

The crew laughed as the captain sat down staring wide-eyed at the huge bowl. "There must be twice as many berries as I brought. Where did you find all of these?"

"Trade secret," Fearless told him.

Captain Johnston saw the humor in their prank and laughed with them. He raised a spoon with a large strawberry in it and declared, "You once were lost, but now you are found," then opened his mouth and consumed the entire berry in a single bite. The berry was cold... it hurt his teeth.

Captain Johnston and Fearless had joined the fire department the same year. Both men were from the "old school"—most of their training had come on the job. Things had changed a lot over the past twenty years, starting with changing names from firemen to firefighters in an age of female employees and political correctness. Both men teased the newcomers that they had learned their trade back when men were men and firefighters were men. Nowadays, they would tell the younger squad members that new firefighters were wunderkinds, snot-nosed kids with two-year associate degrees in firefighting.

Every new crew member, male or female, received a large dose of good-natured ribbing. The older firefighters handed it out mercilessly, but they were good at taking it, too. The younger crew members teased the older ones about having such modest mental faculties that they actually enjoyed walking into burning buildings. The continual banter helped mold the Station 8 crew into a congenial and cohesive group.

Together, they worked hard at staying up-to-date on emergency medical care, hazardous materials, incident management, high-tech rescues, and fire suppression methods, all parts of a mosaic of seemingly endless modern fire and rescue skills.

Fearless was nicknamed because of his reputation for being the first of the Station 8 crew to go into a burning building. He also had a reputation for getting out safely. After following Fearless' hose a few times, new squad members learned to appreciate his bravery. There was nobody else they'd rather follow into harm's way.

Yet, when it had come time to pick a new captain, Johnston was promoted over Fearless because he'd been perceived as being more cautious. That quality had helped save the lives of more than one firefighter. Modestly jealous, Fearless acknowledged the captain's abilities to manage complex emergency and rescue situations. Despite Johnston's promotion, the two remained good friends.

The crew continued to pick at each other in typical, good-natured firehouse fashion. Someone mentioned listening to the Marty and Jones Early Morning Show about the latest GI losses in Bosnia. After the group collectively exhausted their commentary about the the U.S.'s ineffectiveness in managing world affairs, Sawbones asked, "Do you suppose somebody has to ride shotgun on their ambulances?"

Fearless answered, "Wouldn't surprise me a bit." Others chimed in. Fearless stood up and stuffed a magazine under his left arm. As he headed towards the men's room, he called back to the group, "Hold my calls while I'm in the library."

A couple of crew members finished eating and started picking up the kitchen area, busing dishes to the sink, then rinsing them. The captain was savoring his bowl of strawberries, drowned in cream and sugar, when the klaxon sounded. "Shit!" He stood up and carried his berries to the refrigerator where hopefully they would wait for his return.

The dispatcher's voice came over the loudspeakers in the fire hall, "Station 8, Engines 2, 3, and 4, Signal 10-52, one mile south of I-35 cloverleaf on Grand Avenue. Acknowledge, please." The Signal 10-52 code meant a two-vehicle collision. It was nearby, less than two miles from the station. Crew members scrambled to gear up.

Captain Johnston pressed the talk button on his shoulder-mounted radio. "Dispatch, Station 8. Engines 2, 3, and 4 are responding."

The dispatcher came back, "Station 8, a DTA driver reports a head-on collision. Advise Code 3." They would run with lights and sirens.

As he walked by the men's room, the captain banged on the door and yelled, "C'mon, McBundy! Pinch a loaf. We gotta roll."

Fearless' exasperated voice sounded from the other side of the door, "I'm coming." He stumbled out of the restroom struggling to get his pants zipped and suspenders back on.

Captain Johnston climbed into his bunker pants and boots, pulled the power cord to Engine 4, the rescue truck, then jumped up into the passenger's seat. He would put the rest of his fireproof gear on while en route. The station's rookie, Janine, appeared nervous as she settled into the the driver's seat of the large truck. "Take a deep breath. You'll do fine," Johnston told her. Still learning the various firefighters' duties, this was her first week at the wheel of Engine 4. Driving meant she would also be the FEO, or Fire Equipment Officer, for Engine 4 at the accident scene. The captain looked at her, "Let's get going."

The young woman slammed her cab door shut and pushed the remote-controlled garage door opener. She hit the starter to fire up the Cummins diesel engine. Captain Johnston watched a small cloud of black smoke billow toward the ceiling as Janine revved the engine and shifted the transmission into first gear.

The bright yellow rescue unit rolled out of the station and came fully alive with lights and siren. Medic Unit 803, the ambulance, followed immediately behind them. The captain pressed the garage door control and looked back to make sure the door was closing behind them. It was tough enough keeping vandals out of the fire hall without leaving the doors open. He watched as the door opened in front of Engine 2, the big pumper. It carried two thousand feet of hose, sixty feet of ladders, and five hundred gallons of "wet-water," a mixture of water and fire suppression chemicals. Fearless was standing on one foot in his bunker pants, trying to get one of his boots on. The captain laughed when he thought of the expletives that might be flying around in front of Engine 2, especially with no women left in the station. Fearless and Engine 2 would only be a block behind them. Engine 1, the bucket and ladder unit, was not called out for this run.

Captain Johnston began organizing the run in his mind. He thought about how he would merge the duties of the rescue and medic units dispatched from Station 10. Station 8 was closer to the scene of the accident, so they would beat the Station 10 crew to the scene by three to five minutes. He would be the Incident Commander.

Captain Johnston watched the traffic as they drove down the snow-packed road. "Always try to anticipate what the other drivers are doing," he told Janine. They were just blocks from the station when an oncoming driver tried to make a left turn directly in front of Engine 4. Duluth had its fair share of drivers who failed to yield to emergency vehicles. Either they'd try to beat responding units through intersections or they couldn't hear the sirens over their own radios and fan noises. Some were not alert enough to notice the wigwag lights.

"Get out of the way, you idiot!" the captain yelled at the car as he laid on the air horn. If the driver didn't know he was breaking the law, he would receive a harsh lesson about it in the next few minutes. Because of the slippery roads, the driver didn't finish his turn in time to get out of the way.

Janine couldn't stop before she hit the late model sedan in the right rear quarter panel.

"Shit," she said as she turned sheepishly to the captain for advice, orders, or a chewing out. The captain didn't take lightly to dents and scratches on his big shiny trucks.

The captain instructed her, "Keep driving, Janine. I'll call it in." He grabbed the microphone and reported the accident. After a short conversation, which included a description of the vehicle now stopped at the intersection, he turned to Janine and said, "The police will see to it that he gets a hefty ticket for failing to yield to us."

Engines 3 and 4 arrived at the scene within three minutes of leaving the station. "Good." Johnston observed, "Duluth Police already has officers at the scene." Flares were placed and traffic moved to make room for the fire and rescue vehicles.

Captain Johnston finished dressing in his coat, Nomex hood, helmet, and gloves as Janine drove just past the accident scene, jerked the truck left into the oncoming lanes, and stopped in front of the two wrecked cars. Parking in this fashion would use the engines and the wrecked cars as protective barriers against oncoming vehicles. She shut down the siren, set the brakes, jumped down from the cab to chock the rear wheels with two sets of blocks, and began preparing equipment for the rescue.

Captain Johnston jumped out the other side with his self-contained breathing apparatus, or SCBA, hung over his right shoulder. Standing on the ground, he shoved his left arm through the second strap of the SCBA and hoisted it up on his back. He fixed the mask to his face and pulled his helmet on as he prepared to approach the wrecks. The SCBA was a precautionary measure in case of fire.

Engine 2 pulled up next to Johnston and Engine 3. The FEO chocked his tires and moved to the lighted control panel to ready the pumps, while Fearless and another firefighter pulled the hose toward the two wrecks. As they approached the vehicles, the captain clicked his shoulder microphone, "Dispatch, Station 8 is at the scene."

"10-4, Station 8, 0742," the dispatcher confirmed the time of their arrival.

The captain ordered, "All local units switch to fireground frequency." They switched to the preassigned radio frequency where their chatter would not disturb the main dispatch frequency. He began his broadcast, "I see fuel, antifreeze, and debris under and around the vehicles. Better give it a good shot." The FEO charged the line with water and started siphoning the chemically-treated foam. The firefighter aimed a healthy shot of wet-water at the puddle under the car, rendering it harmless before anyone approached the cars. The captain ordered, "Let's get in there and block the wheels." Fearless and three other firefighters moved in to continue stabilizing the scene.

Sawbones parked the ambulance, Medic 803, about sixty feet from the other side of the wrecks. He and Smitty got dressed in their turnout gear and holding their medical kits, waited for clearance to approach the vehicles. A uniformed DTA driver and a second man approached them. They were animated as they anxiously encouraged the paramedics, "Hurry up, 'cause that guy over there is still alive, but he looks really bad. He looked like he was dead... scared the hell out of us when he started moaning for help. He looks like a bloody ghost."

Sawbones tried to explain, "We can't go in until the captain says it's safe."

He knew they would have to wait for Captain Johnston to go through his mental checklist. There was no smoke or fire and a water line was charged at the ready. The site appeared to be stabilized. He watched the captain click his microphone, "Scene looks stable. Okay, Sawbones, you and Smitty can go in."

Sawbones thanked the two men and asked them to please stay back. He and Smitty moved toward the wrecks, she to the smaller sedan, Sawbones to the other. The medic unit from Station 10 arrived and pulled up next to Medic 803. Engine 10-01, a pumper, pulled up on the center line seventy-five yards ahead of Engine 2. Sawbones knew they would locate or "catch" the nearest fire hydrant and provide a continuous water supply via a four-inch diameter hose. Hopefully, it would not be needed. One never knew for certain, especially with fuel leaks and all the crap people carried in their trunks, like gasoline and aerosol cans, ammunition, and fertilizer. If there was a fire, it could kill everyone inside the vehicles in 90 seconds and severely injure fire and rescue workers.

Sawbones watched as two firefighters with large prybars opened the driver's door of the larger sedan. He moved in toward the patient and completed his initial observations in a few seconds. He always said, "It doesn't take long to look at a horseshoe." The victim was unresponsive. He reached into the vehicle with latex-gloved hands to check for vital signs. The patient's lips were blue. There was no pulse or respiration. The old man was strapped in his seatbelt and appeared to be dead, but they were obliged to try to resuscitate him until an attending physician made an official determination.

Sawbones clicked his microphone, "Captain, I have a male, about late sixties, in full arrest. I have a code." He shouted at the two paramedics from Station 10, "Come on, you guys! Bring your Montana blanket roll and a backboard. This one's gotta go, stat!" He checked the patient's airway. Seeing that it was clear, Sawbones began bagging air into his lungs with a bag-valve-mask as they completed a rapid extrication with the rolled-up blanket wrapped around his neck, crossed over his chest, passed under the arms, and twisted together behind his back. In case of whiplash or neck injuries, this extrication method afforded some protection while being very fast. There was no more time for this one. Very quickly, they had the old man out of the car and strapped into Medic 10-03.

Inside the ambulance, a Station 10 medic attached the patches of the defibrillator/heart monitor to the patient's graying body while a second medic started CPR. Sawbones watched the driver grab the microphone through the open cab of the ambulance and heard him call, "St. Mary's Hospital. Medic 10-03...." He informed St. Mary's Trauma Center of the patient's condition and their ETA, or estimated time of arrival. Sawbones closed the rear doors and pounded twice on the side of the ambulance to alert the driver they were clear to leave. As Medic 10-03 pulled away with lights and siren, Sawbones sadly knew the ambulance ride would turn out to be the first leg of the trip to the patient's funeral, with intermittent stops at St. Mary's Hospital and Cease and Deceaste Funeral Home.

He turned back toward the scene of the wreck and watched as firefighters finished blocking the wheels, flattening tires, and hosing the underside of the second vehicle. Two firefighters from Station 10 cut the front and center posts off the compact sedan with their Jaws of Life. Next, they would peel the roof back, like opening a large sardine can. Sawbones thought to himself, *The doors must be crushed shut. Damn! It sure would be nice if Detroit would develop a new Nader bolt that would retract after impact.* The bolts helped keep car doors closed in a crash, but when seconds counted in saving lives after the crash, it sure was a bitch when the only way to extricate a patient from his car was to turn it into a convertible.

Sawbones noted that Smitty had covered the patient with a protective blanket and was assessing his condition through the side window. He walked quickly over and tapped her on the shoulder to let her know he was ready to help and noticed Fearless in the back seat of the crushed car. He must have climbed through the back window to help Smitty. Fearless yelled over the noises of the compressor and the pumper engine, "Top should be off in another thirty seconds."

"What do you have?" Sawbones shouted to Smitty.

Smitty reported, "He's about fifty years old, wasn't wearing a seatbelt. He's sustained head and chest lacerations from fighting with the windshield and steering wheel. Possible broken face and nose. Nosebleed is slowing down. His right lung sounds bad. The other is worse. I'm going to put a cervical collar on him to stabilize his neck. Looks like he has a compound fracture to the right wrist and a possible fracture to the right femur. Probably has internal injuries, but I don't see any major bleeders. Respirations are labored, about ten breaths per minute. His pulse is so weak and irregular that

I can only feel it in his carotid artery. I got him suctioned out and on oxygen. He's pale, cool, and damp. He's shocky—in and out of consciousness."

The two firemen who were cutting the top off the car set the Jaws to the side and waved for the hose tender to water the road down one more time before they removed the patient. The road was very slippery. After each hosing, ice and slush formed on everything the water had touched. With four firefighters helping, the top lifted easily. Though they left it hanging in midair, there was still room to lift the patient out. Sawbones watched as Smitty removed the blanket she'd draped over the patient and instructed Fearless to hold his neck and head while she put a cervical collar on Jarod.

Once the blanket was off, Fearless shouted, "Hey, I know this guy. He owns the hardware store over by the station… name's Martin, Jarod Martin."

Sawbones readied the spineboard and instructed Fearless, "You keep holding his head while we get the board behind him." Gently, they slid the backboard in behind the patient. "We're gonna have to snake his legs out from under the dashboard." They worked in unison to lift the weight of the man around the dash and over the door. Fearless explained what they were doing to Jarod, trying to reassure him that he'd soon be out.

Sawbones heard Jarod moan from the pain of bruised and broken nerve endings being jostled during the lift. They reset him on the backboard and immobilized his head with foam blocks. A couple more rounds of duct tape to secure everything. Thank God for duct tape—the paramedic's answer to baling wire. They strapped him on the stretcher and carefully moved Jarod and their equipment back to the ambulance. Smitty told Sawbones, "I'll start cutting off his clothes. You can start the IV. We'll boogie as soon as he's secured in the rig."

"Sure," was all Sawbones needed to say. He turned to Fearless. "You drive. We'll need two medics in the back. We'll take him to Mercy. Call the hospital and request Trauma Code Status."

Inside the ambulance, Sawbones swabbed Jarod's arm with alcohol and selected a needle. As he searched for a good vein, he said, "Not much to choose from." The veins were collapsing. "Here! I think I've got one." He gave Jarod's arm a stab with the large-bore needle. He slipped the needle out, leaving the cathlon, a small plastic sheath, in the vein. "That should do it." Sawbones could feel the back wheels slipping as they got under way. He taped the cathlon to Jarod's arm, connected the tubing to the bag of IV fluids, and started the IV.

As Sawbones continued his work in the back, he heard Fearless in the driver's seat just ahead of him, calling on the radio, "Mercy Hospital—Medic 803 on channel four."

"Go ahead, Eight-Oohh-Three. This is Mercy."

"Mercy, we are at a 10-52 with a fifty-year-old male. Request Trauma

Code Status." Sawbones coached Fearless as he reported the patient's critical condition. The hospital operator would alert the trauma team. "ETA is ten minutes. We are Code Three."

"10-4, Eight-Oohh-Three. Mercy Hospital at 0750." Fearless hit the siren. It was 7:50 A.M.

Sawbones and Smitty methodically re-evaluated Jarod's condition. Even though his eyes were open, Jarod did not respond to their questions. Sawbones pinched the skin over Jarod's collarbone. He winced. They rated his level of consciousness as a P, meaning he responded to pain. After checking his airway, breathing, circulation, bleeding, and oxygen saturation, they examined him for other injuries. His capillary refill functions were slow. A pinch to one of his fingernails was taking more than two seconds to pink up. Jarod's pulse was 120 beats per minute and irregular. His respirations were shallow and up to twenty-four breaths per minute. There was an ominous rattle in his right lung and still no sounds in the left.

"Better start bagging him, Smitty." She started bagging Jarod with 100% oxygen with each squeeze of the bag-valve-mask.

Sawbones said, "I'm gonna hook up the heart monitor and start another IV—we need to get more fluids in him."

The ambulance headed eastward on Interstate 35 and was nearly to the old railroad depot and the Duluth Convention Center when Jarod's eyes glazed over.

Smitty said, "He's really shocky."

"Yeah, I know." Sawbones leaned over the patient, calling him by name, "Jarod, hang on. Try to stay awake. We'll be at the hospital in a few minutes."

When he lost consciousness, Jarod felt himself leave his body again. The pain stopped—it was instant relief. He couldn't tell if the wave of pain had pushed him out or if he was mercifully being spared by some Higher Power. He found himself looking down at the top of the ambulance. He could see the name, Medic 803, in large black stenciling on the roof of the truck as it moved along the interstate. He moved back inside the ambulance and looked down at the two medics as they worked on his body. One was pumping air into him with some sort of bag. The other was connecting a bag of fluids to his IV.

How would that help? He wasn't in there. Jarod knew he had to get back inside his body. He tried to tell them to look up, but it was just like trying to talk to those guys at the accident scene. Maybe the driver could help. He moved to the passenger seat in the front of the ambulance. God, he knew the driver! Fearless was a customer of his at the hardware store. Jarod tried to touch him, call to him, even hit him, to get his attention. Nothing happened.

His words were not heard. His hands slipped right through Fearless' body! What was going on?

Fearless saw nothing but the road ahead. He felt a chill pass through his arm, then through his entire body. The hair stood up on the back of his neck. He'd felt it many times before. He turned to the back of the ambulance. "You're losing him, aren't you?"

"He's unconscious," Sawbones answered him.

"Hey, you two! I don't want nobody dying on my shift." As an Emergency Medical Technician, Fearless knew it wasn't that simple. It was a superstitious request. Nobody really knew which patient might turn into The Ghost of Station 8. He especially didn't want any ghosts who knew him. He turned forward and muttered to himself, "Everybody's having a good time 'til somebody gets killed. Jesus, I hate it when that happens." Fearless crossed himself and said a silent prayer for the man who had just touched him. Few people ever saw the sensitive side of the most macho man at Station 8. He liked it that way.

Smitty told Sawbones, "Every time I ventilate him, I'm getting more resistance. I think his lung is collapsing. Do you think it's a pneumothorax?"

"If it is, we'll have to take the pressure off so we can reinflate the lung. Here, let me try bagging him for a minute." She handed the bag-valve-mask over to Sawbones. After three breaths, he agreed, "He needs a decompression. We have to release the air trapped between his lung and chest wall."

"I thought so," Smitty gulped. "He's only got one functioning lung as it is." She looked at Sawbones, "You do it." It was obvious she didn't want to try.

Sawbones hated this procedure. Medics can go their entire careers without having to do a chest decompression, but this would be the third for the first-year medical student.

Sawbones swabbed the chest wall with betadine. The brownish-red disinfectant dripped down onto the stretcher. He felt down the right side of Jarod's chest from the collarbone to the space between the second and third ribs and held his finger there. Next, he selected another large bore needle with a cathlon jacket and gently pushed through the tissue between the ribs until he heard a hissing sound from the trapped air being released. "Voila! That should help." He taped the cathlon into place.

Smitty congratulated him, "It's working. Good job, Sawbones. I can feel the difference." She continued ventilating the patient. They shared a look of relief.

Jarod felt himself being sucked back inside his body. The buzzing! There was that buzzing again. It sounded like a yardful of giant cicadas on a hot July afternoon. His eyes opened wide as he was jolted by the pain from the procedure.

"Welcome back, Jarod," Sawbones told him. "I want you to try and stay with us 'til we get you to the hospital."

Tears streamed from Jarod's eyes, but he blinked his right eye in recognition. "Good." Jarod felt Sawbones put a hand on his shoulder and give him a comforting squeeze.

Fearless crossed himself and said a silent prayer of thanks for not letting *this* patient expire on his shift. He pulled the ambulance over to the Sixth Avenue East off ramp and slowly turned left through a red light. They climbed up the hill away from the lake for five blocks, then turned into the emergency entrance for Mercy Hospital.

VI

"Men love to wonder, and that is the seed of our science."
—Emerson, "Works and Days," *Society and Solitude* (1870) (p. 704)

Date: November 24, 1997
Time: 7:30 A.M.
Place: Mercy Hospital, Duluth, MN

Dr. Ben Bradley parked the 4X4 in his private parking spot on the staff level of the Mercy Hospital parking ramp. After a quick workout and a light breakfast at the health club, Ben's mind felt more focused—cleansed from the haunting images which had visited him in his sleep. He locked his vehicle and walked the skyway which connected with all four hospitals and the major health care facilities in downtown Duluth. Opening a door marked Mercy Hospital, Ben entered the mezzanine level of the atrium and reception area.

The atrium, built in the late eighties, was generously decorated in mauves, plums, and grays—a sure sign of that decorating era. It was well accessorized with a small jungle of live plants and trees. Standing on the balcony twelve feet above the ground floor, Ben still had to look up to see the treetops that reached for the ceiling of the three-story-high room. The room glowed from the recessed mercury vapor lighting. In another half hour, it would be filled with natural sunlight which daily bathed the indoor garden through the southern exposure of plate glass windows and skylights. Even in the dead cold of winter, this entrance to Mercy Hospital was very pleasant and offered a therapeutic calm to patients and their families in times of crisis.

Ben walked left to the bank of elevators and pressed the Up button. In a few seconds, the bell rang and one of the four sets of elevator doors opened. He walked in, inserted his staff ID card in the security check, and pressed 4. After a short ride up, the bell rang and the doors opened to a polished and sanitized hallway. He walked to a door marked 421, Trauma Monitoring, and again ran his ID card through the reader slot. The magnetic lock snapped open, allowing him to open the door and walk into the dimly lit room. He draped his down-filled parka over a chair back and set his gym bag next to it. Dr. David Parkhurst, a co-worker and friend, was seated in front of the bank of monitors, gauges, and screens. "Good morning, David. I see you're up early today, too," Ben greeted him.

"Thought I'd check out the new equipment and see if we got anything interesting."

"Mmm, hmmm," Ben mumbled as he reached for the phone and dialed... "Yeah, good morning. This is Dr. Bradley. I'm in room 421... Yes, my pager is on... Any messages? Good. I'll be up here for a while. Maybe thirty minutes." He hung up. The Trauma Monitoring Room, or TMR, recorded everything that happened in the Trauma Center at Mercy Hospital. It contained audio, visual, and equipment sensors that monitored and recorded data on each patient in the Trauma Center. There was a duplicate set of monitors and equipment for every bay in the STU or Shock/Trauma Unit, the operating rooms, and the four intensive care rooms. The TMR records could be copied and sent out to other doctors and clinics. The original records became a permanent part of the patient records by referencing a tape number and footage. The tapes were also used for educational and quality assurance purposes.

Parkhurst peered over his bifocals from a lighted bank of monitors and equipment and teased, "Now Mercy Hospital knows that Elvis is in the building. Or should I say 'God'?" The STU was Ben's turf. The staff accorded him the respect of a god or a rock star; Parkhurst didn't. Ten years Ben's senior, his approach was less than respectful, "How about kicking your stinky gym bag into the closet?"

"Come on, David. It doesn't smell."

"I have to keep you humble," Parkhurst said, smiling.

"I don't know why I let you be my friend," Ben grumbled as he moved his gym bag to a corner of the room.

"Because you need me and you crave the attention."

"Enough of the kidding around." Ben was too controlled to swear. Control was the name of the game. "How did the new equipment work over the weekend?"

"Why don't you sit down, and I'll show you?" Ben pulled up the chair with the parka draped over it and sat down as Parkhurst turned the videotape on and continued. "There were no deaths in the Shock/Trauma Unit over the weekend. All we've got to look at are some tapes of the Electromagnetic Field images of patients being treated and the staff who treated them before they were moved to another section of the hospital or released. Very disappointing."

"Why, Dr. Parkhurst, I am shocked!" Ben twisted the knife as he watched the monitor. "I thought doctors wanted their patients to live."

"You know what I mean, Ben. We already had lots of tape of perfectly healthy staff members before we installed the prototype units into the Shock/Trauma treatment bays and operating rooms. We're still waiting to see what happens with the Energy Field image of a patient in crisis or one who's dying. The only interesting thing we've seen so far is how the EF images change in damaged tissue areas."

"So, an injury did change the image's signal strength?"

"Oh, yes. Stress seems to affect the images as well. We got especially good footage of a mother who was distraught when she brought in her four-year old with a head injury." He advanced the tape and pressed Play once again. He pointed his pen at the monitor. "See, her EF showed nearly as much stress as the child's!" Parkhurst leaned back in his chair and ran his hand over his balding head. "It's all very interesting, but I'm *dying* to watch a patient in a life-threatening crisis."

"Great, then we get to watch *you* die at the same time."

"Aw shit, Ben, you know what I mean."

"It's a bit diabolical to think the machine will work the best when a patient dies."

"Well, that's one of the mysteries of life we're hoping to unravel. What really happens to the EF at times of life-threatening crises and death? Does it escape, evaporate, or dissipate into the atmosphere?"

Frustrated, Ben threw his arms up, "We already know it escapes from the bodies of animals from our lab trials."

"And if it follows, we could suspect the same for humans," Parkhurst surmised.

"Precisely."

"But the human body and mind are much more complex. The Energy Field might respond differently. Once we've identified a patient's EF frequency, maybe we'll even figure out how to prolong his life by pumping in more energy at that frequency while we repair the physical disorders."

"Or maybe we could use it to predict who's going to die before we waste valuable health care resources on a patient who should be wearing a 'Do Not Resuscitate' bracelet," Ben said as he tapped a pencil against his hand and looked straight into David's eyes.

"You can be so cynical, Ben."

"Think of the billions that could be saved. How much do you think the government and insurance companies would pay for a machine that could save that much money?"

"I think we're getting way ahead of ourselves."

"If we just use it as a diagnostic tool, we'll get these machines into hospitals and clinics years before the FDA would ever let it be used for therapeutic purposes," Ben justified. "You know it as well as I do."

They'd spent several years developing the Electromagnetic Energy Field Monitor, or EEFM, ever since David Parkhurst, an electrical engineer and medical doctor, had come to Mercy Hospital after retiring as a colonel from the U.S. Air Force.

"You know, David, you gave a great performance last week." Ben recalled Dr. Parkhurst's presentation to the Mercy Hospital Board of Ethics. Parkhurst had begun by saying that diagnostic machines such as X rays and ultrasounds bombard the patient with electronic beams, sound waves, or magnetic pulses of one frequency or another. Rather than bombardment, the Electromagnetic Energy Field Monitor was the first to consistently observe the natural electromagnetic energy field housed inside a human body. It was as harmless to a patient as a VCR camera.

Ben had watched as Parkhurst had worked his audience saying that every atom, every molecule, has electromagnetic structure which fits somewhere in the electromagnetic spectrum. Since the human body was composed of atoms and molecules, the team theorized that the energy occupying the human body must be electromagnetic. Parkhurst had referred to his diagrams on the easel at the front of the room saying if that structure exists, it should be identifiable; and if they could identify it, they should be able to measure, observe, and even manipulate it. If successful, he'd told them, it could be a major breakthrough in diagnosing and treating diseases and injuries. Mercy Hospital would become known worldwide as the innovator in this field.

Ben had been impressed as David continued by saying that the team had utilized a magnetic echo chamber which reflected the electromagnetic signals to an omni-directional cardioid sensor head mounted over a silver-plated parabolic mirrored surface. The reflected EF image was then converted to a visible frequency on a monitor by a gang of three Pentium computers. In simpler terms, he'd said, it was like a shiny miniature satellite receiving dish that reflected the EF signal into a microphone mounted in the middle.

Parkhurst interrupted Ben's thoughts, "Did you like how I joked with the chairwoman of the Ethics Board when I convinced her to stand in front of the sensor unit for a demonstration?"

"Yeah, she didn't know what you were up to. The whole board was abuzz when the unit identified her frequency and then displayed her EF image within seconds," Ben responded. "They were fascinated as you explained how, like fingerprints, every human body operates on a distinct frequency on the ultragamma wave band. I about croaked when you demonstrated how the scanner could sense multiple frequencies by taking all five board members in front of the sensor."

Ben recalled how, one by one, the board members' ghostly images had appeared on the monitor as the computers identified their frequencies.

Parkhurst nodded in agreement, "Yes, I think seeing their own blue/green EF images on the computer monitor was both exciting and eerie for them. They were surprised that their images so closely resembled a human body with a head, arms with hands, and legs with feet."

"I really liked how the chairwoman said she felt she was looking into Jello," Ben mused.

Dr. Parkhurst had completed his presentation by telling the board that their development team had learned a lot, but they had just scratched the surface. Then he requested permission to mount the units in the bays of the STU. He received overwhelming approval from the Board.

"If we could only get you in front of the regulatory board and stroke them the way you stroked the hospital Ethics Board, we could bypass years of testing. You were brilliant."

David blushed, "I'm not used to hearing praise from you, Ben."

"You deserve it, David."

"Thanks." David changed the subject, "I'd show you more tape, but it isn't very interesting." Parkhurst reached forward and hit the Stop button. "You know how important it is for us to observe life-threatening crises and even death with this machine. I want to see more than a kid with a contusion. That's why we worked so hard to convince the Ethics Board to allow us to install the prototypes in the STU."

Ben's pager beeped for five seconds, then transmitted a message from the dispatcher, "Green team, report to the STU. Code 3. ETA eight minutes. Repeat, green team...."

Ben pushed the reset button and returned his attention to Parkhurst. "The truth is, David, you're more anxious about this EF image thing than I am."

Parkhurst stroked his chin, "Yeah, I've heard the lecture before. You're just looking for another method of diagnosing the patient, but you think I'm on a quest to discover his soul."

"That's pretty much it in a nutshell. David, I think you've set yourself up for a huge disappointment. Science and medicine have gone far beyond souls and gods. This EF is purely electromagnetic in nature, not spiritual."

"Well, I think you're very curious, too," Parkhurst said as he looked directly into Ben's steely blue eyes.

"Absolutely, David. I'm *very* curious. This is medical technology at its finest. We're making history."

"Well, Dr. Bradley, this may be our link to eternity. Don't be afraid if you find your own soul."

Ben averted David's stare. "I appreciate what you're saying, David. I'll accept it as a possibility, but I think we should leave the religious study to the chaplain's staff. Besides, we took an oath to save lives. We can't let our fascination with EF's compete with our purpose for being doctors."

"This EEFM technology is really exciting, Ben. I think we're on the trail of something very, very big. Six months ago, we had no proof that an EF was real. Now... well... We don't have a clue how far this thing could go."

"David, are you prepared to meet your destiny?" There was a mocking tone in Ben's voice.

"Actually, Ben, I think I'm all right with this, no matter how it turns out. There are no ghosts in my closet."

"We've put a lot of time and money into this project, and I'm looking forward to a nice return on our investment. But now, it's time for me to go. The night shift surgeon is ready to be relieved. I told him I'd cover for him for the holiday weekend. He's got family to see in Des Moines, and he's anxious to get out of town. And I have less than eight minutes to scrub for the Code 3." Ben moved toward the door, then looked back, "This may be the case you've so anxiously awaited, but you know I'll be fighting for his life right to the bitter end."

"I'd expect nothing less, Ben."

"Great. Hey, I really need to get into my scrubs and see what's going on." Ben turned away and opened the door to leave.

Parkhurst called out, "Ben!"

"What now?"

"Don't forget to take that smelly bag with you. And remember, drop smelly bag, then scrub."

Ben picked up the bag, "Some day, David. Some day...."

VII

"Trust in the Lord with all thine heart; and lean not unto thine own understanding. In all thy ways acknowledge him, and he shall direct thy paths."
—*Bible* (KJV) *Proverbs* 3:5-6

Date: November 24, 1997
Time: 7:55 A.M.
Place: Mercy Hospital, Duluth, MN

The pager beeped. The call came in. "Trauma alert. Report to STU. Code 3. ETA eight minutes. Repeat, Trauma alert...." An elderly woman was seated at a desk in the small office next to the chapel with her head in her hands. It had been a busy night. One patient died in the cardiac care unit; another died in the hospice unit. She'd made her rounds to pray with apprehensive patients and families who were scheduled for morning surgeries. She'd just sat down for a well-deserved break when her pager summoned her to the Shock/Trauma Unit.

Even though she was not a priest, Sister Celeste worked full time as a chaplain at Mercy. Priests were scarce. Well-trained nuns were getting scarce, too. College educated with a master's degree in counseling, she was a valuable asset in a hospital setting. As a member of the trauma team, however, what she could do for a trauma patient was severely limited. Hospital protocol did not allow her or anyone from the chaplaincy to touch patients while the trauma team worked on them. The threat of infection was the primary reason. She also believed that trauma surgeons and ER doctors didn't like any interruptions in their control of the Emergency Room environment. Many doctors' opinions were that chaplains should only be allowed in the emergency department to give aid and comfort to the patient's family, not to the patient. That aid usually started with phone calls to loved ones to inform them of the patient's condition.

"I'm coming. I'm coming," she said wearily. Sister Celeste hit the reset button on her pager. The bright-eyed, sixty-two-year-old nun wore black slacks and a white blouse with the collar buttoned. A simple gold cross hung on a chain around her neck. She didn't wear a nun's habit; it wasn't appropriate for a secular environment. She wore her name tag with pride—Sister Celeste McFarlane, Assistant Chaplain.

In recent years, the chaplaincy staff had been reduced by twenty percent, from ten staff members to eight. When she retired, she expected her position would not be replaced. Mercy, like other U.S. hospitals, had been hard hit by health care reform. The chaplaincy was not a revenue generating department, so it was fair game for cutbacks; yet it seemed to go from one crisis to another. The fire that burned inside Sister Celeste was not as strong as it once had been. She had seen and experienced many mysteries and even a few miracles during her forty-year career. They sustained her, but she was burning out.

She picked up her Bible and communion kit. A patient might request Holy Communion. In case of emergency, she could give the elements that had already been blessed by a priest. If nuns were going to be placed in death's way and be asked to do a priest's job, accommodations had to be made.

The five-foot-four-inch woman snapped the office light off, genuflected, and crossed herself as she walked into the chapel. She knelt and said a short prayer for the inbound patient and for strength for herself. She crossed herself, stood up, and made a proper exit, genuflecting as she walked out the chapel door to the elevator.

VIII

"Men fear death, as children fear to go into the dark..."
—Francis Bacon, "Of Death," *Essays* (1625) (p. 134)

Date: November 24, 1997
Time: 8:04 A.M.
Place: Mercy Hospital, Emergency Entrance, Duluth, MN

Fearless pulled Medic 803 to a stop inside the emergency garage entrance to Mercy Hospital. As he opened the back door to unload the MVA victim, Jarod said his first words since his resuscitation.

"Jerry," he rasped. "Let me talk with Jerry." Fearless jumped up into the rig and bent over Jarod to listen. Jarod spoke softly into his ear, "Thanks for your prayers, Jerry. I promise I won't haunt the fire hall."

Fearless stiffened as he went pale. Jarod winked at him. Holy Mary, Mother of Jesus! Fearless wondered how Jarod could have known what he'd done, what he'd been thinking. The man had been unconscious, and Fearless was up front driving! He put his hand on Jarod's forehead and said, "I hope you make it, Jarod. I really do. God bless." Fearless quickly made a sign of a cross over Jarod, then jumped out of the ambulance. They pulled the stretcher out the back of the ambulance.

Fearless watched as Dr. Bradley and members of the trauma team began collecting data and taking over functions from Smitty and Bones. As they wheeled the gurney through the automatic sliding glass doors from the garage entrance into the Emergency Care Unit, Dr. Bradley ordered, "Take him directly to the Shock/Trauma Unit, Bay One."

Fearless called out to Dr. Bradley, "Hey, Doc, take good care of him. I know him. He's a nice guy."

"We take good care of everybody who comes here," Dr. Bradley said abruptly.

Bones turned to Fearless and asked, "What was that all about? What did the patient say to you?"

"You don't want to know."

"You don't look so good. You want to talk about it?"

"NO!"

Within moments, Ben and the trauma team had Jarod moved into the STU, off the stretcher, and onto the examining table. Ben's gaze lingered on Jenny Kragun, a registered nurse, as she prepared a fresh bag of IV fluids.

He scolded himself. *Now is not the time to be thinking about her.* He returned his thoughts to the patient as the orderly and a second nurse removed any remaining clothing which might hamper access to the patient. Once his clothing was removed, the two RN's attached new patches for the EKG monitor, a pulse oximeter to measure oxygen saturation of the blood, a urinary catheter, an NG tube into the stomach, and other tubes and leads as Ben instructed.

Wearing a set of scrubs, Ben put his stethoscope to several points on Jarod's chest and abdomen. "I don't like that rattle in his chest. Let's get an airway in him and put him on a respirator. What's the patient's name?" The recorder called out Jarod's name and vital statistics. Ben leaned over the patient and spoke clearly to him, "All right, Jarod, we're going to medicate you before we start treating you. You'll feel a little woozy, maybe sleepy. We're going to put a tube from your mouth into your lungs and use a machine to help you breathe. Any discomfort will only last for a few seconds. Okay?"

Jarod looked up at the doctor. It was difficult to tell if the patient comprehended what he was being told. "Give him one milligram of succinylcholine per kilogram of body weight intravenously. I estimate his weight at... say seventy-five kilograms." The nurse anesthetist prepared, then injected the drug into the IV line.

Ben observed the anesthesiologist and her respiratory team at work. In less than fifteen seconds, 100% oxygen was going into the patient's lungs through the ET, or endotracheal tube, and respirator, carefully monitored by the team. The anesthesiologist announced, "He's on the respirator. We've got a clear airway." If he vomited or his throat continued swelling, they'd be able to keep him breathing.

"Good, we're done with that," Ben declared. "Now, we need some X rays. Let's see what we can do to help this guy." Staff members from the lab waited for instructions as the radiology department began with a fairly standard series of pictures.

Sister Celeste stood inside the doorway to the treatment room, holding Jarod's identification papers and personal belongings in her latex-gloved hands. After helping the recorder locate vital data for the patient's record, she listened for clues about the patient's condition and offered a silent prayer for a positive outcome before beginning the job of tracking down family members. She would not be able to get close to the patient until there was a break in the trauma team's work. Dr. Bradley treated her like a germ factory that contaminated his sterile field.

The recorder stood next to her and wrote all orders and other pertinent discussions onto preprinted forms for a permanent record of everything that was observed and done for the patient. In all, eleven people surrounded Jarod. To the untrained eye, it was pandemonium, but everyone in the room knew their jobs. Each staff person from the trauma surgeon, the captain of the ship, to the lowly orderly served an important purpose. Each knew where to stand and what to do, especially when the captain gave an order.

Jarod Martin was partially aware of all that was happening to him. The lights were bright. He sensed there were people all around him. His chest and face still hurt the most. His abdomen and his neck were next. He had a terrible headache and felt woozy, but at least it was easier to breathe. He felt cold, like he was naked, or maybe it was from being stuck in his wrecked car on a dark and snowy morning.

Ben methodically assessed the patient and called out orders to the staff members for tests and treatments. "I want a full draw, a C-spine, chest and pelvic X rays. We'll take him to CT once we get him stabilized. Place a hold order for two units of blood." The laboratory technician drew three vials of blood for an automatic workup on the patient, including an ABG, or arterial blood gases test, and a type and cross-match for a blood transfusion. Later, the CT scan would scan his entire body for injuries. "I'm worried about his lung. Let's get a couple chest tubes ready to go so we can remove that field fix the medics did."

"I also see some blood in his urine. Let's do an ultrasound of the peritoneal area," Ben ordered. The catheter tube was stained red with blood. "He's probably got other damage in his abdomen. We need some pictures so we can see what we're dealing with. We'll wait to see if he stabilizes before we take any pictures of the left lower leg and ankle. Everybody clear on that?"

"You've got it, Doctor," an RN responded as she moved the ultrasound equipment cart next to the patient.

"And somebody call upstairs and see if the neurosurgeon can come down and take a look at the head shots as soon as we get some pictures."

It was time for the others to scrub for surgery. The patient's golden hour, Mother Nature's grace period, was coming to an end. An accurate diagnosis and fast action might save this patient. He was breathing with the help of the respirator. The double fluids would help keep his blood pressure up, but they needed to get fresh blood into him and find what was bleeding. They'd have to stop the blood loss to save him. Time was their enemy.

Sister Celeste looked up Jarod's phone number in the telephone directory and dialed the number. The phone rang twice before a female voice answered. "Hello, is this Mrs. Martin? Mrs. Jarod Martin? I'm sorry to be calling you so early. My name is Sister Celeste. I'm calling from Mercy Hospital. Your husband has been in a car accident... Yes, it looks very serious...."

IX

Date: November 24, 1997
Time: 8:20 A.M.
Place: Mercy Hospital, Shock/Trauma Unit Operating Room

After a chest tube replacement and a quick trip to the CT scanner, or computerized tomography scanner, Jarod was moved from the STU treatment bay into the Shock/Trauma Operating Room. His vital signs continued to deteriorate. To save time, Ben ordered a large slice CT scan of Jarod's head and torso to find any major bleeds and areas of tissue damage. He'd have to operate with that information plus the initial X rays and portable ultrasound. Fifteen minutes for diagnosis, pictures, and prep was already too much time. The lab had matched Jarod's blood type and hung two units, yet his blood pressure continued to drop.

The trauma surgical team finished scrubbing for surgery while Ben and the neurosurgeon reviewed the computer images. "Well, Ben, what's your diagnosis of the situation?" the neurosurgeon asked.

"I see several areas of concern." Ben pointed at the computer-generated images. "I need to tackle the major sources of bleeding in the abdomen and the liver. The abdomen is distended, there was blood in the peritoneum, the CT scan shows a blunt trauma to the liver, and his blood toxin levels are rising."

Ben continued, "He has several breaks in his face and jaw and a serious comminuted fracture of the femur. If it was just a simple break, it could wait to be set, but if he throws a bloodclot or some bone marrow into the bloodstream, it could be fatal. The orthopedic surgeon will be busy when he gets down here. What do you see in the skull series?"

The neurosurgeon answered, "I see some bleeding in the brain, and he's showing signs of increased intracranial pressure. I plan to drill a hole and thread a monitoring tube to the brain, right here." She pointed to the CT scan. "Then I'll be able to drain some fluid and reduce the pressure that's building."

"Judging by the PVC's he's throwing on the EKG, we can expect heart complications as well." Ben summarized, "We've got a very tough case here, but I don't let my patients go without a fight."

"Ben, your resolve is admirable," she told him, "but you know if the liver isn't functioning, his chances are minimal. The kidneys and then everything else will fail. He'll just crash."

"Your diagnosis sounds a bit callous." Ben felt personally challenged, as though she dared him to let the patient die.

"I'm sorry, Ben. Short of a miracle, I think there's little or nothing we can do, but you call the shots."

"I'll get started with the abdomen while you get going on the head," Ben said.

"You've got it, Ben."

Ben turned to the nurse anesthetist, "I want the patient fully sedated." He addressed Jenny, "Do a fast scrub of the abdomen and drape him."

As Jarod lay on the operating table with his eyes closed, he heard an ethereal voice calling to him through the quiet of his sedated semiconsciousness.

"Jarod. Jarod Martin. Jarod! Can you hear me?"

He couldn't answer because of the tubes down his throat. He projected his thoughts toward the voice. "I can hear you."

The voice spoke to him, "I am here with you, Jarod. I shall stay with you to help you through all of this."

"Where are you?" Jarod inquired.

"I am right here with you. You could see me if you'd open your eyes. Yes, Jarod, it is time. Open your eyes."

Jarod opened his eyes. He could see a very large light shining over his head and an occasional masked face of a doctor or nurse as the trauma team prepared him for surgery. One nurse leaned over him and looked down at him. She wore a mask and cap so all he could see were her beautiful brown eyes, which gave him a reassuring wink.

"Jarod!" The voice was firm.

"What?" he thought.

"Open your eyes," the voice insisted.

"I did."

"Not your physical eyes. Open your real eyes."

"What do you mean? I don't understand." Jarod was perplexed.

"They don't teach you anything around here," the voice scolded. "Close your physical eyes." Jarod followed orders. There was a reddish-pink glow from the surgical lamp as it shone through his eyelids. "Good. Now, I'll touch your real eyes. Can you feel what I mean?"

Jarod felt a warmth about his face. The most intense sensation was in his forehead, between his temples. He felt something stirring inside his head as he opened his "real eyes" for the first time. Initially, he only saw a glowing light hovering over him. He thought it might just be the lamp over the table, but this light was different. It was like a soft and pearlescent globe.

As his new eyes focused on their surroundings, Jarod began to sense a shape. There was a face and a body inside the shimmering light—or maybe the light was emanating from the body. It looked like a man, a very handsome, middle-aged man. Jarod was startled. He opened his physical eyes, but the vision stayed with him as he viewed the comings and goings of the surgical staff in the OR. The man wore some kind of robe or coat. Jarod thought maybe he was a doctor.

"I am not one of them, Jarod," the being said, smiling.

"You can read my thoughts?"

"Yes, my child, that's how we communicate."

Jarod closed his physical eyes. The image of the operating room dimmed, but it did not go away. The being remained, shining before him. "Who are you?" Jarod transmitted his question.

"I am not the One in whom you believe. I am but one who helps. My name is Crusias, and I have come for you."

"But you are so handsome... beautiful." Jarod struggled for a word to describe this... this man. "Why are you in the light?"

Crusias spoke, "The light is my essence, the core of my being." It almost seemed casual when it said, "Where I come from, we are called pure, not beautiful. There are others who are much purer than I. There are some whom I dare not look upon for fear that I would be blinded."

Crusias moved in closer. Jarod felt warmed by the light. It was like getting an all-over tan. He felt warm and loved as the pains in his body began to dissipate.

"I don't want to rush you, Jarod, but we have precious little time to visit. I'm going to give it to you straight." Crusias' voice was comforting, yet firm. Jarod listened intently. "It's time for you to leave your body; time to die, as you call it."

Jarod's physical eyes opened wide. He felt as though he tensed up against the restraining straps that held him to the operating table, yet his physical body remained motionless. He wanted to scream! He felt nauseous.

"Dr. Bradley," Jenny called.

"Yes?"

"The patient's eyes are wide open and his pupils are dilated. Something is going on." She'd seen it many times before. It was like the patient had just realized he was going to die. Ten years ago when she first saw a patient do the same thing, she'd expressed her concerns to the surgeon. It had elicited a comment like, "You just do what you're told. I'll tell you if the patient is getting better or worse." Since then, she'd kept her thoughts to herself.

Ben turned to examine the patient. He looked at the nurse anesthetist. "Isn't he out yet?"

"Just about," she responded. "He'll be fully sedated in a couple minutes."

Ben looked at Jenny and ordered, "Tape his eyes shut."

"We could wait until he's fully anesthetized."

"Jenny, tape his eyes shut now," Ben ordered.

Jenny bent over and spoke softly to Jarod, "I'm sorry, Jarod. Doctor's orders." With two small strips of tape, all of the fear and knowledge of death was blocked from the views of Jenny and the surgical staff.

Having his physical eyes taped shut helped keep Jarod's eyes moist, but it increased his level of anxiety.

"Jarod! Jarod!" He heard Crusias calling.

"Please! I don't want to die," Jarod pleaded.

"Jarod, listen to me! There is nothing we can do. Your body is damaged beyond repair—they can't fix it."

"I'm not ready. I still have things I need to do." The store had to be readied for the customers. The children still needed him. He thought of a million excuses.

"Jarod, look at me with your new eyes. Come on, I know you can do it." Jarod looked up as the being spoke softly. "I'm not some kind of alien. Don't look at me that way." He read Jarod's thoughts. "It's time for you to come home, Jarod. Things don't always work out the way we plan them. Right now, you have a big problem—your body isn't fit to stay in. You've lost a lot of blood, and they can't get more into you fast enough. You've got brain damage. And your liver—well, let me tell you, it's beyond repair. You can try to stay longer, but it will just hurt. You might last another hour, maybe more, but it won't be worth the pain. It's all right, Jarod. You don't need your earthly body."

"Why did they tape my eyes shut?" Jarod asked Crusias.

"They always say it is so your eyes won't dry out. I sometimes think it is so they don't have to commune with your fears or watch as the life energy leaves your body. I think they're afraid, but that's because they can't see the eternal life in your real eyes. Can you still see them?"

"Yes, but the vision is dimmer than it was before."

"That is good," Crusias said. "They will make it difficult enough to get you out. They will use all their power and gadgets to stop you from leaving your body, but their magic is not strong enough to keep you inside when it is time to go. They even have a new machine that can observe your life energy. They will observe your coming-out. One of them is watching and recording us this very minute—there I go, talking about minutes. Where we're going, there is no time or space as you know it. We must get to work."

"Help me, Crusias," Jarod implored. "I'm afraid."

"This will be a lot easier than coming into the world. With all your physical injuries, it just seems messier. First, we must get you out of your body. You've partially done that already. Do you remember the ambulance ride?"

"Is that what happened?"

"Yes, my child, that is what happened. You scared the bejeebers out of that firefighter." Crusias smiled his full countenance upon Jarod, engulfing him in unconditional love, a love much larger than his own. "The next order of business is to get you through the world of death and blackness to the Greatest of All Lights. I shall take you to a world more beautiful than you have ever seen or imagined. You will be reunited with others you have missed, those who have gone before you. On the way, we shall take a look at your life. It should be a thrill."

Jarod conveyed a sadness to Crusias that would fill a book. "Please don't take me yet."

"Didn't you get a chance to say good-bye to your wife?" Crusias asked.
"No."

"And you still love her after all these years, don't you?"
"Yes."

"You shall have a chance to visit her. That's not too difficult. It may be a first for you, but it happens all the time. First, we must get you all the way out of your body. Then, we shall have a couple surprises of our own."

X

"I am a spirit-body. I am a spirit-soul. I am equipped."
—*The Book of the Dead*, (circa 1500 BC)

Date: November 24, 1997
Time: 8:28 A.M.
Place: Mercy Hospital, Room 421, Trauma Monitoring Room

Parkhurst continued observing the control panel filled with monitors and electronic devices in the TMR, three floors above the Shock/Trauma Operating Room where Jarod Martin struggled to stay alive. He wished he could be downstairs helping, yet he knew his work here was also important. He heard the disk drives in the three processors humming and clicking away three feet from him in the quiet room as they monitored the conditions in the Shock/Trauma OR.

The EEFM scanner quickly picked up and deleted the frequencies of staff people as they moved in and out. The surgical staff was settling in for surgery. As they prepped the patient, Parkhurst could tell that tensions were rising as he watched the EF images of the staff members' hands and feet change from a cool blue-green to shades of orange and yellow.

"Let's see," he said to himself. "There are seven signals from seven EF images in the room—two doctors, an RN, the respiratory therapist, the nurse anesthetist, and the patient. That makes six. No way." Parkhurst recounted. The computers clicked away as they did their job. Seven lights glowed on the control panel as seven EF's were displayed on the monitor. There had to be a seventh person in the room. Parkhurst checked the video camera monitor. No one else was in the room. What in the world?

An extra EF, clear, bright, and white, floated at the foot of the operating table. Its features resembled the other human EF's on the monitor. It had a body and extremities, but there was no corresponding human image on the video camera. It couldn't be a surgical staff member of Mercy Hospital. Parkhurst fiddled with the dials, filtering the human frequencies into and out of the computer. He tried to overlay the EF's on top of the video pictures of live bodies to match the EF's with their human owners. The extra image persisted!

It was a very strong signal, brighter than the others. A thunderbolt hit Parkhurst. He practically shouted, "Fantastic! We've got a bogey in the Operating Room!" No one else was in the control room to hear him and share the vision on the monitors. He turned the tape unit to High-Speed Record. Ten times the normal amount of tape would record the event. The

EF at the foot of the operating table shone brightly on the monitor. By God! He was going to get lots of tape of this!

Parkhurst muttered, "How in the world did a bogey get into the OR? It couldn't have just floated through the wall, could it?"

Parkhurst watched as the patient's condition worsened. The EEFM showed the patient's legs fading to shades of black. There was actually *no* life energy remaining in his legs. He watched as the patient's EF image receded from his extremities and became concentrated in the area of the head, spine, and heart.

Elevated pulse, lowered blood pressure, and deteriorating blood gases meant the patient was bleeding to death in spite of two units of blood going at once. Parkhurst looked at the EKG monitor on the control panel. The patient was going into ventricular fibrillation. The crisis was here.

XI

"Or ever the silver cord be loosed,..."
—Bible (KJV) *Ecclesiastes* 12:6

Date: November 24, 1997
Time: 8:31 A.M.
Place: Mercy Hospital, Shock/Trauma Unit Operating Room

Ben watched the EKG monitor acting up. "He's going into V-fib." If he wanted the patient to live through his surgery, Ben had to get the patient's heartbeat straightened out. He ordered, "Shock him at two hundred."

"You've got it," Jenny answered, as she set the defibrillator at two hundred joules.

Jarod felt it start with a cramp, which progressed to a tight pinch in his chest. He rolled his eyeballs under his taped lids as the wave of pain surged through him. "Help me, Crusias! It hurts." Crusias tried to comfort Jarod. "Is this it? Is it time to go?"

"Yes, my child. You must stop your struggling. We have much to do."

"But the pain—it hurts so much!" It was like trying to stop a dam break.

Crusias said, "It won't help to fight, Jarod. You must come with me now."

The pain was so intense, Jarod had no options. "All right, I'll go with you." He trembled as he surrendered to Crusias. He was signing off from the world. Jarod felt a buzzing or vibration, a sense as though he were unbound, and then he felt as if he was floating. He could hear Crusias speaking telepathically to him. It was more like a stream of thought, a formal set of instructions, as Crusias talked Jarod through the process.

Jarod watched as the surgical team crowded around him, doing whatever it was they did. His pain and anxiety were abating—he felt more relaxed.

The voices and thought streams from the people in the OR penetrated Jarod's being. He tried to focus on one which was particularly strong. He saw a woman dressed in black just outside the sliding glass door of the OR. He could hear her thoughts. She was communicating telepathically like Crusias—she was praying! Still busy with Crusias, Jarod had difficulty hearing all the words that came from her into his consciousness.... "The Lord is my shepherd... yea, though I walk through... Thy rod and Thy staff... house of the Lord... look kindly upon your servant. Jarod!" she called out. "Can you hear me? The doctors are trying to help you, but I sense some kind of force has come to help you… listen to it, obey it… friends and family shall be reunited… light, go towards the light, Jarod… the light is power, the light is love… go toward the love… go to the source of power… It is God."

Jarod looked up to Crusias, "That woman is talking to me. Can you hear her?"

"But of course."

"Who is she?"

Crusias smiled. "She is Sister Celeste. She is such a goodhearted and kind woman—she would have made a wonderful grandmother. She has devoted so much of herself to learning about life's many mysteries and to helping others. You'll see her again. Actually, you will see most of them again. Don't be afraid. You're still partially connected. Can you see the cord, the shiny thread of energy?" Jarod's attention returned to his physical body. Crusias pointed to the umbilical-type cord that connected Jarod's essence to his physical body.

"Yes, I see it," he said.

"I shall lift you out of your body. We must try to disconnect you. The humans will try to make this difficult." He raised one arm and passed it between Jarod's energy and his physical body, trying to cut the connection to his body. "I order you to come out!"

XII

"Then shall the dust return to the earth as it was:
and the spirit shall return unto God who gave it."
—*Bible* (KJV) *Ecclesiastes* 12:7

Date: November 24, 1997
Time: 8:32 A.M.
Place: Mercy Hospital, Room 421, Trauma Monitoring Room

Parkhurst watched in fascination as the events unfolded before his eyes. It was incredible! God, he wished there was someone in the room to share these amazing images with him. All five members of the surgical team hovered over the patient, trying to resuscitate him. The scanner continued to observe the seven EF's of the team, the patient, and the bogey. The team was working in so close to the patient that it was difficult to see him and the extra EF image at the foot of the bed.

As the crisis progressed, the patient's image on the monitor faded from red to black in all his extremities and in his torso. Within seconds, it began escaping from the body. As it did, the colored cranial image faded from red to black.

The EF image rose out of the patient's physical body into the air above the operating table. The bogey remained at the foot of the bed. Parkhurst could almost swear that the image of the bogey was interacting with the patient. It had reached out and touched the patient's eyes, and now it seemed to have something to do with the patient's EF rising out of his physical body! Each time the bogey became animated, the patient's EF image came further out of his body. If the surgical team was going to intervene in the process, Parkhurst knew they'd have to be quick.

In the Shock/Trauma Operating Room Ben watched as Jenny set the defibrillator, "Everyone clear?"

"Clear," was the response of all as they backed away. *ZAP!* The patient's body jolted from the shock.

Ben reviewed the tape as the electrocardiograph printed the results of the shock to the heart. "Nothing," he said. "Shock him again at three hundred."

Jenny reset the controls, "You've got three hundred joules… Everybody, clear!" *Zap!* The body convulsed again.

"Still no regular rhythm on the EKG," Ben reported. "Let's try one more time at 360."

Jenny adjusted the defibrillator. "Everybody, clear!" *Zap*! The body strained against the restraints.

Ben exclaimed, "We've got a rhythm!"

Once, twice, three times—Jarod felt himself being sucked back inside his physical body each time they shocked him, as though he was sinking into quicksand. Waves of pain overwhelmed his senses. Jarod wanted to scream at them, "Please, please, just stop! It hurts too much. Just let me go. I must go with Crusias!"

Parkhurst sat alone in the Trauma Monitoring Room, holding onto the desktop in front of the monitoring panel as he maintained his watch. The EF was pulled back inside the patient's body with each defibrillation. The trauma team's efforts succeeded in resuscitating the patient on the third try at T minus 1:32, the time which had passed since the patient coded. Parkhurst could hardly believe he was actually observing the return of the energy field to the body as a result of the defibrillation. It was fantastic! There were EKG and EEG signals, signs of electrical activity in both heart and brain. The dark red EF image had returned to the cranial and heart areas of the patient's body. Parkhurst waited, but the image did not return to the rest of the body.

The bogey EF image lingered at the foot of the bed, not leaving, not moving, but changing to a bluish color around the edges. Parkhurst shouted out loud at the control panel, "Defib one more time! Do it! Come on! Do it again. You've got to get him all the way back into his body!" He reached for the microphone to broadcast his message over the PA system in the OR. How was he going to explain this? Would he tell them that there was a bogey in the room trying to pull the patient's EF out of his body? They'd think he'd lost his marbles. The patient's signal strength was dropping again. He clicked the microphone switch on, "Parkhurst here. Ben, I recommend you defib again."

He heard Ben answer, "That is contraindicated on the EKG, David. We've got a sinus rhythm back."

"Ben, the EF is only partially in the body. Look at your EF monitor. You have to shock him again." Parkhurst watched in the video monitor as Ben looked at the EEFM, then looked up at the camera mounted in the OR.

"Sorry, David, no can do. It's against protocol."

At T minus 2:57, Parkhurst fidgeted as he watched the bogey's color change back to white and become very animated. The patient's EKG went into V-fib again as the patient's EF rose up over the table. Only a small thread of energy remained connected. Suddenly, it snapped out from the body up into the EF image. The EF image in the patient's body went completely black as the EF rose nearly to the ceiling. The bogey closed in on the patient's EF and wrapped itself around it. The combination of the two energy fields shone very strongly on the monitor. The image on the screen and film began to burn from overexposure.

Parkhurst had difficulty seeing anything on the EEFM. He tried increasing the gain on the monitor and filtering out the signal strength, but the brilliant double image continued to burn into the film. Then the screen went completely black. Parkhurst muttered to himself, "We're making history, and I can't get a fucking picture!"

Crusias told Jarod, "Your physical pain is nearly over. You will hear a whooshing noise and experience darkness as you pass through the inside of the silvery cord. Then you will be completely outside your body," Crusias said to him. "This will be the hardest part of your coming out."

Jarod listened as Crusias helped him escape from the bondage of his body.

"Soon the humans will not be able to hurt you any more." This time, Jarod had succeeded in getting out entirely. Crusias told Jarod, "This is going to hurt, but it will be a different kind of pain." With a wave of his hand, Crusias disconnected Jarod's lifeline at the point where the silvery cord of energy was attached to the body. It snapped like a rubber band as it joined the rest of Jarod's EF.

"Ouch!"

"Sorry," Crusias said. "That's the worst of it. They can do as they wish with your uninhabited body. No shocks or medications will draw you back into the pain and suffering. Nothing less than the will of God will do that. You are like a butterfly coming out of its cocoon—you need time to heal, to strengthen, and to adapt to being out of your body." Crusias cradled Jarod in his arms and comforted him. "I must take you to the Source of all strength and power quickly before you lose any more of your energy. Without your physical body to sustain you, you shall remain weak until you are connected to a different source of energy. I must take you to the Light."

Crusias held Jarod securely, "Before we leave, would you like to say something to the members of the trauma team?"

"Could I tell them to stop working on my body?"

"Sure, but it might not help." Crusias held him up over the operating table and showed him how to communicate. Jarod projected his thoughts to them, "You can stop. I'm all right. Thank you."

Jarod was exhausted. Every thought, every movement, every communication took energy. Crusias looked at Jarod, still cradled in his arms. "We must go." Their takeoff through the east wall was no more dignified than Crusias' entry. They flew quickly out of the hospital, through the snowy downtown area, and down along a stretch of freeway near the downtown exits.

Jarod pointed out a car, "There she is, Crusias. That's Betty's car!" Crusias made a low pass in front of it. Betty was driving and looking out the windshield directly at him. Jarod tried to project his thoughts to her, to somehow get her attention, to say good-bye, but he was too weak. She did not seem to notice his effort. As she prepared to turn off the downtown exit ramp onto Fifth Avenue, Betty Martin looked right for traffic before turning onto the ramp. It was no good—she didn't seem to notice them in front of her. Crusias started climbing.

Jarod felt a sadness in his heart as he said, "Good-bye, my love." He watched as the view of the city disappeared. They flew higher and higher into the snowstorm. Jarod looked back toward the city—it had all disappeared in the swirling clouds. He became disoriented until they broke through the top of the snowstorm. The morning sun was bright on the eastern horizon. Thus began the rapture of Jarod Martin.

XIII

"Then a spirit passed before my face: the hair of my flesh stood up;
It stood still, but I could not discern the form thereof; an image
was before mine eyes, there was silence, and I heard a voice..."
—*Bible* (KJV) *Job* 4:15,16

Date: November 24, 1997
Time: 8:35 A.M.
Place: Mercy Hospital, Shock/Trauma Operating Room

The trauma team worked feverishly to resuscitate their patient. They'd lost the pulse—the patient was dying. The EEFM monitor had gone totally black, void of any life signs. It was T minus 4:00 minutes. Jenny was preparing for the next defibrillator shock when she heard it, not with her ears but in the center of her head. The words were clear. "You can stop. I'm all right. Thank you." She watched as others on the surgical team stopped and looked at each other.

"Did you say something?"

"Nope."

"Not me," came the denials.

The nurse anesthetist looked at the others. "Are you sure you didn't hear something?"

"Nope."

The only one left in the room was the patient, and he certainly could not speak. Jenny found herself looking right at him when she heard it. His mouth did not move. He was intubated. His body was lifeless. She was overcome with a feeling of warmth, the biggest hot flash she'd ever had! Then she knew. It would be useless to keep working on the body—Jarod was gone. She softly whispered to the patient, "Fly away, gentle spirit. Fly away." Her concentration broken, she began to cry.

Ben looked up from the patient. "Are we ready to defib again?" Jenny did not move. Ben looked into Jenny's eyes. She was crying. The longer he stared at her, the more her tears flowed. "Jenny, what's the matter with you?" She did not answer. His heart softened seeing her cry, but this was an OR and he had a patient to save. Ben said abruptly, "Maybe you'd better step out for a while." He turned and asked the other RN to take her place as Jenny exited the OR.

There was nothing else for Parkhurst to do in the Trauma Monitoring Room but sit on his hands and grumble. The overexposed tape and monitor burned out at T minus 3:41. The damned thing had had a meltdown when the two energy fields had merged. There was a flash, then nothing. He figured he had about three minutes of good, high-speed tape to watch and analyze. At least he'd be able to demonstrate the escape of the EF from the body. Hopefully, the "bogey" was on tape as well. God! He hoped at least the first three minutes of tape was good. All the other equipment was working, but the patient was gone. He had watched. He knew. It was time to talk with Ben.

Ben reluctantly pronounced Jarod dead at T minus 17:00 minutes in the Shock/Trauma OR. After repeated unsuccessful efforts to resuscitate the patient, it was time to end the surgical team's efforts. After several more defib attempts, the EKG tape remained flatlined. Frustrated, Ben resented losing his patient. Each death was a personal defeat.

Ben removed his mask and cap and said, "Tell Sister Celeste she may come in." The respiratory therapist hit the button to slide the glass door open and invited Sister Celeste into the OR. When Celeste moved inside the doorway, Ben said, "Well, Sister, I guess my job is over and yours may begin. You may now touch the patient if you feel compelled."

"You mean the corpse, don't you?" Celeste snipped at Ben as she walked up to the table where the body lay.

"Don't push me. You know the rules on sterile fields." There was nothing Ben would like more than for her to pick a fight with him.

She backed down. "Yes, of course, Doctor. I had such a strong sense of a presence with this one. I just wished I could have laid hands on him."

"I don't think it would have helped. He was in tough shape," he told her. Ben watched as Celeste made a sign of a cross on the patient's forehead with her thumb and said a short prayer. He'd used all of his skill as a surgeon and lost. Somehow this woman thought she could have helped save the patient. *At her age,* he thought, *she should know better. What good would it do to lay hands on a dead body*? He knew that Celeste would soon be busy ministering to the living. Mrs. Martin would be there directly. The widow would need her help far more than the patient. Sister Celeste gave a final blessing and stepped out of the OR to keep a watchful eye out for Mrs. Martin.

Another surgical team would soon be coming to Mercy Hospital to harvest useable tissues and organs as his donor card had instructed. Some of Jarod Martin's body parts would be flown to hospitals and body banks in the Midwestern States. Eyes, skin, and tendons were the most likely candidate tissues for transplantation to help others have a more normal life. Ben knew that was the gift of life, that something good could come from this tragedy.

Other than visit the widow and dictate the final memos for the patient's case file, Bradley would have little left to do on this case. Perhaps Parkhurst would have some new information on the performance of the EEFM. He stepped out of the OR and noticed Jenny leaning against the wall in the hallway. He checked off another mental note from his list. This one he would address immediately. He walked over to her, leaned on the wall with his arms folded, and began his reprimand, "Jenny, what happened to you in there?"

"I'm not really sure, Doctor. It was like the patient was talking to me... to us. I know it sounds strange, but it rattled me." She looked up at him with hurt in her eyes. "You didn't need to send me out. You know I don't make a habit of it."

He stared into her eyes, her beautiful hurting eyes. *Control yourself, Ben,* he said to himself. *Don't get upset with her like you did with Celeste.* Feelings surged inside him as he watched her—sympathy and compassion for those hurting eyes. He averted his stare toward the floor. "I felt like I lost you in there. I know you weren't the only one who thought you heard something, but you were the only one who lost control."

"I know that, Dr. Bradley." She wrung her surgical cap.

"I don't know what you need, but your lack of concentration and control impacts the efforts of the whole surgical team."

"I understand that, Dr. Bradley."

"Well, if you know that, then you should do something about it. We can't have this sort of thing happening again."

She blurted out, "It seemed like the patient's voice."

"Jenny, the patient was intubated and sedated. His eyes were taped shut. He was restrained." Ben tried to rationalize away her feelings. He wanted her to understand there was no way it could be the patient.

"There was a voice," she offered her outstretched hands, as if she were begging for Ben to understand. "I distinctly remember—like the patient was talking to me."

"Jenny, the patient was in full arrest." Ben punctuated his sentences with his hands. "I thought I heard a voice too, but whatever it was—it was not the patient. I'll admit it was strange. It may have been the PA system picking up another frequency. It could have been a lot of things, but I know it wasn't the patient." His rebuke was mild, softened by the feelings he had for her.

He watched Jenny as she wiped the tears from her eyes. "I know he couldn't possibly have spoken, but I heard this voice in the middle of my head. It said something like, 'You can stop. I'm all right.' Then it said, 'Thank you.' It just startled me when it happened."

"Has this happened to you before?" Ben asked.

"Yes, several times before—I just don't talk much about it. I don't know why these things happen to me, they just do. A lot of other nurses have told me about their experiences, too."

"Why are you telling me this?"

"I don't know, but I feel I need to be open with you. This experience was more intense than the others have been. Maybe I thought you'd be receptive." Ben knew she was embarassed, that she had let her professional demeanor slip. She was at his mercy.

Jenny admitted, "I've tried to harden myself to these things. I guess I was touched by it today. It won't happen again if I have any control over the situation, Doctor."

At the end of the hallway, the arrival of the elevator was announced by a single bell ring. The door opened. Ben watched as David Parkhurst stepped out and walked directly toward them. Ben finished with Jenny, "As unlikely as it seems to me, it could have been real. But even if it is, Jenny, you're too good a nurse to lose control in the middle of a code."

She apologized, "I'm sorry."

Parkhurst was two steps away when he started talking, "Sorry to interrupt, Ben, but you'd better come and see this."

"What do you have?"

"We have some amazing footage on tape. I don't want to talk about it here. You need to come upstairs right away."

Jenny gave a curious look, but Parkhurst didn't offer an explanation to her.

Ben watched as Sister Celeste came down the hall with another woman in tow. As they approached, Ben said, "This is probably the new widow." He was never very good at this. "Jenny, we'll consider this conversation closed unless you would like to continue it later."

"I think I've already said way more than I should."

"I don't know why this occurred, but I think we should just forget it. Okay?"

"Thank you, Doctor."

"Call me Ben. Will you please do me a favor and go get the patient ready for a visitation? I'll talk with his wife for a minute before I send them in."

"Yes, Doctor... er, Ben. Right away." Jenny turned and walked swiftly toward the OR door. Ben was disappointed as he watched her walk back to the OR. *This was no way to be friends*, he thought. *You dummy! You sure didn't score any points today.*

"Ben... earth to Ben! Come in."

Ben turned to his friend and said, "David, you're going to have to wait. I'll have to get back to you later."

"This won't wait for long," Parkhurst answered. "This is important. I'll make some copies of the tapes and interview some of the surgical staff members while I wait for you. Try to hurry—this is really important!"

The two women walked directly to Ben as Parkhurst departed. Sister Celeste made the introductions. Ben noticed Betty Martin's hair was uncombed, she wore no makeup, and her blouse didn't match her slacks. He figured she'd been in a big rush to get to the hospital. Ben said, "Let's find a room where we can sit down and talk." They stepped into the empty family lounge and sat down.

Betty was frantic, "I came as quickly as I could. Why aren't you working on my husband? What's going on? Driving over here, I got this awful feeling I was too late. Please, I want to see him now."

"Mrs. Martin," Ben spoke in a matter-of-fact tone of voice. "I'm sorry to have to tell you this—your husband has died. There was nothing more I could do for him."

Betty put her hands over her mouth to hide her shock as she gasped. "What do you mean?"

"I'm sorry." He knew there was no need to camouflage what the words meant. "Your husband died of complications from injuries he received in an automobile crash early this morning. The time of death was 8:49 A.M."

"What kind of injuries?" she asked.

Ben reviewed the inventory of injuries and what they had tried to do to save him. He finished by saying, "His system was beyond repair."

"Did he speak? Did he say anything to you?"

"To the best of my knowledge, he did not say anything to anyone. We intubated him shortly after he arrived." He wasn't going to tell her Jenny's ghost story. Instead, he explained the process of opening the airway to her.

"May I see him?" she inquired.

"Yes, if you wish. We still have him in the OR. Sister Celeste can take you in to see him." Ben continued, "I'm sure you are aware of your husband's wishes to be an organ donor." It didn't seem to be a good time to talk about harvesting tissues, but it had to be done now.

Betty hesitated, "Yes, I'm aware of his request."

"We'll have some forms for you to sign. I suppose this all sounds a bit uncaring to you right now, but I'm sure you see the wisdom and love that your husband has shown for others through his bequest." He was efficient and to the point as he discussed a few more details. Relations with the families of patients, especially deceased patients, was not something he enjoyed. Ben stood up to go. "I wish there was more we could have done for your husband, Mrs. Martin. I'm very sorry. Please accept my condolences."

"Thank you, Doctor."

"Our Assistant Chaplain, Sister Celeste here, will see to it that you get to say good-bye to your husband. I'm sure she will take good care of you." He reached his hand out to shake hers. It was probably the first and last time he would see this woman. "If there's anything I can do to help, please don't hesitate to contact me." She was preoccupied and did not reciprocate the handshake so Ben withdrew his hand. "Good-bye, Mrs. Martin." He turned and walked out the door, leaving the two women alone in the room.

Celeste let Betty sit in silence for a moment, then she walked over to her, placing her hand on Betty's shoulder. Betty looked up at her. Celeste said, "We really do need to go if you want to see him." She helped her up, then they walked together to the OR. Celeste tried her best to prepare Betty for what she'd see.

Betty's knees buckled as she caught the first glimpse of the sheet covering the remains of the man with whom she had shared her life. Celeste was prepared for her reaction and firmed her grip on Betty's elbow as she felt her swoon.

"You don't have to do this."

"No, no. I must do this," Betty responded. Two nurses and an aide were still cleaning up in the room. They respectfully left as Betty and Celeste approached the table. Celeste pulled the sheet back, exposing Jarod's badly bruised face. The three on cleanup had removed the tubes, washed his face, and even combed his hair. The large cuts on his face were bandaged. He looked like he could have just been resting.

Betty could not hold the tears back any longer. They gushed as she reached to touch his forehead. Celeste knew it was a very harsh reality. Gently, Betty ran her fingers down one cheek, then down his neck. The body was already starting to cool. Celeste heard Betty as she spoke softly to him. "Oh, Jarod, I just never thought it would turn out this way. We had so many things we were going to do together." She glanced at Sister Celeste. "You know, we never even said good-bye this morning. I always see him when I get to work."

"You loved him very much, didn't you?" Celeste observed.

"Oh, yes. He was a big-hearted man, kind and gentle with me, and a good father. Sometimes he worked too much, but he always felt he was building a future for us and the kids. What am I going to do without him?"

Celeste knew there was plenty to do. Betty would need help with all the details—police reports, release forms, hospital bills, insurance reports, funeral arrangements. She knew the people left behind were the ones who had to do all the work. There would almost be enough to keep a bereaved widow distracted; enough to keep her from dwelling on her loss; to fill in the void in her life for the first few days.

"Where are your children?"

"They're away at college. Oh, dear!" Betty fretted. "How am I going to tell them their father is gone?"

"Why don't we go to my office and call them?"

"Oh, thank you, Sister."

Celeste continued, "Do you belong to a church?"

"Yes. We've been members of Our Redeemer's Church for years."

Celeste had worked with most of the local pastors. "I can call Pastor Lockner."

Betty's lips trembled as she looked at Jarod's bruised face. "That would be fine."

Celeste put her arm around Betty's shoulder. "We'll have to go soon. We have to let nurses and aides finish their work. Your husband has some important work to finish, too." Celeste knew the organ retrieval team was on their way.

"I know."

"We can say a short prayer before we go."

"Thank you, Sister. That would be nice."

XIV

*"If there is a God, atheism must strike Him as less
of an insult than religion."*
—Edmond and Jules De Goncourt, *Journal,* Jan. 24, 1868,
tr. Robert Baldick (p. 663)

Date: November 24, 1997
Time: 12:44 P.M.
Place: Mercy Hospital, Room 421, Trauma Monitoring

Ben Bradley walked into the Trauma Monitoring Room four hours after he'd last spoken to David Parkhurst. Parkhurst had difficulty controlling his irritation when he saw Ben.

"Nice that you could make it," was the first thing said.

"I've been a little busy," Ben responded.

"So have I. Plus I've been up all night, and I need to go home and get some sleep." Parkhurst tapped his pencil on the desktop and shifted impatiently in his chair.

"Sorry, David. What do you have?" Ben answered.

"You're going to want to see this. I've got it ready to go. Let's have lunch brought in."

"Great idea. I haven't eaten since early this morning." They ordered sandwiches and a pot of coffee to be brought up from the cafeteria and sat down in front of the control panel. Several video and computer monitors were filled with images of snow, like television screens waiting for the VCR to begin the movie.

Ben opened, "Okay, let's see what couldn't wait."

Parkhurst pressed the Start button, simultaneously starting the synchronized images on the video tape player, the EEFM, and the replay of the readings from the other equipment which had been hooked up to the patient. "Our main feature for today is 'Death of a Patient' in a multi-media presentation. Note the time readout on the monitor. At 8:25 A.M., the EEFM indicates changes in your patient's color and the signal strength in his extremities. The EKG, EEG, and other machines are all consistent. This would be the time the EEFM indicates he began deteriorating to a near-death condition. Those signs did not change, as we suspected, for another several minutes. Here. See?" Parkhurst produced the charts and pointed to the recorder's accounting of the situation.

Ben remarked, "So far, the machine is doing what we said it would do, right?"

"Absolutely." Parkhurst pressed Fast Forward. The motors wound up and the tapes whined as they skipped ahead. "Here you take him into the OR after his X rays and CT scan. I've reviewed all of this. You can do it at your leisure. All indications are that the machine continues to do what we said it would."

He stopped the tapes at his next point of interest. "Here's where you and the surgical staff settle into the OR. Watch the frequency search. The machine is searching for your EF signals. It's accessing... accessing... Bingo! It's got your signal. Watch the video monitors. There's the picture of you and the neurosurgeon on the video, and now your EF image shows up on the EEFM. It picked up your signals very quickly because the computer has the correct frequencies for you, the staff, and the patient. You see six people in the room, right?"

"Yes, I can see it, David. So what's the big deal?" Ben answered with a hint of impatience. What was Parkhurst talking about? "We've seen all of this before."

"You'll see. I just want you to note that up to this point, the machine is working properly." Parkhurst fast forwarded the tape.

Ben fidgeted. "Let's keep moving. I have a busy schedule this afternoon."

"The machine continues to monitor the deterioration of the patient and the changing anxiety levels of the surgical staff members. I have tape of the whole thing, nearly to the end."

"What do you mean, nearly?"

"We're just about to that part. It's right about... here!" Parkhurst pressed Stop. The reels of tape stopped their whirring. "This is where he codes." Parkhurst seemed to be savoring the suspense.

"Come on, David. Turn it on," Ben said, clearly irritated now. They reviewed and discussed the slow motion replay for several minutes, watching the trauma team, the patient, and the extra EF.

"There it is, big as life. Right in the middle of the STU and nobody knows it's there." Parkhurst stopped the tapes frequently to count and compare.

"Wow! You're absolutely sure there's no one else in the room?" Ben was amazed. Now he knew why David had been so insistent.

"Absolutely. I even asked a couple of the team members. I called Sister Celeste at her home number and woke her up. She'd gone home after she'd finished working with the widow. She swears she stood by the door the whole time and nobody else went in the room." Parkhurst extended his hands as he sat forward on the edge of his chair. "But get this—she says she felt a 'strong presence'."

"And you're sure the machine didn't malfunction?" Ben asked.

"That would be a stretch of the imagination since all of the other signals were stable." He continued, "Anyway, that's the same time as the patient started circling the drain. Watch the bogey—I call it a bogey. It touches the patient's eyes or something. Jenny went to put bandages over his eyes while the nurse/anesthetist started the sedative in the IV."

"Yeah, the patient opened his eyes just then."

"Jenny didn't want to cover them right away because he appeared partially conscious, remember?" Parkhurst reminded Ben. "You *ordered* them to hurry up with the anesthesia in the IV and to tape his eyes immediately."

"You heard all that over the closed circuit system?"

"Yeah, Ben. You were a little short with them."

"I'm accustomed to having things my way in there, you know that."

"Yeah, yeah. Well, the patient's vitals really went to hell after that. The EKG, the EEG, everything." Ben watched the monitor. The extra image was clear and strong, almost white in color.

"What do you think it is?"

"Well, I sure as hell don't think it's some sort of anomaly," Parkhurst told him. "I'm not ready for a leap of faith, but it's clearly some type of energy without a physical body, similar to the EF's within our own bodies. The fascinating part about this bogey is that the patient became agitated at the same time this energy source showed up on the scanner. In a less informed time, we might have called it some sort of death vision, perhaps similar to the visions that some people have claimed during near-death experiences. The difference is we've got this one on tape!"

"Don't start getting all spiritual on me now. Let's keep this professional and use reason to describe what's going on here," Ben retorted.

"Maybe you'd better watch the rest of the tape," Parkhurst said defensively.

"All right," Ben said. "Let's speed it up." There was a knock on the door. Parkhurst said, "Maybe that's our lunch. You keep watching while I answer the door." Ben watched the tape while a young staff member, dressed in a white cafeteria uniform, brought in a brown bag with the sandwiches and coffee. Parkhurst gave him a ten-dollar bill and told him to keep the change. The kid told him the bill was eleven-fifty. Ben grinned as Parkhurst muttered a few words about inflation as he dug into his wallet. He gave the kid a five, again telling him to keep the change.

Ben reviewed the deterioration and concentration of the patient's signal. Throughout this time, the extra image endured at the foot of the bed. He made a few notes on the notepad at the console. Ben felt sad. "We're watching this patient die a second time. Geez, David, it was hard enough the first time."

"Just keep watching. There's more, much more."

As he focused his attention back on the screen, Ben was stunned by what he saw. "Each time we defibrillated, the EF was drawn back into the body!"

"Amazing, yes?" said Parkhurst.

"What happens after that?"

"When he coded the second time, he made a total separation from his body. That's also when the damned tape burned on us. Here it comes. Watch this." He turned the replay back to super slow motion.

They watched in silence. After it was finished, Parkhurst shut the monitors off. "That, unfortunately, is all the tape we have. The rest is gone." He paused before asking. "Where do you think we go from here?"

"First, we need to show this to the rest of our development team. Second, we need to figure out how to keep that tape from burning up on us the next time," Ben said.

Parkhurst continued, "If these bogey images keep showing up on our machines, we'd better start thinking about what we're going to say to the rest of the world, starting with the trauma teams who work in these rooms and the hospital Board of Ethics."

Ben hesitated, then admitted, "We all heard or felt something in there at the time the patient died."

"You all heard something?" Parkhurst was excited. "What was it?"

Ben explained what he'd heard and what Jenny told him. "She got a little emotional, and I accused her of losing control."

"You were just kind of sharing your cheerful disposition with everybody this morning," Parkhurst teased.

"I guess you could say that."

"Maybe you need to make a truce with Jenny and Sister Celeste and bring them in on this."

"Aw, David. Why them?"

"What's your problem? Why are you so condescending?"

"All these spiritual affectations are getting to me," Ben said. "I mean, they're *not* scientific. They're just irritating."

"Ben, if some of our staff really can hear or sense these energy fields, we should get them involved in the project. Wouldn't it further the interests of science? Even if it's Jenny Kragun or Sister Celeste?"

"Let me think about it."

XV

"Whoever believes that a winner is one who dies
with the most toys has yet to reach the finish line."
—Author, 1997

Date: Tuesday, November 25, 1997
Time: 6:45 A.M.
Place: Paul Sanderson Home, near Hawks' Ridge, Duluth, MN

The alarm clock buzzed persistently on the nightstand until a sleepy hand reached out and bumped the snooze bar. Paul Sanderson lay in bed wishing he hadn't made plans to go ice fishing with his shipmate, Frank. He'd stayed up 'til after one watching some old rerun war movie. He couldn't even remember the name of the damned thing. His head pounded from the twelve pack he'd drained over the course of the evening. He'd vegged out in the family room of his ranch style home in front of the 32-inch color TV, which was mounted in an entertainment center filled with electronic gizmos and videotapes.

When he'd gone to bed, Peggy, his wife, had pretended to be asleep when he halfheartedly tried to arouse her. Paul looked at her, still asleep, and thought, *If I had half a chance for a quick piece after the kids leave for school, maybe I'd stay in bed and risk some razzing from Frank for being late.* He figured the odds favored fishing by a wide margin, so he got out of bed and stretched, stepped over the pile of dirty clothes he'd left on the floor last night, and stumbled into the bathroom. He left the snooze alarm on, figuring Peggy would be rising at the second buzz of the electrically powered nuisance.

Turning on the bathroom light, Paul took aim at the stool with the seat down, then flushed the toilet. He belched as he looked into the mirror at the sleepy face with the overnight growth of stubble. The smell was reminiscent of last night's tacos and beer. He reached into the medicine chest for a couple aspirins. He thought, *Maybe I should take them with a beer and tomato juice—a little of the hair of the dog that bit me. Heck, I'll just take a six-pack out fishing.* He swallowed the aspirins with a little water.

This Duluth ship's third mate had showered, dressed, and lit his first cigarette when he called, "Peg, I'm ready for a cup of hot java as soon as you can wake up Mr. Coffee." He hit the light switch to awaken Peggy. She covered her eyes and groaned. "I could use a couple sandwiches, too," he ordered.

"The snooze alarm hasn't buzzed. What's your rush?"

71

"I got most of the day off. I told Frank I'd go fishin' with him. I'm not gonna waste it sittin' around here on my ass watching the soaps." He took a long drag off his cigarette and set it in an ash tray on his dresser as he dug into the top drawer. "You know where my wool socks are?"

"The last time I wore them…" Peggy started to answer.

"Just tell me where they are."

"You're getting warm. Just keep looking, dear," she sighed wearily.

Paul searched in the back of the drawer and pulled them out. "Here they are." He took another drag off his cigarette, then sat on the bed to put the socks on.

"Must you smoke in the bedroom, Paul?"

"A man's home is his castle, Babe. Besides, who brings home the bacon around here?" There was no answer. "If this king wants to smoke in his castle, then he does. C'mon, I'm still waiting for my coffee."

"I was hoping you'd get something done around the house as long as you were going to be home for a few days."

"Work on a holiday weekend? Peg, why do you think they call it a holiday?" Paul thought, it really wasn't even a whole weekend. Loaded, serviced, and provisioned, his ship, the *Seawinds*, would set sail the Saturday after Thanksgiving. He had a good job working on one of the big boats. He was gone for long periods of time, but his trips were punctuated by long stays at home, especially during the winter months. "I wasn't even supposed to be home, remember?"

"I know," Peg answered. "I appreciate the captain giving your crew time off to wait out the blizzard."

"I'm glad he held off, too," Paul told her. Since the sinking of the huge ore ship, the *Fritz Gaylord*, back in the 1970's, Paul knew that shipping companies were more cautious to wait out the potentially dangerous November storms that occasionally blew through the Great Lakes Region. Paul did not want to be caught on the next ship that sank in a storm on Lake Superior.

Paul watched as Peggy Sanderson—wife, mother, cook, housekeeper, launderer, and occasional lover—sat up in bed. Her hair and nightgown were tangled from a restless night's sleep. As she swung her legs over the edge of the bed, she pulled down her flannel nightgown to cover her pretties. She ran her fingers through her hair to straighten it a bit, then shuffled over to her closet to get her robe, a worn out yellow terry cloth affair that was comfortable and warm in the cold winter months. She walked out of the bedroom and into the bathroom.

As long as he had to wait for his coffee, Paul thought he might as well get his fishing gear ready. He walked through the kitchen to the back hall, searching until he found his parka and insulated boots in a closet piled high with boots, jackets, sports equipment, and smelly tennis shoes. He opened the door to the garage, turned on the lights, and surveyed the area for the most likely place to start looking for the rest of his gear. Stepping around Peggy's car and the 4x4 with the four-wheeler in the back, he dug into a pile in the corner. Paul moved mounds of prized personal possessions—bicycles and sports equipment the kids had broken or outgrown, lawn and garden tools, boring old games and toys, power tools and appliances that he and Peggy didn't use, even a juicer and food dehydrater stored in unopened boxes. He complained to himself, "Jesus, we've got a lot of stuff around here! I bet I'm still making payments on half this crap." He dug into the pile and found his ice-fishing rod, tackle box, a lifebelt, and a cooler and started packing the truck.

Paul did not consider himself wealthy. It was mass production and easy credit that afforded the American Dream to the common man. He knew he didn't really own the house, the cars, and all of these possessions; he just maintained the right to use them while he made the monthly principal, interest, tax, and insurance payments on two mortgages and the maxed-out credit cards. He talked to himself as he packed his gear, "I should be saving up for schooling for the kids and retirement's only twenty-three years away! My pension won't take care of us when it costs four bucks for a frikkin' cup of coffee. How the hell do I start saving when I can't get ahead of my payments? There's got to be a better way. Maybe some day I'll win the lottery. Can't buy all them lottery tickets and not score big somewhere along the way."

For now, Paul's desire to save was outweighed by his desire to acquire. "Besides," he justified to himself, "it's important for a working father and husband to provide these conveniences for his family." He just wished it all would fulfill the promises that the advertisers implied when they showed happy, sexy, lively people using their products.

It never worked out that way. With all the wonderful gadgets, Paul felt his life as a middle-aged, modestly successful ship's mate and married man with three children seemed to have little joy or excitement. He faced the quiet desperation of a man with a mostly monotonous job that provided just enough to make him itch for more but little opportunity to scratch.

Paul had to continue working in order to maintain his lifestyle. He only had 224 payments left on his thirty-year mortgage, thirty-two payments remaining on the cars, and the sixteen percent credit card payments looked as though they would go into perpetuity.

Finished packing, Paul walked back into the kitchen. Peggy had set out a bowl of cereal and a glass of orange juice for him and was pouring two cups of coffee.

"You don't have to go to work today, do you?" Peggy asked.

"Frank and me told the Captain we'd go in for a few hours this afternoon after we quit fishing. He wants to make sure things are battened down real good, what with the storm coming."

"You couldn't have picked a worse day for fishing," she chided him. "There must be six inches of fresh snow out there." Paul started his breakfast. They visited as Peggy made sandwiches.

"With the barometer dropping, the fish should be biting. Besides, I'll have the four wheeler." He referred to his all-terrain vehicle loaded in the back of the 4x4.

"Honey, I don't think it's such a good idea for you to go fishing. The ice isn't very thick, it's only been frozen for a couple of weeks," she advised.

"Aw, Peg, lots of guys have been out there already. Frank says the ice is a foot thick. Besides, I got a hankerin' for some fresh lake trout." Paul looked out the kitchen window as he took his first sip of coffee. The amber glow of a nearby street light illuminated the snow. "I don't have time to shovel. Doug can do it."

Paul walked a few steps down the hallway, stuck his head into the third bedroom, and snapped on the light. The floor was strewn with clothes, books, skates, a basketball, and CD's of screaming rock stars. "Hey, Dougie, time to get up! I want you to shovel before you go to school." A classic monosyllabic grunt emerged from under the fifteen-year-old's covers as his son rolled over, pulling his pillow over his head. "C'mon, Dougie, rise and shine." He returned to the kitchen where Peggy was tuning the radio.

"The kids might not even have to go to school today," she reported.

"He can still get his butt moving." Paul put his arms around Peg and gave her a hug. "Good morning. How's about a kiss, baby?" She perfunctorily turned. Their lips met. "I enjoyed the part when you moved last night," he griped.

"I just didn't feel up to it," Peggy said. "After I finished the laundry, helped the kids with homework, and went to bed alone, there wasn't much spark left."

"Well, I work hard, too, you know. It hasn't stopped me from getting the hots for you. I might not let you off so easily tonight, my little temptress," he cooed at her. He wasn't trying to be some sort of male chauvinist pig, but he didn't know how *not* to be one either. "I'm not giving up. I'm willing to wait for the best damned…"

She put her finger over his lips. "Shhh! The kids can hear you talking," she whispered to him.

"Oh, all right then." He patted her rear end, then returned to his coffee. "Hey, Dougie," he shouted from the kitchen. "Get a move on it, will ya?"

"I'm up, already, okay?" Doug said, lying in his bed. "Why do I always have to do all the shoveling?"

"You're a healthy young buck. You have enough energy for basketball so you should have enough to help a little around the house, too. Come on, let's get going."

"Yeah, whatever," he grumbled. Footsteps, a good sign. Door slams, a bad sign.

"AND CLEAN UP THAT MESS IN YOUR ROOM!" Paul hollered, then turned to his wife. "That really pisses me off. I hate it when he does that. After all we do for him, it sure seems like he hates me."

"He's a teenager, Paul, and it is *his* room."

"Yeah, but it's still *my* house."

"Don't be too sarcastic," Peggy asserted. "Even when he grumbles the loudest, he still does what you ask of him."

"I sure wish he'd do something about that horseshit attitude." Paul took a cold six-pack out of the refrigerator and stuffed it and the sandwiches in the cooler. "Gotta go, Babe. Told Frank I'd meet him out there before eight. Thanks for the breakfast... and the lunch." He held up the cooler in recognition of her efforts with bread and bologna. "See you tonight."

Paul lifted the garage door, then started the pickup. He backed down the driveway, leaving the overhead door open. Shifting the pickup into drive, he motored out of sight of the house.

After two blocks, he turned right at the stop sign onto Sixtieth Avenue East. A few short blocks down the hill toward the lake got him to Old Highway 61 where he turned left. The road up the North Shore Drive was icy underneath the snow. Traffic was slow, but it was only a couple miles to the spot where he would meet Frank. It would just be a few minutes... might as well turn on the radio... find a good country western station... have another smoke....

XVI

*"The gods do not deduct from man's allotted span
the hours spent in fishing."* —Babylonian Proverb (p. 219)

Date: Tuesday, November 25, 1997
Time: 7:55 A.M.
Place: Lake Superior shoreline, northeast Duluth, MN

Paul Sanderson turned his pickup off Old Highway 61 into the small parking area next to the Talmage River outlet into Lake Superior. Following fresh sets of tire tracks, he pulled in behind a half dozen other vehicles. He recognized one of them. It belonged to Frank Rosetti, his friend from work. Looking across the road, he could see an abandoned resort next to the river. The roadside in front of the resort was posted, "No Trespassing, No Visitors, and No Fishing." Paul knew that the resort wouldn't attract tourists, but the riverbank that ran through the property was a constant lure to fishermen, especially in the spring.

South of the old resort was the Lakeside Castle, a newly remodeled motel and restaurant. Paul would keep that place in view from out on the ice. He and Frank might stop there to warm up after fishing when the bar opened. This part of the Lake Superior shoreline was a popular fishing area. Paul knew that the warmer, nutrient-enriched currents from several rivers and streams attracted baitfish and gamefish in the late fall. His chances of catching a few lake trout were good.

Paul stepped out of his truck. The snow swirled around him in the gusty winds. *Fall fishing is a relative term*, he thought. Winter didn't officially start for nearly a month, but it sure felt like winter. His boots made six-inch-deep tracks in the snow since the rest area was not plowed. Paul looked out over the ice toward the east. He could make out the water's edge in the flying snow. He estimated the ice was solid nearly a half mile out from shore. Beyond that, he could make out the silhouette of a ship sailing into the safety of the freshwater port. Its rigging and hull, covered with snow and ice, offered a ghostly image. He knew the ship was slippery and hazardous for the crew, but God, it was beautiful!

Paul figured he could safely ride on the ice as long as he stayed near the shoreline. He could see a small gathering of stalwart fishermen standing in the wind and snow two hundred yards from the landing. Frank would be with them. It was a good day to take the four-wheeler out for a ride. One of the pickup trucks in the parking lot still had an ATV in the truck box. *I wonder why he walked out on the ice? Probably 'cause the others didn't have four-wheelers,* Paul thought to himself. *I might as well take mine out. It'll be a lot easier than walking. Besides, I can give a few rides out and back.*

Paul pulled his ramps out and hung them on the back of his truck. He jumped up in the box of the pickup and tied his fishing gear to the cargo rack of the ATV. A turn of the key, a little choke and throttle, and the four-wheeler came to life. He let the engine warm for a minute and took the time to put his lifebelt on under his coat. Paul was a hearty soul, but no fool. If he went through the ice, he had no intentions of drowning; but late fall fishing was good enough to take a few calculated risks.

Paul backed the four-wheeler down the ramps onto the snow, shifted the transmission into forward, and turned toward the lake. He revved up the engine and drove down onto the ice. He headed out toward the small gathering of fishermen, leaving a tire trail in the snow behind him.

When Paul got out to the group, he shut off the engine. The lake was nearly silent but for the wind, their own voices, and the sounds of the ice creaking under the wind and pressure of the new-fallen snow. It was peaceful and quiet, hard to believe they were barely an eighth of a mile from the shoreline.

"How're they biting?" he asked the group.

"Just a couple so far. It's a lot slower than I thought it would be," Frank replied.

"Any keepers?"

"I got a three pounder," Frank lifted the fish to show it off. It would make a nice trout dinner.

Another fisherman looked up from his seat by his fishing hole, "Not very good weather."

"No shit, Sherlock!" one of the others exclaimed.

"Hey, Paul," Frank called out to him, "you been gaining weight this fall?"

"Not particularly, but thanks for asking."

Frank explained, "The ice creaked a lot when you came out on your four-wheeler."

"How much ice is there?" Paul asked him.

"My hole is about eight inches deep." He gestured to the hole he'd drilled in the ice and was now fishing through.

Paul calculated as he spoke, "Six to eight inches ought to be plenty of ice. You know if it's even in thickness, two inches of ice can hold like a Sherman tank or at least a truck or somethin'. I read that someplace."

Frank grinned as he teased Paul, "Not much to do at night when you're out working the boats, huh? Might as well bone up on little-known facts."

"Just trying to help you guys with your continuing education credits."

Frank's line showed signs of life. He jerked his pole to set the hook and began pulling up a fish. "Come on, Paul. Get a move on. You can't catch fish by talkin' about it." He pulled up a two pounder through the hole in the ice as the small group continued to fish, drink beer and coffee, and tell stories.

Paul had only been there for half an hour when he heard a large cracking sound as it thundered under the ice between them and the shoreline.

Frank paled as he turned to Paul, "Did you hear that?"

"I felt that one! Maybe we'd better get out of here." Paul questioned Frank, "Did you bring your cell phone?"

Frank looked up as he was packing his things, "Yeah, I hope we don't need it."

"Let's get out of here," another said. "We're probably okay, but we don't want us to be the 'idiots' the Coast Guard has to rescue from an ice floe this year."

"I'll lead the way with the four-wheeler," Paul told the others.

"You be careful."

"I got my lifebelt on—I ain't gonna drown." Paul hopped on his machine and started it. Slowly, he drove straight toward shore, stopping after fifty yards. He could see a crack running parallel with the shoreline. Standing on the four-wheeler, it appeared to Paul to be about a two-foot separation. He turned the machine around and went back to the group. "Houston, we've got a problem. The ice is broken clean off at the crack. There's open water. We can't get back to shore," he explained to the group.

They agreed to proceed carefully on a path parallel with the crack until they found a place where they could cross. Paul would scout in front of the group with his machine. If the ice was broken clean off and floating out into the lake, things would get out of control in a hurry.

Paul followed the opening a third of a mile south and east, toward deeper water, as the crack led him away from the shoreline. In some places, there was four feet of open water. He located the end of the separation nearly a quarter mile out from shore, twice as far out as where he'd started. Paul figured the ice had to be weaker and thinner a quarter mile from shore. If it had broken where it was eight inches thick, it could break here any time. If it did, the only thing that would keep them from floating out into the lake would be the ragged edges of the ice pack binding on the edges of the floe they were on. He waved to the others to hurry.

His friends were nearly half the distance to Paul when he thought to turn his machine around to go back and retrieve one or more of them. As he began to turn his ATV, the wind-stressed ice gave way under his machine. A new crack opened out toward the open water as Paul and his machine broke through the ice. Paul tried to rev up the engine, but the screaming ATV disappeared below the surface with its engine and lights still on.

Paul let go of the machine as it sank. God, the water was cold. Damned cold! Colder than a witch's... well, it was really cold. His arms flailed in the water as he struggled for his next breath. He felt his limbs begin to stiffen, but he didn't sink. *Hey*, he thought, *the lifebelt worked*!

The hole he'd fallen into was ten feet across. *Keep your wits*, he instructed himself. He kicked and thrashed his way to the edge of the ice and grabbed for something solid. Facing the shoreline, he grabbed for the edge of the ice. Each time he tried, his hands and arms slipped back into the water. Three times, four times he tried. *Come on, Paul, you can do it*, he coached himself. On the fifth try, he swung his right arm out of the water nearly level with the ice and left it flat on the ice. It worked! His arm remained on the edge so that he could hold his head up and out of the water. If only he could climb out. Keeping his arm up on the ice, he felt in his pocket with his other hand for something that might work as an ice pick. Nothing. Better just hold this position until the guys got to him. His teeth started chattering.

He looked back toward the rest of the group. They were getting closer to him, but Paul realized he was hanging on the shore side of the gap. Ten feet of open water separated him from the rest of the group. Breathless from the cold, he tried to call to the others. He saw Frank talking on his cell phone. Paul figured the only way they would be able to help him was for him to let go and swim across the hole to the others. Frank and two of the other men stopped twenty-five feet away from where Paul hung on to the edge of the ice. "C'mon, you guys! Help me! I'll swim across to you."

"Don't do it, Paul. We can't get to you. There's six inches of water in your tracks. We'll *all* go swimming."

"Shit! What do you want me to do, tread frikkin' water 'til I freeze to death?"

Frank called out to Paul, "How're you doin'?"

"Jesus, Frank, I'm cold. Get me out of here."

"We can't get to you," Frank told Paul. "Unless this ice shifts, we're all gonna have to wait 'til help gets here. I called 911. They're on the way. You gotta hold on, Paul. You just gotta do it."

"If you don't get me out of here pretty damned quick, I'm gonna sing like a choirboy for the rest of my life," Paul said, trying to make light of his dilemma.

Frank knew Paul was cold. He could see Paul's blue lips and his convulsive shivering from twenty feet away. "Keep talkin' to me, man. And whatever you do, stay awake."

"I'll try. D-Did you call the Lakeside C-Castle?"

Frank was embarrassed that he didn't think of calling them. It was right across the road from them, barely a quarter mile away. Perhaps someone there could help them. He dialed information. "Operator, this is an emergency. Please give me the number for the Lakeside Castle? You'll connect me for a small what? Shit!... I'm sorry, lady. Yes, I'll pay the charge. Please! Just connect me." There was a short silence.

After three rings, a voice answered, "Lakeside Castle. Will you please hold for a minute?"

"Please! Don't put me on hold. This is an emergency."

The voice was impatient, "Look, I've got people standing here waiting. It will just be a minute or two."

"Hey! Don't put me on hold!" Frank shouted. "I've got a man through the ice in front of your place. Can you see out on the lake?"

Frank could hear the man ask someone to wait. "It's snowing pretty hard. What am I looking for?"

"I'm waving at you," Frank answered. "Can you see me on the ice?"

"Holy Mother of Mary! Yes, I can barely see you. Have you called 911?"

"Yes, they're on the way. Do you see the guy in the water?"

"Is that what it is?" the voice answered.

"We can't get to him. The ice has cracked. We've got slush and open water between us and him. Do you have someone who could come out and throw a rope or slide a ladder to him to help pull him out?"

"I don't know if…."

Frank interrupted him, "Come on, mister. You'll be saving a man's life. Please?"

"I'll see what I can do. Stay on the line."

Frank hollered, "Paul, someone's coming from Lakeside to help. He says he's gonna try something. Hang on!" After ten minutes in the frigid water, he knew Paul's body had cooled many times faster than if he'd been exposed to air. His body temperature would drop at a rate of nearly one degree per minute. "How are you doing?" There was no answer. "Paul! Talk to me!"

"I fawanna fop jibbering," Paul's speech was slurred.

"DAMMIT, PAUL! TALK TO ME!" Frank thought, *God, he's not going to make it. He's losing it, becoming withdrawn.*

Paul spoke very slowly, "I… finally… stop… jibbering."

"How do you feel?" Frank asked.

"Feel sweepy… need nap."

"Paul, don't go to sleep. Do you hear me? Don't let go of the ice, and don't go to sleep. Keep talking with me."

"Whabba should… talk about?" Paul asked.

"Anything you want. Just hang on. Help will be here soon. Can you hear the sirens? They're getting close."

"I don'… hear 'dem."

Frank could hear the sirens and see the wigwag lights as a rescue vehicle approached from the north on the old highway. In the distance he could hear more sirens approaching from the south. He wondered if the 911 operator also notified the Coast Guard. Even if they sent a boat, it wouldn't arrive for at least thirty minutes. As he scanned the shoreline, Frank saw a strange-looking apparition running out across the ice from the Lakeside Castle in... in... Holy Cow! Frank could see it was a man running clumsily in snowshoes and bright yellow rubber boots. Frank watched as the man closed in on them. He was wearing a bright orange life jacket over a purple parka and was carrying an aluminum ladder and a large rope coiled around one shoulder and an inner tube around the other. Frank nearly laughed as he watched the unlikely rescuer work his way toward Paul. He looked ridiculous, but Frank could tell this Boy Scout was prepared for action.

XVII

"Neither earth nor ocean
produces a creature as savage and monstrous
as woman." —Euripides, *Hecuba,* circa 425 B.C.
translated by William Arrowsmith (p. 700)

Date: Tuesday, November 25, 1997
Time: 9:10 A.M.
Place: Lake Superior shoreline, northeast Duluth, MN

Paul was frustrated, and he was having difficulty communicating with Frank. He'd been in the cold water for too damn long. He felt his heart slowly laboring in his chest. Why was everyone else so confused? Why didn't they just help him?

He saw a woman kneeling near him on the edge of the ice. She was crying and washing something in the icy cold water. Washing and wailing. Crying and cleansing. He tried to call out to her, "Hey, lady, stop crying. Come over here and help me, please."

The others thought he was just talking to himself. Frank yelled to him, "Hey, Paul! Who are you talking to?"

"The labee ober dere. I aked her to hep me."

"Paul, there's no one there." Frank turned to his friend, "Dammit, he's losin' it." He looked over to the landing. Firefighters were scurrying to unload their supplies and equipment from the rescue truck now parked there. It would still be a few minutes. They were a third of a mile away and would have to get to them on foot. The strange-looking apparition with the ladder and rope was closing in on them. "Hang on, Paul. Whatever you do, don't let go!"

Paul focused on the lady kneeling at the edge of the ice, "Why do you cry?"

"I am mourning those who have died in the lake."

"What are you washing?" he asked her, not so much with his voice as with his mind.

"I am washing the blood from this shirt. I must prepare it for one who will join the others," she answered.

"Woman, will you help me?" Paul reached out to her.

The woman stopped washing the shirt and looked directly at Paul. "If I help you, you must do as I say."

"I'll do anything you ask of me," he responded. "Just get me out of this freezing cold water."

"Then let go of the ice and come with me before the others can hurt you," she beckoned to him.

"The others… they told me to hang on," Paul answered.

"Then I must continue with my work." She returned to her scrubbing, ignoring him.

"Please, lady, I'm so cold. Stop washing that thing and help me. I'll do as you say."

"That is good." Paul watched her lift the dripping garment out of the water and inspect it. "It is ready," she announced.

"What do you mean? What is it ready for?" He was curious.

"The nightshirt is ready for *you*!"

Paul watched the woman stand and walk toward him. Her long red hair and her bedclothes flowed as the wind blew through them. She had no shoes! Why was she barefoot on the ice? She spoke intensely to him, "Hurry, my precious, you must not let them hurt you. You must let go. Only then may I help you. Only then, can you sing with me."

Startled, Paul Sanderson saw a purple and orange man sliding a ladder toward him. The man called out to him, "Grab the ladder!"

It seemed to Paul that Frank and the others were floating farther out… fading away. He watched a man with a ladder reaching out to him, "Come on, I know you can do it. Grab the ladder and hang on."

In a fog, Paul thought he heard the funny purple and orange man say, "He's not responding." He watched the man, as he kicked off his snowshoes and crawled out on top of the ladder toward Paul until he was directly over him. Paul heard him say, "I'm going to put this rope around you and try to pull you out. You gotta try and help me. Hang on to the rope. Can you do that for me?" He wrapped the rope around Paul's torso, under his arms, then made a knot. He pinched Paul's cheek to get his attention. "Can you hear me, Mister?"

Paul flinched, "I… hear." He held the rope, but lost his grip on reality.

He heard the siren calling to him, "Paul… O, Paul. Come to me, my precious. Let go of the ice. Do as I say, and I will take you to my bosom and hold you forever." He felt the rope tightening around him, then heard the woman scream at him, "Do not hold on to the rope, Paul! He will take you away from me. Come to me now, my precious! Let go!"

Paul observed two strange creatures wearing bright yellow space suits. He wondered what planet they were from.

Frank watched as two firefighters arrived at the scene. They wore bright yellow suits made for cold water rescues. If a firefighter fell into the water, or had to jump in, the suit would keep him afloat, warm, and dry. One of them had towed a small toboggan filled with supplies. The other towed a rubberized raft. A third and a fourth rescuer remained a hundred feet closer to shore, connected to the first two by nylon tethers. One called out to the man crawling on the ladder, "Hey, you, get out of there. We'll take over."

Frank watched as the man crawled away from the hole on top of the ladder, put his snowshoes back on and called out, "Come on, guys, I got a rope around him. Help me pull him out." He uncoiled about twenty more feet of rope and slid the ladder a few feet away from the hole. Frank thought the man was doing an incredible job. The firefighters and the man from the Lakeside Castle were ready to pull.

Frank watched Paul hanging limp at the end of the lifeline as one of the firefighters called to Paul, "All right, mister, you gotta help us now. We're going to pull you out on the count of three. Ready? On my count. One, two, three." They pulled. Paul popped out of the water onto the ice, barely moving. The firefighter nearest the hole grabbed a knot in the rope. Stepping carefully onto the ladder, he slid Paul's body away from the hole. When they got twenty feet away from the hole, they untied the rope and lifted Paul onto the toboggan and checked his vital signs.

"Hey, mister," the firefighter asked, "are you awake? Talk to us." He spoke with Paul for a few seconds as they did a quick assessment. The second firefighter clicked his microphone on, "Dispatch, this is Rescue 6. I have a cold water rescue victim. Male, about forty. He is confused and incoherent. Pulse is weak and slow. We have a short toboggan ride before we can load. The Medic unit hasn't arrived yet. We still have a half dozen others stranded out on the ice. They appear to be dry and stable so far. We'll attempt a rescue with the raft. Rescue 6, out." Next, he called over to Frank and the group, "Is anyone injured over there?"

Frank put his hands to his mouth and called to the firefighter, "We're just scared. Is Paul all right?"

"He's got a bad case of hypothermia," one answered.

"Do you have an ambulance coming?"

The first firefighter called back, "Station 8 is sending an ambulance and another rescue crew."

"Is there anything we can do?" Frank hollered.

"You just stay there. We'll get this man in first. Then we'll start shuttling you guys across the open water in the rubber raft."

Frank mumbled to himself, "'Stay where you are?' The guy has a sense of humor. We're not goin' anywhere. God, I'm never gonna live this one down."

Frank watched as the two firefighters wrapped Paul in the hypothermia blanket they'd brought out with the supplies. Without further delay, the second firefighter took off on a brisk walk toward the landing with the toboggan in tow. When he reached the third and fourth firefighters, he handed the toboggan off to one and returned, his safety line still attached.

Under the wind pressure, Frank could hear the ice floe continue grinding its way loose from the shore ice. The first firefighter turned toward Frank with a coil of rope, "I'm going to throw this line to you and you can pull the raft across the opening. One at a time, we'll pull you across the water. It'll take a while, but we'll get you all across safely."

"Thanks, we really appreciate it," Frank answered as a flood of relief overcame him. "I'll tend the line on this side and help get the others across."

"When you get across here, you better thank this fellow, too." The firefighter pointed to the man in purple.

"When this is over, I'm gonna buy you all the biggest steak dinners in town," Frank promised.

Medic 803 and Rescue 804 arrived at the parking lot. As Sawbones jumped out of the ambulance, he could see the third firefighter jogging toward the landing with a patient behind him on a toboggan. Sawbones, Smitty, and Fearless were ready to transport. Rescue 804 had two more firefighters in rubberized rescue suits and another raft. They helped carry the patient up the ramp and load him into the ambulance. Then the three firefighters began working their way back out to the rescue scene where they would stay until the fishermen were safely off the ice.

Medic 803 was ready to go. Sawbones pulled the doors shut and called, "Giddie-yap, Fearless. Let's boogey."

Sawbones could feel the ambulance slip as Fearless shifted into gear, hit the lights and siren, and pulled a U-turn onto the highway. The back tires of the ambulance skidded as they searched for traction on Old Highway 61. He heard Fearless put in the call, "Mercy Hospital. Medic 803 calling."

A voice came in clearly over the sounds of the siren, "Go ahead, Medic Eight-Ooh-Three. This is Mercy."

"We are inbound, Code Three, with a severe hypothermia case. Request Trauma Code Status. ETA is ten minutes."

"Medic Eight-Ooh-Three. This is Mercy. Confirm Trauma Code Status for severe hypothermia case. ETA ten minutes."

Smitty started removing the patient's clothing. "Gently," Sawbones reminded her. "Treat him like he might break into a thousand pieces. We'll cut whatever doesn't come off easily." They wrapped him in dry towels and blankets and started an IV of saline solution through a tubing that was wrapped in heat packs to get warm fluids into his body. "We don't want him to start warming up in the ambulance. The shock could throw his heart into V-fib or a complete arrest. We just want to stop his body temp from dropping any further." It was best to take those risks in a medical center that was fully prepared for such crises.

Smitty observed, "His body temperature is down to seventy-nine degrees; pulse is forty-two and weak; respirations are very shallow. What little he's said so far confirms that he's in an irrational state. He keeps mumbling about some woman. He says she wants him to go with her."

Paul Sanderson was afraid. It was difficult to stay awake; he felt so tired. Every time he closed his eyes, the woman was with him, hovering just over his head. She wasn't crying anymore, she was furious. She stayed in his face, "I told you I would help you. All you had to do was let go. Damn you! I would have done the rest." Her face transformed into that of an old hag with very rough and scaly skin. She hissed at him, "I guess we'll have to do this the hard way. You're coming with me whether you like it or not."

"Who are you? What do you want with me?" he asked.

The old hag spoke to him with several voices in unison, as if she were possessed by multiple personalities. "We are many. We are the legion of spirits from the lake. We have come to claim you as our own. You shall come with us. You are not protected, you have not been claimed. We have come to take you to the lake where you belong."

Paul thought his mind was playing tricks on him. "Who are you?" he persisted. His eyes opened wide. He had to stay awake. He had to fight this. If he didn't, he feared she might take him to God knows where. Her image persisted. The old hag continued to metamorphose into something more horrible, into some kind of serpent. She coiled herself around him. He felt her squeeze against his body. He could barely breathe. He was going unconscious. In a desperate attempt to free himself from her, Paul struggled against the restraints that now held him in the stretcher.

"Ged away fum me! Go way... Pease, go way!" Paul called out loud, as he tried to shake the oxygen mask from his face.

Paul could see Sawbones' face as he leaned over to look directly into his eyes. "Hey, hey, mister. It's all right. Nobody's trying to hurt you. Just relax. We're trying to help you."

Paul looked wide-eyed with panic into Sawbones' eyes. He tried to communicate with the man, but the words failed to form in his mouth. Paul tried to warn him. His insides screamed out, *She's turned into a serpent. She's so horrible! She's huge! She's gonna take me with her. Don't let her take me! Please, help me! Save me!*

Sawbones put his hand on Paul's forehead. "Calm down, mister. We'll have you to the hospital in a little bit. It's just the effects of the cold. You're going to be fine." Sawbones looked up at Smitty, "Do you think he's on drugs?"

Paul heard her say, "If he is, he's high risk."

The serpent coiled its long neck above Paul's face as it spoke to him, "Why do you talk to them? They can't help you. There is only one with enough power to save you, and He has not claimed you. You are free for the taking. You shall come with me." The serpent opened its great mouth. Paul could feel its fangs wrapping around his head. He tried to scream. Everything around him went black.

"He's unconscious," Bones said.

"Or he's leaving us," Smitty said. It was time to run through the checklist of vital signs. *One, two, three, four—check the patient out once more. Five, six, seven, eight—gotta try to change his fate.*

As he drove, Fearless broke into a cold sweat. It wasn't that hot in the ambulance. The rig temperature was set a little over room temperature. Still, he felt a deep and penetrating chill. It was as if there was some sort of evil presence. He couldn't explain it; no one would believe him anyway. It was probably just superstition. He crossed himself and said a Hail, Mary... or two.

XVIII

Paul had no idea how long it had been since he'd dreamt about being swallowed by the horrible serpent. It had to be a nightmare. He felt as though he was in a place that was dark and cold. The smells were so absolutely disgusting that he became nauseous. If evil had a smell, this would be it. The sensations made Paul nervously suspicious that he was not in control. That scared him until he retched.

He felt as if he was moving—moving through some terrible place—some vile and disgusting tunnel.

There! Off in the distance, through his confusion, he could see lights. They flashed in tones of blues, reds, and yellows. Compared to the place he was moving through, it was very bright. Paul clung to the hope that he was moving toward the lights, away from this vile-smelling darkness. Whatever awaited him at the end *had* to be better than this repugnant place. The light grew brighter. Go to the light....

Out he popped. He was still in Duluth! The snow was flying. He was moving. There were cars and trucks everywhere. He looked around to get his bearings. He was outside the ambulance! He was moving along Interstate 35 toward the downtown, floating above the ambulance. What was holding him up in the air? The last thing he remembered was the huge head of a horrible serpent trying to swallow him whole! It was like a bad dream. At least that was over. He tried to look around. Maybe he could figure out why he was floating.

Struggling for his breath, Paul felt something squeezing tightly around his body. He looked down. Whatever he was looking at was certainly not his own body. It looked more like the scaly body of a snake wrapped around the blood-stained nightshirt he recalled from his dream... Ohhhh, shit! He looked skyward, face-to-face with his worst nightmare.

The serpent looked down at him and smiled an evil smile. "Did you have a nice nap? While you were s-s-sleeping, I was busy extracting you from your useless carcass. They can have it—I don't care. I only want you, my little puppy dog. I shall claim you, and you shall be all mine."

Paul struggled to break free, to get back in the ambulance, to get back to the safety of his own body.

The serpent hissed at him, "S-S-Stop your s-s-silly thoughts. S-S-Sit s-s-still." The serpent squeezed its coils tightly around Paul until he stopped struggling. "Now, Mis-s-ster S-S-Sanderson, we could waste your time and mine, riding around on top of this s-s-silly little can, waiting for them to let you go. Pers-s-sonally, I'd rather take you to your new home. We're going to s-s-spend a lot of time together, s-s-so we might as well get s-s-started. Besides, I hate this-s-s place. You humans are s-s-so pathetic. Everyone is s-s-so busy chasing around from one place to another, yet not one of you knows where you are going. Well, things will be different for you today. Any ques-s-stions before we go?"

Paul thought to himself, *What do I ask? I haven't the first... clue.*

"Ha!" The serpent gave out a great laugh. "That's what I thought you'd s-s-say."

"You know my thoughts?" Paul asked.

"I know everything that you think and do. You are like a part of me, and you shall s-s-serve me well—it is the des-s-stiny of those who are unclaimed in *my* lake, *my* town. You are all *my* s-s-souls. I get all the unclaimed ones. I know everything that happens in this town, s-s-sometimes before it happens." The serpent gestured with its head. "Now, we must be off—my skin is s-s-starting to dry. This-s-s cold weather offends me greatly."

They flew up above the ambulance, above the city, in a giant arch back toward the lake, back to the hole in the ice from where Paul had just been rescued. As they dove at the hole, Paul could see the rescue operation. Most of the fishermen were safely across the gap in the ice, which had grown to thirty feet. His friend Frank was in one of the rafts being pulled across. Paul tried to signal to him. Frank looked up toward them as they flew to the place where Paul had fallen into the water.

"They cannot s-s-see either of us-s-s. There is no help for you." They hit the water at breakneck speed, but there was no splash! The first thing Paul saw once they were in the water was his four-wheeler lying on the lake bottom. The lights were still on! Maybe Frank could...

The serpent looked down at Paul. Its eyes pierced his essence, slicing into his soul like a cold piece of steel. She spoke, "You are s-s-so pathetic. Even in death, you love your meaningless possessions more than your own life. When I am through with you, you will wish you had not wasted s-s-so much of your life satisfying your physical desires. You were bored with the life you were given. You was-s-sted the precious time you were given! You s-s-spiced up your life with the mind-numbing monotony of picture boxes, gluttony, and overconsumption. You are lost and unclaimed, little man, because you did not know where you are going. You never did! Did you hope? Did you pray? Did you s-s-seek your Master? Did you teach the ways of life to your children?

"Worry no more about a good life, little man," she continued. "Today is a day of celebration. No longer are you lost. No longer must you wander the earth unclaimed, for today I have claimed you. You are mine, from this-s-s day forward. Do not try to think, little man. You will never find your way back.

"I assure you, little man, you shall never be bored again! You shall dwell in fear with me in the dark depths of your own ignorance and confusion. You will drink deeply from the lake of tears. I shall eat your flesh and torment your s-s-soul a thousand times. Nay! I shall torment you ten thousand times until you call out in des-s-speration to your God. But only I shall answer, for I shall be your god, and you shall come and dwell with me. Together in my world of shadows and darkness, we shall take the communion of the doomed. You shall be all things to me: my s-s-slave, my child, my s-s-servant, my s-s-supper. Come fly with me."

The serpent laughed a horrible laugh as they moved out to deep water. Paul could see the dark outline of the underside of the ice. The surface became brighter as they moved out past the ice, then faded once again into darkness as they traveled deeper, deeper.

Paul sensed that he was choking... or drowning! That's it! They were underwater and he couldn't breathe.

"Get used to it," the serpent said. "You've taken your last breath."

Paul saw nothing but the green glow of the serpent's body as they swam through the darkness. Paul gagged and choked on the cold lake water. He stopped struggling against the will and strength of the mighty serpent. Even if Paul could break the crushing hold it maintained on him, even if he could escape into the darkness, to where or what would he escape? He would surely perish. The serpent said little as they sped to only God knows where... to where God knows not. They traveled a long time and a great distance in a dimension where time and space have no meaning until they came to...

It started as a dull greenish glow in the water. As the serpent homed in on it, Paul could see that the glow was coming from an old ship. It had some sort of slimy residue smeared on the sides of the ship. It was an old wreck, covered with rust, lying on its side in the mucky lake bottom. They drew close to the bow. The name! Paul could see the name!

"Little man, why does that excite you?" the serpent asked. "You know not where you are. Is it that you can give this-s-s place a name? Does the name on the bow, *Lord Perry*, ring a bell for you? You foolish little man. This long-forgotten wreck of an old ore boat was lost with all hands on board in an early blizzard years ago. No one claimed them either. They are my little s-s-sailors, just as you shall be. They do my bidding, as you shall.

"S-S-Soon, you shall lose the thrill of knowing the name of this-s-s place. You shall learn its real name."

They moved straight to the door of the pilot house and into the room.

Paul could feel the iron-tight grip loosen around his middle. With the crushing now removed from his chest, he mistakenly felt that he would perhaps be able to "breathe" better. The only thing that changed was an increased sense that he was choking and drowning.

The serpent shackled him to the captain's wheel. "You will s-s-stay here with the others. Do not try to es-s-scape." The serpent swung its great tail around its head and lashed Paul's backside. The sting of the lashing hurt like nothing he'd ever experienced during his days alive. Then he heard her stern warning, "If you even think to escape, that will just be a small s-s-sampling of how much I enjoy teaching you the lessons of s-s-submission."

Paul thought he could see movement in the dimly lit room. He was afraid. The serpent spoke in a hissing tone, "You s-s-stay here with your new friends-s-s. It is a good day. I mus-s-st go fetch another." She beckoned the others, "Come out, my little ones-s-s. Do not be afraid. Come and meet the pretty one. Come, show him how we do things around here. I shall return s-s-soon." The serpent left the ship and disappeared into the water's darkness.

Paul sensed the shuffling of shackled feet approaching from the shadowy corners of the room. Three bodies, greatly decomposed, approached him. They were dead sailors. What little flesh they had left was held together by their rotting clothes. One of them eyed Paul with eyeballs that were only partially in their sockets. Heads and hands were bare bones.

"Has no one claimed you?" one of them asked shyly.

"I don't know. I guess not. I don't even know what it means, except that's what the serpent told me."

The second sailor approached, more gruesome than the first. He pointed a bony finger at Paul's face, "You look like a fresh one. When did you die?"

Paul panicked, "Is that what this is?"

"Don't piss me off, Mate. Answer my question."

"I'm sorry. I didn't know I was dead."

A fourth one came toward him from out of the shadows. "How did you think you got here then, you little prick?"

"I'm sorry. I really didn't know."

"Well, this ain't heaven, you little peckerhead. And you ain't gonna be so pretty for long." They all laughed as they tried to hold themselves together. Spitting some disgusting phlegm, he continued, "Who are you? What's your name, pretty boy?"

"Paul, Paul Sanderson. Who are you?"

"We're the crewmembers of the *Lord Perry*. We sank in an early winter storm many years ago. What year is it?"

"It's 1997," Paul told them.

"What day is it up topside?" another asked, thoughtfully rubbing his bony chin.

"If it's still the same day, then it's November 25th," Paul told the sailor. He turned his rotting face to the others, "It's our sixtieth anniversary, mates." Dumbfounded, Paul asked, "You've been down here for sixty years?"

They ignored his question, "I bet old scalehead has brought the pretty one to us for our anniversary dinner, to celebrate the day our employer sent us to our deaths in the great Thanksgiving blizzard of '37."

"Yeah, yeah," the others agreed as they moved in, clacking their choppers.

Paul tensed up. He knew he would lose with four-against-one odds, especially when he was shackled to the pilot's wheel, but not without a fight. How could he fight for his life if he was already dead? It made no sense. None of it did. The thought of being eaten by these foul creatures made him ill.

Paul shouted at them, "Don't come another step closer, you rotting zombies!" One of them raised a billy club over Paul's head.

"Ah, my pretty one," the first mate mimicked their master. "Now we are zombies. Why, I oughta crack you one and teach you a little respect." He began to laugh. They all laughed. All but Paul.

"What's so damned funny?" Paul asked.

The ship's steward spoke, "It's the only time we ever have any fun— you know, when a fresh one comes." As his jaw moved, a piece of loosely attached flesh bobbed up and down in the water in front of his face.

"Why's that funny?" Paul saw no humor in the situation.

The steward continued, "Because you're all scared shitless when she brings you down here to Davy Jones' locker. We ain't gonna eat you. We're just her slaves, just like you're gonna be. *She's* gonna eat you! And since you're already dead, you'll get the pleasure of watching her do it. She'll suck most of the juice right out of you, 'til you're but a fraction of what you are now. If you're lucky, she'll make a slave out of you like she did to us."

The second mate spoke, "You'll work with us, painting the ship with her green, glowing excrement, tending to her eggs, and sustaining yourself on the leftovers. When you have nothing left to offer her, she'll pack you into the hold with the rest of the lost souls on board and keep you there, in the darkness, for the rest of time."

"How many souls are there?" Paul asked.

"Maybe a couple thousand," said the first mate. "I can only guess. I'd say she brought more'n five hundred with her when we sank. She just keeps bringin' more. I've heard her talk about other ships, too."

"Who is this serpent? What is 'her' name?" Paul asked.

"We dare not say her name aloud. If you put your ear to my lips, I might whisper it to you." Cautiously, Paul leaned toward the first mate, who whispered in his ear, "She is the one they call Smoane. She's a minor lieutenant of the great serpent demon of the sea, the one who is known as

Leviathan. Don't let her catch you calling her a minor demon. She's just like a few petty bureaucrats I used to know back in my alive days. Goddamned egotists, they were. Give 'em a little power and it all goes to their heads."

Paul mused, "It's worse since you were there."

The second mate spoke, "You won't have to worry about it anymore. You'll be up to your armpits in serpentine—that's what we call it. She's a cruel master. If you don't do her bidding or if you try to escape, it will just be worse."

"I must escape from here," Paul cried. "I must go back. I don't belong here. I don't even know if I'm really dead."

The first mate smiled a gap-toothed smile with less than half a lip. "We all felt that way at first. Sixty years later, we're still here, trapped. She keeps us here against our will. No one has escaped—no one even tries. Our captain tried to organize a mutiny shortly after we sank. The Smoane found out about it and all but destroyed him. What's left of him is corked in a whiskey bottle in the bottom of one of the holds."

"No one has dared oppose her since then. She tells us we are prisoners of our own evil ways, neither loved nor remembered by our families," the steward added. "She says we're unclaimed. Only an act of the One whose name I dare not say will save you, me, or the others. He can do all things. Even thinking the name before the beast has brought swift and painful punishment. No sirree, Paul Sanderson, better not even think that name."

"We are the crew without hope. We died unnecessarily. No one heard our cries sixty years ago, and no one hears our cries today. No one remembers. There is only pain and suffering. When the beast has no more use for us, when we are spent, the only thing we look forward to is a long rest when we are cast into the endless darkness of the ship's hold with the others."

"I must get out of here. My family needs me," Paul told them.

"Stop talking! Don't even think about these things. They'll only bring you pain. You know she can read your thoughts. Stop this foolishness and accept your fate before she returns," the first mate commanded.

"I can't accept this. There must be some hope."

The steward spoke, "The only hope is if you can go back to your life—back into your body—or be claimed in death by a greater power than her. Without one of those, there is no hope. That is why we're all here, no one claimed us. No one knew of our deaths until long after we were gone. No one cared. We didn't have anyone who really loved us, and we didn't care. Hell, that's why we put out to sea in the first place. At least when we were gone, we weren't fighting with our families and friends, if you could call them that. Now no one remembers us."

The second mate rattled on, "Ten thousand years will pass, and we all

94

shall still be here. There is no hope. You must forget your foolish ideas, or we'll all be in trouble."

"The people, the medics, they were trying to save me. They were taking me to the hospital." Paul looked out the window of the wheel house and thought he saw a green glow shimmering in the distance, in the darkness and murk.

"You must stop this talk, now!" The first mate peered out the window. "Do you see the light getting brighter off the bow? The master returns. In a moment, she will be close enough to read our thoughts. Blot out all thoughts of escape from your mind. Fill your heart with fear. Do you understand me, mate? She likes it when we are all afraid."

XIX

"For unto whomsoever much is given, of him shall much be required." —*Bible* (KJV) *Luke* 12:48

Date: Tuesday, November 25, 1997
Time: 9:57 A.M.
Place: Mercy Hospital, Shock/Trauma Unit Ambulance Entrance

Fearless stood waiting next to Medic 803. In the enclosed and heated emergency garage, the ambulance started to thaw, dripping the ice, salt, and dirt which had accumulated from the run to Talmage River. He watched Sawbones and Smitty as they returned with the stretcher to the ambulance and began repacking their equipment to prepare to return to the fire hall. Fearless turned to them and asked with concern, "Do you think he'll make it?"

"Don't know," Sawbones answered. "He was nearly dead when we turned him over to the Shock/Trauma team."

"What was he talking about?"

Smitty answered, "It was like he was hallucinating before he went unconscious. He kept asking us to save him from some monster or something—kept saying, 'Don't let it take me!'"

"What do you suppose he meant by that?"

"I don't know, Fearless, but he sure was scared of something," Smitty replied. "It's like he was on a bad trip, but it's probably just the cold. His body temp was down under 80 degrees Fahrenheit. He'd been exposed to the water and cold for thirty minutes while he was being towed into land. We were lucky to slow down the loss of core temperature. They'll have a tough time saving him."

"Well, I sure got a bad feelin' about that one. I want to shower when we get back to the fire hall."

"Aw, Fearless, you're just being superstitious again," Bones said. "I didn't notice anything."

Smitty added, "It would be interesting to find out what he thought was after him. I've had a couple cases where the patients claimed to have scary death visions. Most of the ones that talk to me say they saw loved ones, angels, or even God. I mean, if their visions are real, they're quite comforting. As scared as this poor fellow was, if something was there, it really must have been bad."

The Shock/Trauma Treatment Bay bristled with activity as Ben kept everyone busy with orders. They needed to get the patient rewarmed, but there were many risks in the process. Due to cold diuresis, or the fact that Paul Sanderson had been involuntarily urinating almost continuously since he'd fallen into the water, Paul's body fluids had concentrated in the center of his body. This caused a complex depletion of blood volume, vital minerals, and blood pressure, while simultaneously raising cardiac enzymes to alarming levels. The team started forcing fluids.

"Dr. Bradley, we're breathing for him." Jenny announced they had the patient on the cardiopulmonary resuscitator and respirator which would breathe for the patient and do chest compressions automatically.

"Let's have a listen." Through his stethoscope, Ben could hear crackling sounds with each breath. "We've got a high risk of ARDS here," Ben said, concerned about adult respiratory distress syndrome. "Let's do a surgical prep and drape for the groin area. I'm going to insert a pulmonary artery catheter so we can monitor and control the patient's hemodynamics." Ben would be able to pump warmed blood into the heart. "What are his vitals?"

"The latest reading shows a blood pressure of 80/52 with an irregular pulse of sixty. His core temperature drop stopped at twenty-five degrees Centigrade, or seventy-eight point two degrees Fahrenheit. He remains unconscious with pupils dilated," said Jenny, calling off the stats.

"We're going to have to live for this patient until we get his temperature up to thirty-four degrees Centigrade, then we'll try to convert him back over to a sinus rhythm." Ben knew there was no sense in shocking the heart until it was warm enough to continue beating on its own.

"Let's finish prepping him so we can get the Bair Hugger on him and get his body temperature back up," Ben ordered as an orderly stood ready with the preheated blanket that resembled an air mattress.

A nurse checked the thermostat control. "Room temperature is up to seventy-eight degrees, Doctor."

"Good. Let's start another warm IV. I want him to get a strong dose of broad spectrum antibiotic and some heparin so we can put him on bypass. Are there any allergies listed on his ID card?"

"No allergies listed," the recorder answered.

"Get two units of fresh frozen platelets and four units of red blood cells ready," Ben ordered. "Are we getting any reports from the lab yet?"

"Yes, he has cardiac enzymes of 6500 and Glucose levels of 220."

Ben knew that the cardiac enzymes were as high as if Paul had suffered a heart attack. The glucose levels indicated that the cold temperature was blocking the release of insulin into the system, keeping his sugar levels high and mimicking a diabetic condition. Trying to balance all of the different systems was very tricky. "He's way out of whack. It sure doesn't take long for the body to get all screwed up, does it? How about his ABG's and his electrolytes?"

"We don't have those numbers yet," Jenny answered.

Ben bellered, "How long do you think this patient can wait for me to hear those numbers?"

"I'll go see what's holding them up," the lab technician answered.

"I need that lab printout, stat!"

"We're doing the best we can," he replied tensely as he turned to go to the laboratory to get the information.

Ben knew the numbers were coming quickly, but zero was the best turn-around time for the patient's sake. As the tech walked out, the X ray technician walked into the room and slapped the film into the lighted viewer on the wall.

Ben walked over to examine the pictures. "Looks like we have a real problem with the lungs. There's a small diffused pulmonary edema right there." He pointed at the area where the fluids were building up in the lung tissue on the film. "Let's hope it doesn't get any larger. We'll need to monitor that spot very closely."

The lab technician returned in less than two minutes. "Here's the lab report, Dr. Bradley."

"Finally," Ben said as he read the chart. "It looks serious, but the worst numbers are his pH, potassium, and sodium readings." Ben addressed the radiology technician, "Did Dr. Parkhurst brief you on the operation of the EEFM?"

"Yes, Doctor."

"What does the EF image look like?" The technician turned to the portable monitor to view the screen. Only the images of the staff members' EF frequencies were identified.

"Well, Doctor, if I'm reading this thing right, there's no signal identified for the patient."

"Are you sure it was fixed?" Ben's tone was accusatory.

"Well, sir," the technician gulped, "everyone else in the room has a frequency identification except the patient."

"Damn," Ben said in frustration. "Call Parkhurst and see what we're getting on the monitor upstairs."

The technician dialed. There was no answer, so he dialed a second call to have the doctor paged. Within two minutes, Parkhurst was on the line. The technician spoke with him briefly. Holding a hand over the phone, the technician reported, "He says that he's getting the same picture on the lab monitor… Holy cow! Did you see that?"

"Is that your professional opinion?" Ben was sarcastic as he turned to watch the monitor.

"I'm sorry, sir. Did you see those new images show up on the monitor? It's like they appeared out of thin air!" The technician pointed to two new images that had just shown up on the screen. They were in a corner of the room.

Ben looked at the corner of the room, but there was no one. "Did Parkhurst see that?"

"I'll ask him."

"Just put him on the speaker phone." The technician hit the switch for the speaker and cradled the headset.

"David, what's going on here? Didn't you get this thing fixed?"

"Ben, your guess is as good as mine. The machine should be working fine. I tweaked the resistors and fused it so we can turn the gain way up and still get an image. There is no EF identified for the patient. Maybe one of those bogey EF images belongs to the patient. If not, my guess is that you are working on a corpse."

"Not funny, Parkhurst."

"How soon can you defibrillate him?"

"Not for another thirty minutes." Ben's answer was not encouraging.

"We'll know if one of those energy fields belongs to the patient if it tries to reattach to the body on its own. If not, I hope they'll wait around for you to defib." Dr. Parkhurst continued, "In the meantime, I'm going to get some high speed film of this."

"What will that do?"

"We'll get this one in super-slow motion."

"What do you suppose this business with no EF in the patient means?" Ben asked.

"I really think it means the Energy Field has left his body," David's voice came over the phone speaker.

"That's probably no good, right?" Ben searched his mind for other explanations.

"That's affirmative, Ben."

"Well, what we see on the monitor makes no difference in how I treat this patient. We still need to jump through the hoops. I know we save precious few with body temperatures this low, but we have to try. Those bogey images could be 'angels of death' come to claim their next victim. Even if they are, we still stick with protocol."

In a matter of minutes, Ben had inserted tubes into the femoral vessels to and from the heart and started pumping fresh, warm blood. He knew they would need to strictly control the temperatures to avoid forming bubbles. "Set the blood flow at 3.5 liters per minute. I don't want his body to warm up faster than one degree Centigrade every four minutes. If he hasn't converted over to a normal sinus rhythm by the time he gets to thirty-four degrees or ninety-three degrees Fahrenheit, we'll try to defibrillate him. In the meantime, Sister Celeste and any immediate family members who show up may have a short visit."

Satisfied that he had done everything that could possibly help the patient, he said, "All we can do now is wait."

The two energy fields identified by the EEFM monitor remained in the corner of the room. Crusias and his companion, Winnifred, were engaged in their own consultation.

"Oh, dear me," Winnifred said. "We must be late."

Crusias was flabbergasted. "I can't believe it. It's been so busy during this awful snowstorm that we just can't keep up."

"I wonder what has become of our patient."

"Well, there's no sign of him here, Winnie."

"He can't be gone—it's not supposed to be his time. That's why we're late! We had an imminent coming-out to care for first. It wasn't time for this one," Winnifred fretted.

"It appears we've missed him," said Crusias. "Or worse yet, we've lost him."

That just made Winnifred more upset. "We shall be held responsible. Here we are, assigned to help the humans and now we've lost one. What shall we do, Crusias?" She wanted to cry. Crusias could still sense the rise in her emotions. "I mean, here we are, in a position of responsibility, and we start losing our charges. This will not set well with the High Council. We'll never get our wings this way."

"Don't go getting your tunic all in a bind. We'll think of something. Somehow, we'll get through this." Crusias was businesslike. "How about making yourself useful instead of just floating there?"

She looked at him, "What do you want me to do? I'll do anything to find him and get him back."

"Go over and see what the recorder has on the case."

"You know the humans are watching us on that machine and talking about us. If I walk over there, that woman will get all nervous and upset."

"Maybe it will do her some good. Let's give them a little surprise."

Winnifred moved over behind the recorder. Looking over her shoulder, she reviewed the paperwork. "The report says he was picked up by the Talmage River bridge. It says he's a hypothermia victim. He fell through the ice when he was riding his all-terrain vehicle on the ice, and according to this, he was hallucinating before he went unconscious. It says to check for drugs. So, Mister Know-It-All Crusias, what do you think happened?"

"Hmm," Crusias pondered. "Hallucination...near-drowning in the lake." He looked at Winnifred. "I have an idea, but first, listen to what they're saying about you."

Jenny was watching the EEFM with the radiology technician and blurted, "Look, one of the images has moved over behind the recorder!"

The recorder turned to face the vision that showed up on the monitor. "There's nothing here," she declared.

"Yeah," Jenny said, "but look on the screen."

Seeing the image positioned behind her unnerved the woman. Again, the recorder looked behind her but saw nothing.

"Jenny, the patient is over here," Ben reminded her. "He still needs our help. I expect you to maintain control in this situation. We'll worry about whatever kind of anomalies or electrical disturbances we might be getting on the monitor *after* we've saved the patient." The team resumed their work on Paul.

Winnifred was standing behind the recorder. "Crusias, look what I've done. I've frightened this poor woman. Now, are you going to share your theory with me, or do I have to torment you, too?"

"Oh, all right, Winnie. Did you ever know this human to do hallucinatory drugs?"

"Well, he has used alcohol and far too much tobacco. Tobacco is such a disgusting habit," Winnifred opined. "Both of them interfere with the human's abilities to connect with our dimension, but they're not like the other drugs that send them off on trips to the other side. They're such zombies when they get here, they don't know that they've come across."

"Come on, Winnifred. Concentrate. Do you ever recall this human using hard drugs?"

"No, Crusias, I don't."

"Well, maybe we should assume that he didn't start using them today either."

"You're probably right," she concurred.

"If they say he was hallucinating, but he wasn't on drugs, what else could cause this bad experience?"

"I don't know, but the humans like to shroud their other-worldly experiences with names like 'drug-induced hallucinations' or 'brain malfunctions.' The one I like the best is 'metabolic disturbance'."

Crusias agreed, "It sounds like a cosmic disturbance. It's really just a big name for the doctor to use when he's blowing hot air through his surgical mask because he doesn't know what's *really* going on."

Winnifred continued the thought process, "If it actually *was* a bad experience, the humans would like nothing more than to blame it on being drug-induced."

"Well, Winnie, maybe we'd better take it seriously." Crusias paused for a moment before he asked her, "Who do you know that's the meanest spirit in the whole lake? Who would try to take a human before his time?"

"You don't mean the old Smoane?" she said, extremely agitated.

"None other."

"But Crusias, she's a bottom feeder. I thought she only got the unclaimed ones that die in... in... Oh, dear me."

"In the lake. Precisely. This Sanderson fellow has been a tough customer, has he not?"

"Yes, Crusias, you're right on that account. He's not a bad person. But, he's definitely not been claimed."

"We were not there to protect him when he fell in the lake. Maybe the old Smoane is just being a little too anxious to snatch a new prize."

"Oh, no!" Winnifred began fretting again. "If the Smoane has him, it may already be too late. That poor, poor fellow. Even if we could get him back... Well, I don't want to think of the emotional scars he'd get from this experience."

"Well, Winnie, let's go on a little fishing expedition and see what we can catch. When was the last time we tried to be 'fishers of men'?"

Winnifred's eyes sparkled as she winked at Crusias. "I think you are on to something, dear Crusias."

"I told you we'd think of something."

Winnifred added a precautionary thought, "Before we go, we'd better secure permission to do an encounter. We should ask for reinforcements— the Smoane is not one to be trifled with."

"We don't need help if we can't find her and the human."

"But if we find the human is in trouble, you know we are not to encounter evil without a warrior escort," Winnie warned.

"I've confronted her before," Crusias claimed. "She is evil, but she's not too smart."

"She might recognize you or try to trick you."

"If the human is in trouble, we must hurry. We cannot waste another nanosecond. Why don't you go get help while I start searching?"

"All right, I shall go for help. I'll return very soon, but you must promise me, Crusias, that you will not get in over your head, that you'll wait until we catch up with you."

Crusias turned to leave. "Hi ho! Away we go!" This had the smell of adventure.

Winnifred cautioned him, "Be careful! Save your singing for later. The Smoane is very dangerous. If she has the human, this will be a difficult mission." She turned to leave the STU with Crusias.

In a flash of less than one frame of film, they were gone! The energy fields disappeared from the room and the EEFM. Although the recorder appeared relieved, Ben wondered if the patient really was dead.

XX

"How does one kill fear, I wonder? How do you shoot a spectre
through the heart, slash off its spectral head,
take it by its spectral throat?"
—Joseph Conrad, *Lord Jim,* (1900) (p. 216)

Crusias made a beeline to the northeast from Mercy Hospital toward North Shore Drive. He could not see where he was going after he got into the clouds. Visibility was severely limited and ceilings were down to less than 1000 feet. He missed his approach and had to cruise under the clouds for half a mile before finding his target area. On his approach, he noticed a large ice floe floating out into the lake and a gathering of people and vehicles on the shoreline. He stopped in their midst to listen for clues. Two firefighters were talking about some kind of machine as they were loading their equipment into a rescue truck. The first firefighter said, "The last guy we took across, name was Frank, said the hypothermia case dumped his four-wheeler in the lake. I betcha the Minnesota Department of Water Resources is gonna make him retrieve the machine, or he'll get fined for polluting and illegal dumping."

The second firefighter responded, "It seems so crazy, you know. Here's a guy who will be damned lucky to survive. If he does, they'll prosecute him if he doesn't get his machine out of the lake. He'll be lucky to even find it after everything freezes well enough to go searching for it. If he doesn't survive, they'll probably go after his widow."

"Yeah, like prosecuting the guy will make the lake cleaner."

"I wonder how many ships have pumped their rusty and oily bilges into the lake over the years without being fined by the DWR, even after it became illegal."

"Yeah, give me a break," the other said.

That was all the information Crusias needed. The machine—it was still on the bottom. He could start by finding it. He moved toward the edge of the ice, then dove under the water. He patrolled the edge at a depth of six feet until he saw the lights. They were dim; the battery was dying, but the headlights still glowed underwater. Crusias began circling the lake bottom, searching for some clue, some trace that might explain what happened to their charge.

It wasn't long before he found a small deposit of slime, still glowing green on the lake bottom. Crusias moved in to examine it more closely, touching it. He could feel himself weakening as he contacted the negative energy, extracting positive energy from his own essence. The green glow died away as the two charges cancelled each other. Crusias knew there were very few sources of this type of discharge. It didn't take a rocket scientist to figure out what had left the disgusting sludge. Crusias was pleased with himself. "Aha! Smoane, you old miscreant! I have a trail."

Crusias thought following the trail of slime was like tracking a submarine with an oil leak, except the trail of the Smoane was a heavier-than-water sludge that stayed on the lake bottom rather than floating to the surface.

It took Crusias some time to figure out the direction of the trail. He found three more small deposits on the lake bottom by moving in ever-widening circles from the previous dropping. After the first half mile, it was easier to follow the droppings in a straight line to the northeast. Either the Smoane was not worried about being followed, or she did not realize she was leaving a trail. Perhaps she was just careless after not being challenged for many years. It didn't matter. The only thing that mattered was to get to the human... in time.

The trip to the darkened depths of Lake Superior was but a blur before Crusias could see the dim green glow of the sunken ship lying on its port side in the mud. As he approached, he could feel the dampening effect of the negative aura that surrounded the ship. The closer he got, the more he could sense other energy forms that were like signals. There were hundreds, perhaps thousands, of them coming from the ship. From a distance, they were camouflaged by the strong negative energy of the green-glowing ship. The strongest signals, both positive and negative, came from the pilot house. The others, very weak, emanated from inside the hull of the ship. Crusias spoke softly to himself, "Smoane, you slippery old eel, I have found your lair. How long has it been? How many years? How many souls have you tormented since last we met? Well, this time you've gone too far."

He moved in closer to the ship. The hull was split near midship. A single stack was broken off and lay on the lake bottom. As Crusias cautiously moved up to the deck, he could see that the railings and cabins were heavily rusted underneath the revolting layer of glowing slime. In an eerie way, Crusias thought the green-lit ship was beautiful.

Cautiously, steadily, Crusias jockeyed to get a view into the wheel house through one of the windows. He reminded himself... do not touch the ship. Do not touch the slime, the layer of serpentine that glowed about the entire ship. Touching it could have devastating consequences.

Crusias hovered near a small porthole on the side door. Yes, yes! There he was, the human, the yet unclaimed one they called Paul Sanderson! In the dim green glow, Crusias could see that he was chained to the wheel. The Smoane was circling him, tormenting him, striking him with her tail. Crusias needed a plan.

The verbal abuse the serpent heaped on her fresh victim was enough to endure; but even worse, each sentence was punctuated with a blow from her scale-clad tail. "You are nothing." Paul received a blow to the face. "You are s-s-scum." Another blow to the midriff. "I don't even know if I want to eat you." The Smoane struck him in the groin. "You are s-s-so pathetic you wouldn't make decent s-s-serpentine." On and on, she continued to abuse and brutalize the new arrival. "Who or what are you, that you think you should be able to was-s-ste my time? I should beat you for eternity, you worthless piece of shit." She hit him again. "I s-s-sense you hope for es-s-scape. I told you never to do that!" She hit him over and over. "Never! Never! Never think of that again, you miserable little wart." The Smoane paused from her ranting and raving and, pointing her nose to the front window of the wheel house, she took a sniff. "Aha! I s-s-sense an intruder nearby."

Crusias knew she would discover him soon. He had to do something. "Think!" he said to himself. "Think of something quickly." Perhaps he could distract the Smoane. He knew he was not strong enough to fight her. Left alone, there would be little left of Paul to return to the hospital. It was time for action. Crusias moved into direct view through the front window of the wheel house. He shouted out, "Hey, you bloated old maggot, long time no see."

The Smoane looked out through a hole in the moss-covered window. "Who dares to come to this-s-s place?" she asked.

"It is I, you old hag," Crusias responded.

"You are either very brave or very foolish." Her eyes glowed a phosphorous green, and she gave a wicked smile when she spotted the intruder. "Come in. We're having a party."

"I'm not foolish, Smoane." Crusias knew he could not go into her lair. The negative energy would sap his own strength and he'd be rendered helpless.

"How is it you know my name, little one?"

Crusias replied, "Many years ago, you tried to take one of my charges." He wagged his finger at her. "Tsk, tsk, I thought you had learned your lesson." Crusias was illuminated by the bright green glow that came from the Smoane's eyes.

"S-s-so you are the one who s-s-spirited my dinner away in the dark of night. You caused me much anguish. Tell me quickly, before I destroy you, what do you wish of me?"

"I have come to return your prisoner to his body. It wasn't the human's time—you had no right to take him."

The Smoane roared. Bubbles boiled upward from her mouth. "I get all the unclaimed s-s-spirits. Go away. He is mine."

Accusatorily, Crusias pointed at her and spoke forcefully, "You took him before his time. You must go by the rules."

Haughtily, she raised her head and howled, "Damn you and your rules!" Her voice echoed through the ship. "This-s-s is not the cosmos-s-s, you fool!

This is *my* ship, *my* kingdom—I make the rules here." Again she lashed at her prisoner, still chained to the pilot's wheel. "This pathetic little man is here as my guest. He desires my company. He s-s-stays."

"We shall see about that. I'll return with help."

"You are bluffing, little one. By the time you return, there will not be enough left to rescue. I can s-s-suck him dry in an instant," she sneered. "Bring a bucket with you—I'll be glad to make a s-s-small deposit for you to take back home." She laughed, making a deep throaty sound.

"If I bring help, your disgusting little kingdom shall be destroyed, and you will be missing your tail." Crusias knew if he left, Paul Sanderson would be lost. He needed a break in the faceoff.

"If it is a fight you desire, I, too, have friends in high places. It would be bes-s-st for you to leave quietly and s-s-say nothing to your kind."

Crusias knew the forces of positive and negative were delicately balanced. If Winnifred brought warriors, they could overpower her, but the Smoane, too, could muster reinforcements. There were many on the side of Leviathan.

"Both s-s-sides would experience losses. For what? One worthless unclaimed piece of shit? It is far better you leave this place and never return."

The Smoane knew she would have huge expenses if she enlisted help. Her allies would only stand by her side for a stiff fee—on a contingency basis, of course. They'd learned that from counselors who'd come over. It would cost her one third of the precious cargo she had locked in the holds.

If this being brought help, the Smoane could lose her ship, its crew, and her entire collection of captives. She'd find herself starting over. The human wasn't worth that much. But, if she could catch the other being... if she could catch Crusias, she'd be rewarded with two meals and a beautiful bucket of shiny green serpentine. If she could take this being now, the High Council wouldn't even know where he was. They could search throughout the universe. They could confront her, but she would deny ever seeing this miserable fellow. The human would be dead and buried, her claim legitimized. There would be no threat to the Smoane and her kingdom. It was worth a try. She formed a plan in her mind. "All right, you miserable little creature, you can have him back. Here we come."

Smoane released the shackles that bound the hostage to the wheel. She hissed softly to her prisoner. "No s-s-sudden moves, my little one, or I shall take you first. You will never know the joy of s-s-serving your new mas-s-ster. You'll be gone in one quick bite."

As she pushed him into the doorway, the Smoane read new thoughts coming from the crew in the dark corners of the wheel house. Her confrontation with this being was giving them ideas. Smoane sensed thoughts of hope for the new one. They were thinking of helping this Paul Sanderson, thinking if there was hope for the new one, then maybe there was hope for some of the crew as well. The old Smoane hissed at them, "I shall deal with you later. This-s-s will cost you dearly." Her smoldering eyes narrowed into slits.

Crusias could also hear the thoughts from the crew. He sensed despair, the end of hope. The saddest day in a person's existence is when he experiences the end of hope. In that moment, in that single glance from those evil eyes, Crusias knew the first mate had lost all hope. His demise was imminent. The Smoane would obliterate them all, delivering them to the end of their miserable existence. Their spirits would be sucked dry, and they would end up in the hold of the ship with the others for eternity.

"You are so wicked. Why do you treat them so badly?" Crusias asked the Smoane.

"They are mine. Take this-s-s little one and be gone. I shall attend to the res-s-st of them as I s-s-see fit."

Crusias sensed a new spark from the first mate's essence. If he had no more hope, then there was nothing left to fear. Damn the Smoane! Damn her straight to hell for all of eternity! The first mate ran at Paul as if he were a defenseman on a blitz, and hit him squarely, popping him out of the doorway. In a single moment, the mate committed a final act of bravery and selflessness. He shouted, "Paul, remember us when you get out." Then he turned to face his destroyer.

"AAARGH!" The Smoane roared with rage. She smashed the first mate square in the teeth with a ferocious blow from her tail. Crusias watched as teeth, bones, and an eyeball took flight. The first mate's body parts bounced off the back wall, then fell toward the starboard wall of the room.

The moment of brief distraction was the break Crusias had desperately needed. He snatched Paul by his blood-soaked shirt and flew away from the ship to the southwest, through the deep, dark waters. Fly, little birds. Fly as fast as you can. The water bubbled and boiled in their contrail. Looking back, Crusias could see a green glow. The Smoane was not far behind. Better move up to the surface... might go faster... find help.

Crusias climbed several hundred feet out of the depths of the lake. He broke to the surface, hydroplaning through fifteen-foot waves with sleet spraying off the tops. With Paul in his arms, Crusias rose above the waves into a quartering wind. It was difficult to see anything through the heavy snows, flying nearly horizontal over the lake. Paul gasped his first breath of air, still not quite understanding his condition.

"Who are you?" Paul asked.

"I am a friend who has come for you. We'll talk later. Now, we must hurry."

If only I could see the shore, Crusias thought, *or the lights of a city, we could seek shelter and safe harbor. We could find help. Perhaps we could find Winnifred and the help she sought, for they would surely have followed the same trail. But wait. He and Paul were above the water and they would be tracking on the bottom. They would miss each other! Oh, Master,* he pleaded, *we need their help.*

Crusias looked down. The water beneath them boiled green. The Smoane! She'd nearly caught up with them. Her body sliced through the water like a torpedo at warp speed, quick and deadly with a phosphorus green wake behind her. The Smoane had her eyes on Crusias. He could feel the hatred. Killing them would be kind. The Smoane was bent on obliteration. Soon she would rise out of the water to confront them. Faster, must go faster. Crusias strained with every ounce of his strength. If only Paul could help....

It was now or never. "Come, my friend," Crusias implored. "You must help."

"What can I do?" Paul asked.

"You must help us fly higher and faster."

"But... but, how can I do that?"

"Do you ever remember flying in your sleep?" Crusias asked.

"Yes, but that was just a dream." Paul looked with consternation into Crusias' face. Crusias could see the question forming. "Wasn't it?"

"And if we ever get you back to your body, where you belong, I suppose you will say this, too, was a dream."

It startled Paul, "You mean...?"

"Exactly," Crusias said. "This is not a test."

"What do I need to do?"

"I want you to remember the feeling you had when you thought you were dreaming about flying. You are pure energy—you no longer have your body to hold you down. Quickly, before the Smoane catches us. We must couple our minds together and fly away from this terrible place, up high into space. She will not follow us there. I know you're short on flight time, but you must do it."

Two minds *can* think alike. Crusias sensed their essences merging. Though Paul was weak, his mind focused on escaping from the Smoane with Crusias. Their combined energies glowed as they gathered power. Then, as one, they slingshotted through the clouds faster than a rocket, leaving the raging Smoane far behind. "I knew we could do it. Look at you, Paul! You can fly!" The earthly view diminished.

Crusias heard Paul's thoughts, *This is fantastic!*

Crusias spoke, "Yes, my child. This is but a foretaste of things to come once you are claimed. You humans waste so many resources trying to conquer space with your physical bodies. It is pure foolishness. You are all capable of becoming space travelers—it just takes practice. Because you deny your own essence, you wait until your physical death to discover the most important part of you. Only when you have no choice do you leave your physical bodies behind."

Paul watched the backside of the moon shrink as they traveled far from his tormentor. "Where are we going?" Paul asked.

"We're going to the Master." The ever-brightening light seemed more like it came to them, rather than them traveling to it.

A voice came from the light, "Crusias, give me the child."

Crusias bowed down to his knees and gently placed Paul before the Master.

"You were foolish not to wait, young Crusias. You could have lost your own soul as well as your charge."

"I am sorry, Master. Please forgive me. He was in my care, and I felt responsible for recovering him."

"We shall deal with you later. Fortunately, all appears to be resolving satisfactorily. As we speak, Winnifred and her escort are encountering the Smoane. There is a great fight, but they shall be victorious. We shall win the day."

"Will she be hurt?"

"Winnifred will be fine. I shall instruct her to meet you back at the place of the host body. You must hurry, for there is much to do. Go and prepare for the trip back." Crusias departed to make preparations.

Paul heard the voice beckoning to him, "Come, my child. I shall open your eyes." Paul was immersed in total love. In a flash, in the wink of an eye, he saw many wonderful visions. It was like a movie of his life. The experiences were piled one on top of the next as though he could simultaneously view several scenes. He saw friends and places and remembered things from his childhood that had faded away from his conscious memory long ago. He saw many beautiful places. He was washed in the pool of forgiveness. His blood-stained cloak was changed into a pure white raiment. His wounds were healed, and he received a gift of renewed strength and courage. Then the Light told him he was ready to go back to his body, his earthly life.

"This place is so beautiful. Can't I stay?"

"It is not your time. You must search to find yourself and your purpose. Your recovery will be slow and painful, but you still have much to do with your life. If you do not, you will be destined to repeat your experience." Paul felt the voice shake him to the very core of his being. "The next time depends on you. Crusias will not come for you. There is only one way for Me to claim you."

"What must I do?"

"Let Me into your heart, and remember…."

"What must I remember?"

"You will know when the time is right."

"What will happen to the others? Who will rescue them from the Smoane?"

"Those things will be done all in their own time. Do not fear the Smoane. She will not bother you again."

The Light vanished as suddenly as it had appeared. Only Crusias was left beside Paul; he turned to face Crusias, knowing it was time to return.

XXI

"The fall of a leaf is a whisper to the living."
—English proverb (p. 415)

Date: Tuesday, November 25, 1997
Time: 10:55 A.M.
Place: Mercy Hospital, Shock /Trauma Unit

It took thirty minutes for Peggy and Douglas Sanderson to get to the hospital. School was cancelled. The weather forecast indicated conditions would continue deteriorating. The children were at home starting their Thanksgiving holiday early when the call had come about Paul's accident. After the Chaplain's office called, Peggy frantically asked a neighbor to come over to take care of the young ones. She appreciated Douglas' company as they drove to the hospital. The roads were getting worse.

They met Sister Celeste at the Emergency Department reception area. "Mrs. Sanderson? Hi, I'm Sister Celeste." They shook hands. "Who is this young man?" she inquired.

"This is my son, Douglas."

"Nice to meet you." She offered her hand, which he took.

Peggy fretted, "Where is my husband?"

"You may see him very soon, but first, I want to visit with you a little bit about his condition. Please, come with me." She led them into the family waiting room where they were alone. Celeste filled Peggy and Douglas in on Paul's condition, especially the part about his fibrillating heart. She tried to prepare them for seeing their loved one attached to life support.

"The doctor is doing everything he can to warm Paul's body up to where he can physically function on his own. You must understand, hypothermia is a very serious condition."

"You say he's been warming for nearly a half hour? Why does it take so long?" Peggy asked.

"They raise his temperature slowly so that he doesn't sustain any further damage."

Peggy asked, "When will they try to restart his heart?"

"It's not really 'restarting' the heart. His heart is having irregular beats so it is not pumping blood under its own power. They're going to try and get a normal rhythm by shocking the heart. They call the process defibrillation. They expect to try it when his body temperature gets back up to ninety-three degrees Fahrenheit."

"What is his temperature now? How much longer will they have to wait?" Peggy's mind was filled with questions. Only a few came out.

"I checked just before you got here. If my math is right, you know, converting from Celsius to Fahrenheit, he should be at about eighty-eight degrees." She looked up at the clock on the wall. "They might be ready to defibrillate him in about fifteen minutes. We can go now if you're prepared to see him."

Peggy walked out the back door of the family waiting room with her son and Sister Celeste, down the polished corridor to the Shock/Trauma Unit bay where Paul lay partially covered by the Bair Hugger and surgical drapes. Tubes and wires seemed to be going from everywhere on his body to machines, bottles, and bags surrounding the table. The room was filled with the sounds of monitors and artificial life support systems mechanically beeping, hissing, and suctioning. Eight doctors, nurses, and technicians were attending to her husband and monitoring the equipment in the room. It was difficult for Peggy to imagine a single bodily function that was not being sustained by some kind of device.

A nurse reminded them to be very careful not to touch or bump any of the equipment or lines. Sister Celeste introduced Peggy to Dr. Bradley, then asked nervously if it would be permissible to touch him. Ben nodded his approval. "Just don't touch anything else."

Peggy moved in closer, but Douglas held back.

"You can talk to him," Ben encouraged them. "He may be able to hear you."

Peggy stared at the lifeless body. He looked so pale. She touched his cheek, then his forehead. His skin felt cool and dry. It was difficult to imagine life existing inside. Her eyes welled with tears. *Is this it? Is this how it was supposed to end? It can't be.* She looked over to Celeste. "I don't know what to say."

"Tell him you are here, that you love him. Tell him you want him to come back. Talk about the children."

Again Peggy faced her husband, "Paul... it's me, Peggy. I'm here for you. Doug is here, too. Can you hear me?" She turned to her son, "Honey, say hello to your father." Douglas was silent.

Peggy turned back to her husband, "Paul, you've got to come back. I need you—we all need you. Can you hear me?" She waited, desperately hoping for a response. There was none. "I don't know what to say, Paul. You've just got to come back from wherever you are." She looked at Celeste, "I don't know what else to say. Can you help me?"

Celeste moved in closer. "Maybe we could say a prayer. Are you a religious person?" She moved in closer with Peggy. "We can pray together."

Peggy responded, "I don't know if we would know how to do it, Sister. It's been many years for me, since I was a child. And Douglas, well, he hasn't been very interested." Peggy was in a life-or-death crisis and felt totally unprepared for the awesome demands on her.

"It can't hurt to try. I'll be glad to help." She seemed so positive to Peggy. "Douglas, would you like to come and help, too?" she asked.

"No."

"Why not?" Peggy asked her son.

"I just don't want to," was his answer.

"Douglas, your father really needs to know you care about him. You should tell him now, honey," Peggy pleaded.

Douglas folded his arms. His eyes were red. His insides were all jumbled up. Unresolved feelings stirred inside him. Anger, denial, a sense of impending doom, fears of abandonment and death, a struggle for independence, an abundance of testosterone—every emotion that makes a teenager tick. There was no sense of proper time and place. He asserted himself, "I said no, Ma." He turned and walked out the door.

"Douglas! Come back." Peggy felt abandoned. She turned to Celeste. "I'm sorry, Sister. I don't know what came over him. I can go get him, bring him back."

"We can go sit with him later. There will be time for that. Right now, we must hurry." Again, Celeste asked, "Will you pray with me?"

"Yes, Sister, yes."

Praying and laying their hands on his head seemed so strange, so foreign to anything Peggy had ever done, but Sister Celeste encouraged and helped her. Celeste placed Peggy's hands on her husband's forehead and softly pressed them down with her own. If there ever was a time that her husband needed her love and support, it was now. Whether Paul Sanderson lived or died, Peggy wanted him to know that he was loved by her and the children.

The words came falteringly, then became more resolute. Peggy did not know if their prayers would help or not, but it was some comfort just to be doing something.

Celeste prayed that Paul would know he was a child of God. She prayed for forgiveness of sins, for healing, and other prayers for the sick. It seemed like only a brief moment before Dr. Bradley interrupted.

He offered his assurances to Peggy that they were doing everything they possibly could. They had experience in hypothermia cases. Dr. Bradley had studied and treated several similar cases over the years. Their techniques were sound, but there were no guarantees since his core temperature was as low as any they had saved before. The women would have to leave. "It's almost time for us to defibrillate him," Ben announced.

Peggy spoke as she softly touched her husband one last time, "Paul, you've got to come back. There's so much we have left to do. I love you."

Celeste took her out of the STU and guided her back to the family room. Douglas stood in the room, facing the corner. They would wait there until they got word on the defibrillation attempt. For them, an eternity would pass in the next twenty minutes.

Dr. Bradley was all business as he updated himself and the team with the patient's latest vital statistics. "Set for 100 joules and stand clear," he ordered. "Now!" *Zap*! The electric charge coursed through Paul's chest, shocking his heart. Ben looked at the EKG. No change.

"Ben," Parkhurst called down on the intercom. "There's a new EF image showing up on the monitor."

"Do you have a frequency?" Ben stepped back from the patient and looked into the screen of the monitor located in the STU. The radiology technician pointed to the bogey that Parkhurst was talking about.

"Yes."

"Does it belong to the patient?"

"I have no idea, but the frequency is the same as one of the two bogeys that were in the room before."

"What do you think it is?" Ben asked.

"I don't know, Ben. Whatever it is, it's just staying in the back of the room."

"What do you want me to do, talk to it?" Ben asked sarcastically.

"I think all we can do is watch it, Ben."

"Well, I'm getting no response from the defibrillation. I'm going to let him warm up one more degree and defibrillate again in about two minutes."

Parkhurst said, "Ben, I don't think the patient's EF is there... and if it's not there, you're not going to be able to do a thing."

"You're going way out on a limb now, David." Ben's eyes narrowed as he snapped back at the words that came over the intercom.

"Hey, Ben, it's not my fault. The image is on the screen—the frequency is the same as before. I just don't know if it belongs to the patient."

"Well, dammit," Ben asserted. "Wherever he is, he'd better hurry back, or I'll have to pronounce him dead."

In the corner of the STU, Winnifred was most unhappy to hear the conversation. After all the trouble they'd gone to; after anguishing over the fact they'd lost their charge; after facing and soliciting help from the fierce warrior; after fighting the Smoane; now, the doctor was going to give up?

Quit? It cannot happen that way! Two minutes! Crusias had two minutes to get back with the essence of this man if they were going to save his life. There was little she could do but wait. Her image remained motionless on the two EEFM monitors.

XXII

"There must always be a struggle between a father and son,
while one aims at power and the other at independence."
—Samuel Johnson, quoted in Boswell's *Life of Samuel Johnson*,
(July 14, 1763) (p. 603)

Crusias and Paul made their approach to the Duluth area. They'd come into earth's orbit from the east over the Atlantic Ocean on about the forty-eighth parallel. They tracked directly over Newfoundland, over the St. Lawrence Seaway, to Quebec, Canada. Too far south. Crusias adjusted his flight path a bit to the north. There, that was better. Lake Huron was south of them. They passed directly over Sudbury. That was the last time they would see old *terra firma* until they dropped through the thick cloud bank.

The storm covered a five-state area. Crusias would have to estimate where they should try to drop down through the clouds. Although he could handle the complexities of celestial navigation, a five-state-wide storm system reduced Crusias to navigating by the bootstrap system. Airline pilots were better equipped to fly through storms. Unlike an airliner, if Crusias missed an approach or landing, the error would not be fatal, but it did mean extra time.

He estimated ten more seconds of flight time at their current airspeed and course. He reduced his airspeed and dropped down into the cloudbank. As they neared the ground, he would have to slow down—it's just the way it was. Light speed wasn't very effective when you were trying to find landmarks. The ceilings were low, and Crusias needed to take a look. Visibility was not much past his nose until he broke through the clouds, and even then, it was down to half a mile and sometimes less.

At least it was daylight. Crusias could see they were over water. They dropped lower, lower, until once again they were just over the large waves. Expecting to be over Lake Superior, he continued to fly in a straight line to the west until he spotted the craggy western shoreline of the lake. Crusias moved onshore to find a landmark. It came soon enough. Crusias recognized the Split Rock Lighthouse.

Paul spoke, "We missed Duluth by more than fifty-five miles."

Crusias responded, "Not bad, considering the weather."

"How long before we get there?" Paul asked.

"A couple of minutes in earth time." Crusias turned southeast. He followed the shoreline as they traveled down the North Shore Drive. The miles melted away as they passed Gooseberry Falls, Two Harbors, and then made their final approach to Duluth. At sixteen hundred miles per hour, the last twenty miles was a blur.

He began tracking the highways, following Old Highway 61, and then Interstate 35 into the harbor and downtown area. As they passed Brighton Beach, Paul asked, "Where am I?" Crusias understood that Paul meant his body.

"Just stick with me, kid. I'll get you there." Crusias' eyes sparkled. He was pleased with himself. This was adventure! The smokestack of the old Fitgers building loomed large ahead of them as Crusias pulled a hard right and hopscotched up to the hospital area. He made a beeline for the emergency entrance of Mercy Hospital. Paul tried to warn Crusias that the door was closed, that they had to open it... too late!

Once they were inside, Crusias moved directly to the STU bay and once again, passed right through the door. "No problem. Doors, walls, mountains, planets—they're all the same." They stopped in the back of the room next to Winnifred.

Crusias' grin was ear to ear. "I hope we're not late."

Winnifred looked at them, then said with displeasure, "Sure is nice you boys could make it back. Dr. Bradley is talking about giving up on you." Crusias surveyed the scene in the STU as the doctors and medical staff prepared the patient for another defibrillation attempt. "You're not a moment too soon. They are going to try another defibrillation in a couple minutes."

"A couple minutes? We've got lots of time." Crusias made the introductions, "Paul Sanderson, this is Winnifred, my partner 'til the end of time. She's been working very hard on your case, too. Winnifred, say hello to Paul Sanderson." They communicated briefly, then they touched and their minds and hearts met.

Crusias asked, "Are any of his loved ones here?"

Winnifred answered, "His wife and son are with Celeste in the family waiting room." She looked at Paul, "It's not going well for your son. He is very confused. You'll need to help him when you get back."

"Well, let's go see them," Crusias said.

Paul moved across the room, through the wall, and to the hall with Crusias and Winnifred. Quickly they passed into the family waiting room. Paul saw Peggy seated in a chair on one side of the room. She was crying as she watched the scene unfold between Sister Celeste and Douglas.

Douglas was crying as he tried to express his feelings to Celeste. "I don't hate him—I don't know what I feel. He's gone so much. And when he's home, we just seem to fight all the time."

"Why, Douglas?"

"I don't know! I guess maybe some of it is that he still treats me like I'm a little kid. Like he can just tell me to do stuff, just 'cause he's the father."

"And if he comes back, what would you like most to tell your father?"

"Maybe I'd say something like, 'Show me how to be a man, don't just tell me.'"

Celeste put her hand on the young man's shoulder. Crusias' thoughts went to Paul, "You see? Your work is not done. There is still much you need to do."

Watching the scene from the corner of the family waiting room made Paul sad. He loved his wife and children, but he just didn't seem to know how to do or say the right things. It seemed like an eternity had passed since he'd left home to go fishing. How could he have taken such important relationships for granted? How could he have treated his family as if they were his employees or worse, as his possessions? He realized how meaningless his life had been when it centered around his material belongings. After nearly losing hope of ever being with them again, Paul began to see a better way. He turned to Crusias and said, "I think I'm starting to understand."

Crusias smiled at Paul and said, "If you really try, you can make contact with them."

"What can I do?" Paul asked.

"Try calling out to her."

He called to his wife. "Peggy, can you hear me? Peggy! It's me. I'm coming back." She did not respond.

Winnifred seemed impatient. "Now, Crusias, you don't have time for parlor tricks. Besides, you're being mean. Tell him what he must do so we can take him back to his body."

"Please, Crusias, tell me," Paul pleaded.

"You can send your thoughts to her if we touch our hands to her head and communicate at the same time."

"Crusias, we do not want to miss his re-entry opportunity," Winnifred insisted.

"I promise, we'll go quickly. We really should let Paul take this opportunity."

"Oh, I suppose so. Even if it takes a few seconds, it's such fun to surprise the humans," she said.

"Good," said Crusias. "Now, Paul, you take my hand, like this." He guided Paul with his own. "Now, we'll place our hands on her head and send your message." Together they bridged the gap between realities as Paul Sanderson called out to Peggy in the family waiting room.

Paul watched the back of Peggy's neck turn to gooseflesh. She could hear him!

"He's here! Douglas! Can you feel it? Can you hear him? Your father is here! He just called out to me."

"Mrs. Sanderson, are you sure you weren't just daydreaming?" Sister Celeste asked.

"I'm not having a dream—I'm wide awake. He just touched me on my head and called my name!"

"What did he say?" Sister Celeste asked her.

"He said, 'Peggy, can you hear me? Peggy, I'm coming back. I love you.' Can't you hear him?"

Douglas looked at Sister Celeste. "Do we have to hold her down or something?"

"It's okay, Doug. Try to understand how upset your mother is. I can get a doctor to prescribe a sedative for her if she needs one. She'll be fine."

"You're right," Peggy asserted. "I am fine. Paul's coming back." Peggy drew in a deep breath through her nostrils like something was in the air. "Oh my God!" she practically shrieked. "I can smell him! It's unmistakable. Nothing else smells like that." Peggy called out to her husband, "Paul! I know you're here." She stretched out her arms and turned around several times in a circle as she called out his name.

Paul watched as Celeste crossed herself and looked skyward, "Lord, this woman needs more help than I can give her. Mrs. Sanderson, I want you to calm down. We can say a prayer that he will come back, but you must understand how critical his condition is."

"I hear what you're saying, Sister, but I know this is my husband. He's in this room with us!"

Paul knew that his wife could sense his presence. She heard and even smelled him! Now she was calling to him. He looked at Crusias, "This is amazing!"

Crusias nodded his agreement and lifted Paul's hands, ending the communiqué between them and Peggy. "We must go now, or it will be too late." Off they headed to the STU.

As suddenly as it had begun, it was over. The feelings, the sense of being surrounded by love, even the goosebumps disappeared. "It had to be him." Peggy held the sleeve of her sweater to her face. "I can still smell him on my clothes—here, Doug, smell." She offered her sweater to him. With an embarrassed look, Douglas took a short whiff. "Can't you smell him?" she asked.

"I'm not sure, Mom."

"He's back! Doug, I just know he's coming back to us!"

Ben's mood was not nearly as positive in the STU. He was having a "discussion" with Parkhurst over the speaker phone. "Come on, David!

122

We've got the body temp up another degree. We're ready to go. We can't just wait around for this Energy Field to show up. You're telling me you think you saw the patient's EF in the room?"

Parkhurst was defensive, "I'm telling you, Ben, three bogey EF's were identified up on the monitor. Two of them are the same frequencies that were here before. One is the very same frequency that was here the other day when the tape burned out. I've sat here and watched the whole thing. Everything is still up and running. The new filters and resistors are holding up. The machine identified their frequencies. Two new ones came into the STU and stayed a short while in the back of the room with the one that was there earlier. Then, they all just took off."

"Well, David," Ben said with growing impatience and a little sarcasm, "if you're so sure of yourself, where do you suppose they went? What are they doing that's so important that they couldn't wait around for us to get this resuscitation going? And what makes you think we should delay the defib and wait for the EF to show up?"

"According to the equipment, everyone in the room has an EF signal but the patient. I'm hoping the patient's EF just came and left with the others. It's just a hunch, Ben, but I really think you need an energy field *plus* a body before you have a patient."

"I can't afford to take the chance that you're wrong, David. I'm going to shock him now." He addressed the staff people in the STU, "All right, everyone, we're going to give this another try." Ben looked right and left at the staff people surrounding him and the patient. All eyes were trancelike and focused on him. "What's everybody staring at? It's like you're all mesmerized. Come on, people!" Ben clapped his hands. "We've got a patient to save." The group jerked back to action—alert, but on edge.

"Jenny, what's the cardiac monitor showing?"

Jenny responded, "He's still in V-fib. The bypass equipment is keeping him alive."

"Give me some fresh defib pads." A nurse placed two new pads on the patient's chest and reconnected the wires.

"Set the shock for 200 joules," Ben ordered.

"Check, 200 joules," Jenny responded.

"Everybody clear."

They responded, "All clear."

Ben looked down at the patient's face and spoke to him, "Come on, little buddy, you can do it." He'd used this saying before in many difficult surgeries. Ben had only told David the story of his own near-drowning and how they were the first words he remembered hearing when he was resuscitated. He liked to think it was his doctor who had said it to him. The staff thought it was just for good luck. Ben said they didn't need luck with him at the helm. Only

Ben really knew how intense he felt as he called to his patients.

Checking his own position to make sure he was clear, Ben returned his attention to the patient. "Fire one." Jenny hit the switch. The patient's body jerked as the shock passed through his chest and heart.

Ben looked up at Jenny, "Well?"

Jenny reported, "Patient is still in V-fib."

"Still no pulse." The others gave terse comments on the changes they noted. "Let's set the shock for 300 joules." Jenny adjusted the power control. "Everybody clear!"

The EEFM was humming away. Three frequencies and images came up on the screen. The radiology technician and Parkhurst's voice over the speaker system spoke almost in unison. "Hold on, Ben, they're back on the monitor!"

"What the…?" Ben turned toward the EEFM monitor on the equipment cart. The three bogey images were back on the screen. He, too, could see the three energy fields against the back wall of the room. "Are they the same frequencies?"

"Yes," Parkhurst answered.

"David! What should I do?"

"Don't move, Ben. Don't shock him yet. Just stay there for a second. Let's see what *they* do."

Crusias looked at the other two. "See, I told you we would be back in time."

"With not a moment to spare. Look, they've already started without us. Don't they know they can't do a thing without the patient?" Winnifred sounded frustrated. "They can't even get *that* part right."

"Winnifred, you must bear with the humans," Crusias told her. "They don't understand all of this, but they will know much more after this day." It was a fair assumption on Crusias' part. "All they can see is a very crude picture of us on their machine." Crusias broke into a grin and began to sing, " 'He's just like a surgeon'…"

"I know the song, Crusias. You want me to lighten up." Winnifred continued, "It's just that we've worked so hard to get this one back. It's been difficult because of this silly blizzard, and now the humans don't know whether to watch their machine or the back of the room."

"Ah, yes, dear Winnifred. That is why we call it adventure." Crusias looked at Paul, "Are you ready to go back to your family?"

"Oh, yes," Paul responded enthusiastically.

"Before you re-enter your body, I shall help you to relax, but it will still be painful." Crusias placed his hand on Paul's head. Paul, too, raised his hand. Crusias paused while Paul whispered something to him, then lay back. Crusias covered Paul's face and induced a hypnotic state.

"What did he tell you?" Winnifred asked.

"He thanked us for helping him get another chance." Crusias' EF signal almost sparkled on the EEFM monitor. "Winnie, it's times like this that make this job worthwhile."

"What are you going to do now?" she asked.

"I'm going to float over there to the table next to the good doctor and slip our patient back into his body."

"Crusias, you're such a showoff. You could just release him. You know he'd go back by himself when they shock him. He has a natural affinity to his body's genetic structure."

"I thought a little showmanship might be exciting for the humans. C'mon, Winnie, help me slip him back in. Make sure you brush up against a couple of them."

Amazed at what he saw happening on the monitor, Parkhurst grabbed the microphone and blurted to the people in the STU. "They're moving! All three of the EF's are moving toward the table. Can you see anything?" he asked from the control room.

"Only what's on the monitor. There's nothing visible in the room to explain the images," the radiology technician responded.

The EF's split up. One moved straight toward the table through the nurse anesthetist and the lab technician, both standing opposite Ben and Jenny. The other two images floated near the patient's head, moving in between Ben and Jenny. The lab technician squealed, "I feel all goosebumpy, like something just touched me. What's going on, Doctor?"

"Oooh!" Jenny peeped. She got an immediate hot flash as an image streaked through her mind. For a split second, she imagined she saw a sleeping form being fed by two translucent hands into the body that lay on the table before her. She thought to herself, *No! This can't be happening again. Just keep it to yourself, Jenny.*

Parkhurst called, "Do you sense movement around you?"

"Yes," the two chimed.

"No," Jenny denied.

"NO!" Ben Bradley exclaimed.

"They're right on top of you. God, Ben, look in the monitor."

Ben felt his right arm warming. The feeling moved to his shoulder, to his neck, and then to his head. The hair on the back of his neck straightened.

"David, I'm getting a sensation of warmth on my right side." He didn't say anything about the hair. "I'm watching the monitor. They're approaching the patient. One of them is moving into the patient's body. What do you want me to do?"

Parkhurst's voice came over the speaker. "It *must* be the patient's energy field. It looks like the other two EF's are putting the patient's EF back into his body! I think you should wait until they're clear before you shock."

"This isn't very professional, David," Ben told him. "But just to amuse you, I'll wait for your imaginary friends. I'm waiting... I'm waiting. If you can hear me, I will shock in ten seconds." Ben counted backwards. "I will shock in five seconds. Everybody clear."

The staff responded in unison, "Clear."

Winnifred and Crusias backed away. Crusias looked at his partner and smiled. "Winnie, I think he's back inside. All that remains is for the humans to shock him."

Winnifred looked heavenward, "Praise God." They both beamed brightly with a sense of accomplishment.

"God, Ben!" Parkhurst called, "I think they can hear you. They're backing away."

Ben continued his countdown, "Five, four, three, two, one. Now!" Three hundred joules of current jolted the patient. The body jumped on the table. Paul Sanderson's eyes opened as wide as pie plates.

Jenny watched as the heart monitor started beeping. "We have a regular sinus rhythm! Pulse is seventy-eight."

"Blood pressure?" Ben started through the checklist.

"BP is ninety-five over sixty and rising," another responded. One by one, they reported their readings to Ben.

"Congratulations, everyone! We've got him back. I don't have a clue what happened here. The patient will have a long recovery, but he's going to make it."

Jenny looked skyward and softly said, "Praise God."

XXIII

"...your old men shall dream dreams, your young men
shall see visions:" —*Bible* (KJV) *Joel* 2:28

Date: Wednesday, November 26, 1997
Time: 2:30 A.M.
Place: Mercy Hospital, Duluth, MN

Ben finished dictating the final orders on his patients' files for the day. It seemed appropriate to begin each file with "It was a dark and stormy night...", as it reflected the conditions that persisted outside the hospital. The transcriber would edit out the comment.

After two days, Ben thought the blizzard was getting monotonous. Local weather broadcasts forecast two more days of the same, saying that snowplow crews were out and working overtime, trying just to keep the main streets and highways open. The back streets and alleys were a lost cause. Broadcasts warned people that even if they could get out of their own driveways, they risked getting stuck somewhere else—in a parking lot, on an inclined street, at the neighbor's, or in the middle of the road.

Ben knew that Mercy Hospital, like other vital services, was having trouble getting their staff in and out for their shifts. Those already in the hospital doubled up on shifts to cover for people who could not get to work. Elective surgeries and procedures were cancelled. Mercy Hospital's top management had requested that no one leave unless a replacement arrived. There were only two ER doctors and no other general surgeons in the hospital, so Ben stayed.

Ben needed a rest after a busy day even if he couldn't leave the hospital. He found an available staff sleeping room near the emergency department. It was small and clean. Other than the fact that it had no window, it reminded Ben of a small dormitory room. It had a single bed, a sink with a large mirror, a desk and chair, and a bathroom with a shower. He took off his shoes and hung his lab coat on the chair. He shut off the light and lay down on the bed. *Tomorrow will be Wednesday*, he thought. *No! It is already Wednesday... or, is it Thursday? Damn!* He hated being so tired and busy that he lost track of the days.

Ben let his mind drift over the events of the day. The hypothermia case this morning was interesting and disturbing. What were those images? They seemed to even have personalities. Why, that was virtually impossible!

If their EEFM machine really did work, he and his development team would have much to discuss, not the least of which would be the probability that they all were going to be very rich from selling the patent rights. Ben thought that *he* especially deserved to be wealthy. He'd poured a small fortune into the EEFM project, to say nothing of the time he'd invested. The EEFM-1 cost him at least the price of a new home, probably more. Maybe now his financial horizons would improve. After practicing medicine for nearly twenty years, he didn't have a lot to show for all the money he'd earned. But then, most doctors he knew didn't. When one of the staff doctors got burned on some investment that was going to make him rich or shelter her from income taxes, they'd always say, "Oh, well, lucky at medicine, unlucky at finances."

At least, the EEFM project had been a much more interesting venture than investing in cattle futures, ex-wives, railroad cars, or river barges. Maybe now it was his turn to be rich, powerful, and eccentric. People beyond the emergency department would offer him a more appropriate level of dignity and respect. They had a new "mousetrap." Buyers should start beating a path to their doorstep.

Ben didn't fully understand what they had observed on the monitors, but he was convinced it was important. His medical training had taught him that death was the end of a human being, but now they were observing evidence that the essence of a life force was electrical. Could that electrical energy possibly be what some called the soul? Could that energy come and go from the body? How could that energy hold itself together outside the body? They'd not seen anything like this case during the initial equipment tests, but of course nobody had died during the trials.

Ben smiled in the nearly total darkness of the room as he thought of being interviewed on national news programs. "Here's the man who saved billions for Medicare and health insurance companies...the man who just sold his shares of the EEFM project for tens of millions..." Ben was really going to enjoy being wealthy. He promised himself that he would not become juvenile and self-centered like some of the famous sports figures and rock stars he'd seen interviewed on late night talk shows. To them, having a multi-million dollar contract meant they didn't have to grow up. Ben's mind drifted as he neared sleep.

"Ben! Ben, wake up," a voice whispered to him.

"Wha... What?" Ben asked groggily, "Is it time to get up?"

"Ben, you know it's not about the money. You've known that all the time."

"What are you talking about? Who are you?"

"Don't you remember me, Ben? You're my best buddy. You said you'd never forget me."

Ben sat up and struggled to see in the darkened room. "Jim? Is that you, Jim?" Jim's image materialized out of the darkness.

"The one and only, the original. How've you been?"

"Ohh, fine, I guess." Unbelieving, Ben tried squinting. He tried to shake the sleep off.

"Ben! It's really me. Let's do something together."

"I don't know, Jim. I don't know if I can. I mean, I'm all grown up now. I don't know if I'm supposed to play anymore." Ben didn't know what to say.

"I know that, Ben. You grew up to be a doctor. I'm just a…," he paused.

"What, Jim? What are you now?" Ben asked as he searched the darkness.

"Well, I grew up some, too," Jim answered. "I want you to come with me, Ben. I want you to see something."

"Where are we going?" Ben asked.

"Just take my hand," Jim said as he reached out his hand and grabbed Ben's. Jim's hand felt real and solid to Ben. "You'll know when we get there."

Ben sensed that they were moving. Multicolored lights shimmered in a swirl of clouds. Jimmie's image solidified.

"It's Jim, not Jimmie. Don't you remember anything?"

"Yeah, Jim. I'm sorry. I didn't think I said it out loud." Ben watched as the vision cleared. It was Jim! He had aged too, just not as fast as Ben. Though the man before him was fully grown, there was no mistaking the image for anyone else but Jim.

"I can hear your thoughts, too."

"Really? Wow!" Jim had a certain glow about him. Ben couldn't quite put his finger on it, but he almost seemed to radiate light from within. He was beautiful—perfect in every detail.

"Thanks, Ben. You don't look so bad yourself."

They came out of the clouds and approached a small lake. Ben recognized the old neighborhood of his childhood days. Everything looked nearly the same, except now there were houses built up all around the lake. Newer homes filled the spaces that once were vacant lots. It was unmistakable. This was where he had lived as a child! They approached from the air. Ben could see his old house and where Jim had lived. He could see the hill where they'd gone sledding. They landed on the shoreline where they'd played as children. What an incredible dream!

"Go ahead, pinch yourself."

"What?"

"You don't think this is real, do you? Go ahead, pinch yourself." Ben hesitated. Jim let go of Ben's hand and grabbed a handful of his cheek.

"OUCH! That hurts, Jim. Why did you do that?"

"Just told you."

"Did not."

"You still think you're dreaming."

"Okay, okay, you win. Where do we go from here?"

"This is where we're going—to a peaceful place. Look around you! There's a bench over here. Let's go sit down."

It was a beautiful summer afternoon. Everything was bright and warm. The leaves were full on the trees. Birds were flying and chirping. Several ducks were swimming with ducklings following behind them. A muskrat left a small wake as it swam beside them in the still waters. The sky was bright and blue, yet there was no sun. "God, Jim, I haven't been here in years." The memory was still painful. "I used to come down here and just sit, wishing we could relive that day, you know, before the... the..."

"The accident. I know. Ben, I want you to look right at me. It's okay. Really, I'm doing just fine."

Ben turned to face his childhood friend and blurted awkwardly, "Boy, you look great!"

"Thanks, Ben," Jim laughed. "I still sense you're having trouble believing this is real. Here, I have a little surprise for you." Jim turned toward the old house and gave a whistle. A black Labrador bounded over the top of the hill. "Come, Missy, come," he called to the dog. She ran down the hill toward them and nearly knocked Ben over when she got to him.

Ben frolicked and rolled around in the warm grass with the dog for a few minutes. She grabbed a stick and laid it at Ben's feet. Her tail wagged furiously as she stared, first at the stick, then into Ben's eyes. Her eyes spoke volumes of love and enthusiasm. *Throw the stick, dammit!* her bark insisted. Ben leaned over to pick up the stick. The dog's eyes were riveted to it. Ben made a large sweeping gesture, pretending to wind up for the throw, then stopped. Missy barked intensely. Ben understood her thoughts, *C'mon, throw the stupid stick!* Ben threw it for her. The stick spun end over end as it flew through the air. Ben laughed as he watched Missy scramble up the hill after it. How could he not laugh? It was a joyful reunion.

Ben and Jim settled down on the bench. Missy came up next to them and sat down. Ben scratched her behind the ears as he listened to Jim.

"You saw something important on your machine yesterday. You have pictures of something that men and women have had a hard time understanding for centuries. The machine is quite remarkable—the least you can do is believe your own eyes."

Ben protested, "But I'm not sure what I saw. The images could be a sort of mass hallucination or hysteria. They could be anomalies or the result of an equipment malfunction. They could be angels or beings from another planet or dimension. They could be almost anything."

"They're energy forms, the same kind that you see inside yourself on the machine. The only difference is they don't have physical bodies—they're pure energy. Isn't that energy what you were always looking for?"

"Well, yes, but I never dreamed it would be like that."

"Oh, I think you did. The point is that you're trying way too hard to structure the incidents to fit your view of reality."

"I'm a surgeon, a scientist, Jim. That's what I'm trained to do."

"Ben, what you saw is the way it is. It doesn't need or try to fit your perspective. If you really wish to understand, you must fit into its reality. Do you get it?"

Ben shrugged, "I'm not sure. What do you mean, Jim?"

"Your scientific perspective of the life energy force must change. Accept the visions you see on the monitor for what they are. Don't explain them away or make them fit your preconceived perspective of reality. They can't conform. They are what they are."

"How did you know I was trying to explain them away?"

"I've worked on the project with you."

"No way, Jim!"

"Really, I was with you when you had your dreams. You know, Ben, we never stop learning—our work never ends."

Ben thought to himself, *I must wake up. This isn't even a dream—it's a mistake. I need to go back to sleep.*

"Go ahead, Ben, pinch yourself again," Jim scolded. "You sure are stubborn, even after seeing things that many people never see before their own coming over. Can you have a dream where you tell yourself it's not a dream? Can you make yourself go to sleep so that you stop dreaming? That's an oxymoron. All the pain you can possibly inflict on yourself will not change the reality of this experience."

Ben continued to doubt his senses, "That reality being...?"

"Ben, do I look like I'm dead?"

"No."

"According to the current limited views of science, I shouldn't be here, right?"

"Right, this is just a dream."

"Listen, Ben. The energy which is nurtured inside your body during your physical life continues as an identifiable energy form after it leaves your body."

"Life doesn't end at the time of death?"

"Bingo! Except we don't think of it like that from our perspective. We call it coming out, rebirth, separation." Jim continued, "Physical death comes stalking. None of us can escape it, but ready or not, eternity comes stalking at the same time. Have you studied for it? Are you prepared for finals? Have you made your peace? It doesn't matter, Ben—it still comes."

Ben frowned, "Those sound like nonmedical issues to me, Jim. Why don't you give this speech to a priest or a philosopher?"

"You understand much more than you let on, Ben. You say you only understand matters of the body and not matters of the heart. Yet, you regularly revisit your own near-death experience, the one we shared in the pond." Jim gestured to the lake before them. "I always hoped you understood that. You promised you would remember, that you would never forget me. When you became a doctor, you tried to forget me, but it didn't work, Ben. Regardless of your belief or disbelief, you'll still face the same experiences. I still come to you in the night. You haven't forgotten. You and everyone else will face the same experience when you come over."

"I'm sorry I've tried to forget. The memories hurt."

"I know you were trained to ignore the messages and visions from the other side of life, not to believe. Part of the reason you chose a medical career was because you thought your medical training would protect you. You thought the hurt would go away. It didn't stop your compulsion to work on this project. Did you notice that this EEFM project proves the exact things that you were trained not to believe?"

"Why me, Jim?"

"Because you've been there. You've been to the edge and back. You know a little of what it's like. Mankind needs hope in an age of incredulity. Why *not* you, Ben? You and your staff can observe and record evidence on your machine to demonstrate that physical death is not a plague. There's a lot of it going around, but it's not the plague."

"Why not give it to a priest or a holy man?" Ben repeated the question, hoping for someone else to be chosen.

"Religious leaders work even harder than scientists to make peoples' experiences fit their definition of reality. Answer this question—if there are one hundred leaders from one hundred different religions from one hundred countries, which one will resist the temptation to fit the experience into their view of reality? Which of the hundred would be the one who will not say, 'We are the one true way. All who come through us shall be saved for eternal life. All the rest shall surely perish.'? Which one of the hundred is right? Quite frankly, Ben, no one who has come across cares a whit how many angels can dance on the head of a pin."

Jim continued, "As a doctor, you understand that all your work ultimately fails. You don't like that fact. You don't like to admit it any more than the next doctor, but you do admit it. I've heard you say it in your own way."

"Say what, Jim?"

"You say your patients don't die. They just go away. What you mean has everything to do with the staff wheeling the body to the morgue rather than the EF leaving the body, but you admit it."

Ben was flabbergasted, "You've heard me say that?"

"Of course. I'm not always with you, but I've heard you say it."

"Not always? What do you mean?"

"Hey, Ben, it's okay. Only the Master can do that. Sometimes I come for visits or to work with you, but I'm not assigned to you like your guardian. A lot of the time I'm busy with my own projects. Crusias and Winnifred are the ones who work at Mercy Hospital. They're the other two frequencies you observed on the monitor. Someday you'll really be able to see them, but for now..." He told Ben their EEFM frequencies so he would know who they were.

"Winnifred and who?"

"Crusias."

"Those are very strange names."

"They are very old family names."

"You're not kidding me, Jim?"

Jim made an X across his chest, "Cross my heart and hope to die." He laughed. "Hope to die... I just kill myself."

Ben understood the joke. It was the situation he didn't get. Once again, the doubts came over Ben. "This isn't real. It can't be. It's nothing but a dream. It's a dammed dream."

"I swear, Ben, you could run into an angel right there in the hospital, be carried away in your own rapture, and not recognize it. What do you think you felt today when Crusias bumped against you in the STU? Did you think it was just a hot flash? It's not PMS, and you're not going through your change in life."

Ben sat still, just gazing into the pool. The quiet surface had a mirrorlike quality.

"You've been selected, Ben. You're it. You and all of medical science know you cannot save a single person from his appointment with eternity. You know that everyone must cross the great chasm of death. We are like unborn chicks—we can't stay in the eggshell forever. If you study eggshells and treat them to be harder, to last longer; if you work hard to lengthen the incubation period, the chick must still come out of the shell. It's the same for us. When it's our time to come out, we must. And like the chick, when we come out, our shells are abandoned.

"Ben, if you really wish to succeed in treating your patients, if you and science want to ultimately succeed in your work, you must also study the life forces, rather than just the shells. Don't be afraid to study the nonphysical side of medicine—it's the foundation of being human. Don't fear it in your patients or in yourself.

"When your patients come back with recollections from the other side, listen to their stories. Don't try to take the experiences away from them by dismissing them as hallucinations or psychological and medical abnormalities. Just because their bodies lay in their beds doesn't mean they didn't take the trip. You don't need to be a priest, Ben; you just need to be a *whole* doctor treating *whole* patients."

"If I'm to do that, I'll need more help, Jim."

"You have a fine staff, including the one you call Sister. They're a good start. Share with them. You'll have as much help as you need, and I'll keep up with my side."

"Start what? When? I thought we'd sell the patent rights to the machine and enjoy life for a while."

"You can start by accepting what you saw on the machine today. Learn about how that should affect how you treat your patients. Then you can teach others."

"By learning about the EF as well as the physical body?"

"Precisely, Ben. You're starting to understand." Jim stood up. "I'm afraid our time is up. They're ready to call you for surgery. You must go back."

Ben followed his friend's cue and stood up. Missy sat still, watching them. She seemed to understand what would happen.

"Won't you take me back, Jim?"

"I know you can find your way back. Besides, we can meet here again once you know how to do it."

"I would really like that, Jim."

"Good. Let's meet soon. You can tell me all about your progress. If you need to call me before that, my frequency is…" Jim gave him the numbers.

"How do I get back, Jim? You've got to help me."

"It's easy, Ben. Just walk into the water and gaze into your reflection on the lake. You'll know what to do after that. Oh, there's one more thing."

"What's that?" Ben waded into the edge of the water and looked down at his feet. He could see the reflection of his face. It was very strange. There were no ripples in the surface as he walked deeper and deeper.

"You can learn to love again."

"But… but…" He turned back to look at his friend, but Jim was gone. The entire park was enveloped in a swirl of clouds and sparkling lights. Ben reached into the clouds. "Jim! Where are you?"

"You didn't lose me. I just changed."

"Jim! Don't leave me!" Ben felt like a lonely child.

"Good-bye, buddy. Don't be afraid."

Everywhere Ben looked he saw bright sparkles of light. He sensed he was moving. Jim, Missy, and the beautiful park were gone, replaced by the clouds and the thousands of points of sparkling lights. He looked forward again. He felt as if he was floating through the light until he caught a glimpse of something. It looked like a door… a window… or a mirror. It was a dark place in a world of lights and clouds. Ben sensed that he should go toward it, willing himself to move. It worked! At first, he moved slowly—then, faster and faster, until the lights became a blur. The opening grew larger, larger. He wanted to stop before he hit it, but he flew through it as though it didn't exist.

XXIV

"O Lord, if there is a Lord, save my soul, if I have a soul."
—Ernest Renan, *Priere d'un Sceptique* (p. 163)

Date: Wednesday, November 26, 1997
Time: 6:45 A.M.
Place: South of Duluth, MN, Interstate 35, Northbound lane

Jeff Arneson knew it would be difficult traveling today. The forecast the night before was for the snow to continue into the third day. Rush hour traffic into the city would move at little more than a crawl. Jeff was pleased with his decision to leave home early and beat the rush. His wife, Danielle, sat beside him in their five-year-old luxury sedan. Two sleepy and hungry children were strapped into child-protection seats in the back seat.

In their early thirties, Jeff and his wife each held professional jobs with corresponding incomes. Danielle was a real estate loan officer in the Northern States National Bank which was owned by a large midwestern bank holding company. Jeff was an attorney with a prominent state-wide law firm. A specialist in real estate, he had always admired the luck and genius of people like Chester Congdon, the attorney who had bought and sold the Iron Range earlier in the century. Jeff knew few large deals like that existed, at least not since the sale of oil rights on the North Slope of Alaska. Accordingly, Jeff conducted his career utilizing the concept of serving his clients well and keeping an eye open for bargains that might allow him to accumulate great wealth over the span of his working years. His first years had confirmed his expectations. Jeff's net worth was impressive, and he was accustomed to paying cash for his toys.

The Arnesons could afford one of the beautiful old homes in Duluth, but they were money pits to remodel and heat in the harsh Minnesota winters. Most of them were also built on small lots. Instead, they had opted for an eighty-acre hobby farm and a stately new home within commuting distance of work. Eighty acres offered privacy, a large lawn, and room for horses and dogs. They'd built the large, energy-efficient home in the middle of a picturesque grove of trees a few miles beyond Thompson Hill. The commute still offered ample opportunities to enjoy the view of Lake Superior.

On mornings like this, Jeff thought it would have been nice for Danielle not to have to work, but the tender traps of house, boat, cars, horses, and other accessories of success still clamored for their combined incomes. Getting to work every day was part of their formula for success. Jeff knew that Danielle enjoyed her work at the bank much more than housekeeping and cooking—she was a '90's woman.

The children would eat breakfast at the daycare center. Jeff and Danielle would try to eat uptown before getting to work. After a couple miles of snowy roads, they turned onto the Interstate 35 ramp and merged into the traffic behind a two-and-a-half-ton hospital supplies truck and a fuel transport tanker/trailer being pulled by a yellow Peterbilt semitractor.

Even with some ice and snow on it, Jeff thought the freeway was in better driving condition than the local roads. The plows had been through once during the night, and the early morning traffic kept some of the snow blown off. They met a gang of MNDOT snowplows working their way south and west in the opposite lanes.

The car was warm. Danielle unbuttoned her blue wool coat and loosened her scarf. "It would have been nice to have a cup of coffee before we left, especially after that awful dream I had last night. I never really got back to sleep after that."

Jeff glanced at her. She looked so professional in her gray suit and high-necked white blouse. Jeff appreciated her conservative style of dress, since it camouflaged her trim figure. The circles under her dark brown eyes were all that detracted from her well-manicured looks. "It'll be worth it to beat the worst of the traffic into town," Jeff responded. "What did you dream about?"

"Oh, I know it's silly, but I dreamed that I saw my father again."

Jeff's fingers tightened on the steering wheel, "Damn it, Dani. He's been dead for over three years. You're going to have to get over it."

"I know that. Don't be upset with me, Jeff," she replied defensively. "I can't control what I dream about, can you?"

"No, I can't either, but Jesus Christ, it seems like you can't let go."

Danielle grabbed Jeff's forearm and dug her fingers into his right arm through his coat. "I've told you not to swear in front of the children."

"Guilty as charged," he said as he pulled upward on his tie with his right hand. "Take me to the gallows."

"Oh, Jeffrey, you know what I mean."

"I'm sorry, but I keep forgetting. I just get tired of hearing about your father after he's been gone for so long."

"Would you rather I didn't tell you about my dreams?" Danielle huffed at him. "Maybe that would be better."

"That's not what I want either. You know that."

"And you know I believe that Papa's still alive in some form of afterlife."

"Yeah, yeah, I know. You've told me before. I still don't believe it, but I appreciate you working on my case. You know, you're going to have to give me evidence that will stand up in court. Otherwise, I remain a skeptic." He quizzed her, "So, what happened in your dream?"

136

"Well, he warned me I should stay home, take the day off. He said something awful would happen. I almost decided to stay home with the kids."

"You don't think it really meant anything, do you?"

"My logical mind tells me it was just a dream, but it seemed so real."

"Maybe you should wake me next time so I can corroborate your story."

It was useless to pursue the subject, "Maybe I'll have to do that next time." Danielle changed the subject. "I have a loan closing at 11 o'clock and a departmental meeting at 4:30. Hopefully, it will be over by 5 o'clock."

"I'll try to meet you at the door to the parking ramp on the skyway at 5:15. We'll start Thanksgiving a little early." Jeff turned his attention to the road and said, "I can't see around these trucks to pass them. I don't think we're going to get by them before we get to the hill."

Each time the trucks hit finger drifts on the highway, swirls of snow billowed up behind them, obscuring Jeff's vision. As they approached the crest of the hill, the trucks downshifted, resulting in a deceleration to forty-five miles per hour. The hospital supply truck skidded. Its brake lights flashed in the swirling snow as the driver worked the brakes and turn signal and pulled into the left lane in front of Jeff.

"I wish these guys would all stay in the right lane," Jeff griped. "Now we'll be stuck behind them all the way down the hill." Jeff could see several other cars and pickups close ranks with them in his rear-view mirror.

Danielle turned her head. Her long, shiny, well-brushed hair danced on her shoulder as she did. She looked at him through her still-tired brown eyes. "Now is not the time to be aggressive, Jeffrey. It'll only take a few more minutes to get into town. We don't go to church so you can take more chances."

Jeff glanced quickly into her eyes. Her reprimand irritated him, but he knew she was right. Their sedan was heavy and handled well, but Thompson Hill was treacherous in bad weather. He slowed down for a moment and let the gap between them and the trucks increase to about four car lengths. Another car pulled up next to them in the right lane.

The rainy fall weather had hampered construction on Interstate 35. Normally, construction work would be completed prior to winter, but it seemed as though it had rained two days out of every three for the last month. Construction equipment was still scattered along the edges of the freeway. Although both northbound lanes were opened for the holiday weekend traffic, a long row of blaze orange barrels sat on the right shoulder. That plus the new ribbons of guardrails down the center and sides of the road gave the freeway a closed-in feeling that made Jeff feel claustrophobic.

The top of Thompson Hill was like the edge of a giant bowl that stood several hundred feet above the shoreline of the port area and helped shape the Duluth skyline. The accumulations of snow and ice were heavier on the inside of the "bowl" as the wind burbled over the edge, dumping heavy snow over the downtown district and port area, reducing visibility. As Jeff drove over the top of the hill, he had difficulty determining whether it was low clouds or fog that restricted visibility to a quarter mile. It made little difference—the effect was the same.

Were it a clear morning, they could have enjoyed the breathtaking panoramic view of the Twin Ports Harbor and Lake Superior from the top of Thompson Hill. Today the snow and clouds blew out of the northwest down the hill toward the lake, creating a crosswind to the inbound traffic in the predawn darkness. The only view they would have during their approach to the city would be that of the trucks ahead of them and flashes of the craggy rock outcroppings through which I-35 was cut.

Jeffrey Arneson and his escort of trucks and passenger vehicles approached the Skyline Parkway/Spirit Mountain off ramp and began their descent into the city.

Joey, the younger child, started fussing and resisting his seat belts. "Dani, do something!" Jeff ordered.

"He doesn't like being confined," Danielle answered.

"Well, it's not a good time for him to throw a tantrum."

Their daughter, Melissa, a four-year old, tried to console Joey. Danielle pleaded unsuccessfully with the two-year old, "Come on, Joey, be a good boy." He only cried louder.

"Can't you do something about him, Dani?" Jeff complained to his wife.

Danielle answered, "He's tired and hungry, too."

"It's really irritating. It's hard to concentrate on the driving with him fussing right behind me."

Danielle reached into a knapsack for some crackers. She tried to hand him one, teasing him with it to get his attention and calm him down. The handoff didn't work. "Oh, shoot," she said as the cracker fell onto the seat, out of the child's reach, giving Joey something else to cry about. Danielle unbuckled her seat belt so she could turn and hand the cracker to him. She offered the box to her daughter. "Here, Melissa, you share these with your brother."

At that same moment, Jeff moaned, "Oh, God!" Barely visible ahead of the trucks, Jeff watched an old blue compact car go into a spin in front of the trucks as it came off the entrance ramp.

The brake lights flashed brightly on the yellow Peterbilt with the tanker/trailer as the driver hit the airbrakes and instinctively jerked his steering wheel to the left to avoid the car. It didn't help. He struck the blue compact squarely, bouncing it ahead of his truck.

The braking action caused the wheels of the tanker/trailer to break traction from the road. The tanker/trailer pitched to the right toward the new guardrail, taking several blaze orange barrels with it down the slippery shoulder of the freeway. As it impacted the guardrail, the attached Peterbilt smacked the old blue compact a second time. The two outside tires on the tanker/trailer exploded from the pressure of trailer against the guardrail, leaving a plume of sparks from steel grinding on steel as the trailer searched for weak spots along the guardrail.

The hospital supply truck was sideswiped by the yellow Peterbilt which hit its right front corner forcing the smaller truck into the center guardrail. The tanker/trailer jackknifed sideways and continued sliding along the guardrail.

There was neither time nor traction for Jeff to stop or avoid the accident. His sedan rear-ended the hospital supply truck. Jeff hardly noticed that the single driver's side airbag deployed. It popped open, then deflated in the blink of an eye. Jeff heard Danielle scream as he watched her catapult into the dashboard and saw her head hit the rear-view mirror.

At the same time as Danielle went flying, Jeff saw the car to their right as it went hood first under the tanker/trailer until the windshield and roof of the car struck the belly of the trailer, ripping the roof off. The left rear wheels of the Peterbilt hit Jeff's car from the right, forcing it to nosedive into the center guardrail. Jeff hit his head on the steering wheel, then felt himself being ejected through the windshield as it shattered into a thousand-piece jigsaw puzzle held together by a coat of plastic laminate. Outside the car, Jeff was suspended ten feet in the air over the hospital supply truck. Horrified, he watched the rest of the accident unfold before him.

After a two-hundred-foot ride down the steep and slippery slope, the blue compact turned sideways as it bounced off the Peterbilt and started rolling down the roadway. The guardrail severed under the pressure of the fuel tanker/trailer, allowing the rear wheels to move to the outside of the guardrail and the tank to ride on top of it. The next fifty feet of guardrail worked like a power grinder, slicing an eight-foot-long gash in the bottom of the stainless steel tank. Several thousand gallons of gasoline received a fresh breath of oxygen. As the fuel spilled out from the tank into the plume of sparks, it ignited with a flash reminiscent of a napalm strike. Burning fuel spilled out onto the road along the old stone retaining wall ten feet outside the new guardrail. The Peterbilt with its burning tanker/trailer, the old blue compact, and the car with no roof slid another fifty yards down the guardrail in a giant conflagration before stopping short of the curve in the road.

Jeff watched as two more vehicles rear-ended his own and twelve more cars and two pickup trucks plowed directly into the crash scene. The two trucks and two cars were caught in the fireball. The burning fuel formed a fiery river as it flowed down the freeway. Some fuel found its way through openings in the stone wall and cascaded in flames down into a ravine.

The sixth car in the lineup was one of the lucky ones. The female driver managed to stop her four-wheel-drive vehicle before driving into the fireball after being rear-ended by a pickup truck. At first, she feared she might be sitting in her own blood. She discovered that only her pride was injured when she realized the wet spot on her dress and the driver's seat was where she had urinated. She picked up her cell phone, called 911, and waited in her car, trembling and crying until help arrived.

XXV

"Now therefore why should we die?
For this great fire will consume us..."
—*Bible* (KJV) *Deuteronomy* 5:25

Date: Wednesday, November 26, 1997
Time: 7:00 A.M.
Place: Duluth Fire Station 8, Duluth, MN

Captain Johnston and the crew at Station 8 had been awake since six in the morning when the administrative order was broadcast for all ten fire stations throughout the city to chain up their vehicles. "Chain up" meant the crews had to spend fifteen to twenty minutes in each station to put chains on the drive wheels of all their emergency vehicles. The chains provided added traction on the snow and ice for days like this. Snowstorms added extra burden to everyone's work. Everything from turnout gear and vehicles to the building and bathrooms suffered from the salt, sand, and grit that Duluth offered in the winter.

In its third day, this storm was getting old. The city plow passed by before the administrative order arrived, leaving a fresh two-foot-high pile of snow on the end of the driveway. That pile, plus the overnight accumulation of another four inches on the driveway and sidewalk, had needed their attention. Two firefighters had finished shoveling and had hung up their shovels and jackets before breakfast.

Captain Johnston completed his report on the two runs that Station 8 had made through the night. The rescue truck and Engine 2 were called out before midnight to put out a fire that had started in a creosote-soaked chimney that should have been cleaned out long ago. Medic 8 and Rescue 8 responded to a single car incident with a drunk driver who spent the night sobering up in the county jail. It was too quiet—the crew had even gotten a couple hours of sleep!

Johnston made an inspection of trucks, equipment, and firefighter gear while crew members chained up their engines. Something caught the captain's attention as he checked the firefighters' gear.

It was time for breakfast—everyone was hungry. The kitchen area buzzed with activity and conversation as Johnston walked in carrying a turnout coat.

He saw Fearless sitting with George Tyler, one of the older firefighters. At age fifty-three, Tyler's three daughters had made him a grandfather several times, honestly earning him the nickname Gramps. Grandchildren plus his gray hair made him the Station 8 target of every old joke and prank in the book. After twenty-five years on the force, Gramps had confided in the captain that sometimes he felt so worn out that he wondered if he should take early retirement, a condition he could ill afford even with a pension. Some days, he'd told Johnston, just putting on his gear was an effort.

Captain Johnston addressed the group, "All right, everybody, listen up." He waited for the conversation and hum of activity to subside. "I just spent the last few minutes inspecting the rigs and gear. There are a few problems." He could hear the moans rumble through the kitchen.

Sawbones asked, "Hey, Captain, can't it wait 'til after breakfast?"

"Come on, you know we're due for an inspection at any time. We want everything to be shipshape, rain or shine."

"How about raging blizzards?"

"That, too. Whining and complaining won't get the work done. You all know our motto. Let's hear it."

Fearless piped up, "Cleanliness is next to impossible." The kitchen filled with laughter.

"Cute, Fearless. Real cute." He cut them some slack. "Anyway, we've got some work to do after breakfast to get things shaped up around here." Johnston reviewed the items that were on his list, and now he was down to the final item.

"I checked through everyone's turnout gear and noticed one of the suits seemed to be a little heavier, like about fifteen pounds heavier." It was time for the joke to end. "Gramps, you've been complaining about being tired lately?"

"Well, um, yes, Cap'n," Gramps hesitantly responded.

Grins broke out at the kitchen table. Johnston suspected some of the smiling faces were accomplices—the rest probably knew about it.

"Maybe this has something to do with it." Captain Johnston unfolded the coat and turned it upside down. A pile of sand formed on the floor. When it finished running out from the lining in the coat, the captain said, "Must be nearly eight pounds of sand in here." Gramps' face started getting red as his blood pressure rose. "I found about the same amount in the pants. Gramps has been carrying quite a load around with him." By adding a pound of sand at a time, Gramps would hardly notice the extra weight. "I don't suppose any of you would like to confess?"

Fearless patted their victim on the back, "Good try, Gramps. I s'pose you were bucking for a disability claim."

"It's a little late to be getting into shape for the Olympics," another blurted. Then the laughter started.

It appeared that Gramps didn't know what to do. Should he be mad about carrying all that extra weight around for the last few weeks?

Or...Johnston knew Gramps had pulled the same joke on some of the others. Usually it was the greenhorns that got the old "sand-in-the-suit" trick. Gramps broke into a grin. "I guess you young whippersnappers want to see me have a coronary."

Fearless slapped Gramps on the back, "You're too ornery for that."

Sawbones whooped above the laughter, "I guess we're never gonna get the old geezer to retire."

Johnston laughed. They had gotten Gramps good. He knew their work could be very stressful since people suffered and died every day. Firefighters and medics saw them under the worst circumstances. Humor was a positive way to let off steam. There were other, less appropriate releases. Each member of the team searched for their own coping methods—some exercised while others looked into the bottom of a bottle too often.

Captain Johnston set Gramps' coat down on top of the sand pile. "As soon as a couple of you are finished with breakfast, you can clean up this mess and go through the checklist." He poured himself a steaming hot cup of java, grabbed a piece of whole wheat toast from the table, and dunked it in the coffee on the way to his mouth.

The buzz of activity lessened when Fearless and Smitty walked out to the garage with coffee cups and the captain's "fixit" list. Others, too, went about their duties, which left Sawbones and two others to clean the kitchen and sweep up the pile of sand. Johnston visited with Gramps for a few minutes while they finished their coffee. He would double check Gramps' gear to be sure everything was back to normal.

They were nearly finished when the klaxon alerted the crew of the incoming dispatch. "Station 1, Station 7, Station 8, Station 10, signal 10-52 on Interstate 35. Northbound lane at Entrance Ramp Two-Four-Niner. At least one truck and several passenger vehicles. Fire involved. Repeat...." Johnston already had the information written down. Ramp 249 was at the top of the hill coming into Duluth. Knock on wood, there had never been a serious accident up there. Today was a lousy time for one.

The captain figured this was going to be a bitch. He hollered out to the crew, "All right, kids! Let's roll!" As he pulled on his bunker pants and boots, Johnston could hear doors slamming and garage door openers grinding. He surveyed the fire hall. Engine 802 and Medic 803 were ready to roll. He watched as three firefighters climbed into the bucket and ladder unit. Small clouds of dark smoke billowed toward the concrete ceiling as the diesel engines came to life.

Janine rolled Engine 804 before Captain Johnston had his door closed. As they pulled out from the station, the captain punched a button on his portable mike, "Engine Eight-Zero-Four to Dispatch."

"Go ahead, Eight-Zero-Four."

"Station 8 is responding. ETA is approximately six minutes. Over."

"Ten-Four, Station 8, at 0712. Copy six minutes to ETA. Over."

Johnston listened to the other stations responding to the call on the radio. They, too, were getting under way. Station 8 beat the others out the door by half a minute. They would be the first engines to the scene unless Station 10 could get up Thompson Hill Road directly to the freeway overpass. He thought to himself, *The early bird gets the... today, it could be the shaft.* Another thought came through. He punched his microphone again.

"Dispatch, Engine 804 calling."

"This is dispatch. Go ahead."

"What's the status of Air-One? Over." Air-One was the local medical helicopter stationed at Mercy Hospital. It was proper protocol to check, even if the weather might not permit flying.

There was a delay between transmissions. It probably meant the dispatcher was checking on another channel. The response came thirty seconds later.

"Dispatch to Engine 804."

"Go ahead, Dispatch."

"Mercy says Air-One is grounded due to weather. Over."

"Thank you, Dispatch. 804 is on the side."

Johnston actually felt relieved. It would have been a miracle to have the helicopter flying in this kind of weather. Neither the FAA nor the pilots liked the idea of their rotors icing up in a snowstorm. Iced-up rotors had a tendency to take the pilot and crew directly to the scene of the crash—their own. Johnston never did like the idea of a giant blade rotating close to his head, though he had to admit that a helicopter was very handy when they needed to get a trauma code patient to the hospital quickly.

One by one the Station 8 units turned at the intersection to the freeway and began the short climb up the entrance ramp. They could not drive faster than thirty miles per hour with their chains rattling and jangling on their wheels, but the weather was bad enough that Johnston appreciated the traction they provided. They had to go up Thompson Hill. Two miles to go— four minutes.

The radio crackled again. "Dispatch to all units responding to 10-52 on I-35." The dispatcher did not wait for a response. Captain Johnston listened intently. "We have a report from sheriff's and Minnesota Highway Patrol units at the scene controlling traffic. Gasoline fires are confirmed. MVA includes two trucks and up to twenty passenger vehicles. Main fire involves a fuel bowser that is ruptured and burning on the guardrail. Implementing Level One MCI response. Use extreme caution. Over."

Johnston knew from the broadcast that law enforcement people were on the scene trying to get traffic out of the way for emergency crews. A Level

One MCI response status meant emergency fire, rescue, law enforcement, and cleanup crews would be arriving from the cities of Duluth and Proctor. The St. Louis County Sheriff's Department and Minnesota State Highway Patrol would also be there. Highway departments would send trucks with plows. Gas station wreckers would be called. Even the Air National Guard Fire Station would send their specialized foaming truck for fire suppression. Like emergency teams around the country, the teams in the Duluth area were all well rehearsed for Mass Casualty Incidents.

Engine 804 was a quarter mile ahead of Engine 802 when they heard the next transmission.

"Dispatch to all units responding to 10-52 on I-35. Station 10, Engine Ten-Ooh-One reports Thompson Hill Road is impassable. They will turn around and come up on the Interstate."

"Just fine," Johnston told Janine. It would take Station 10 another fifteen minutes to get turned around... if they didn't get stuck. Just *damned* fine. He hoped the Proctor units could get there quickly or Station 8 would be on their own for a while.

They were less than a half mile from the accident scene when traffic started blocking their way to the orange glow they could see through the snow and fog. Janine turned and exclaimed, "Holy shit, Captain!"

Johnston confirmed her description, "This looks like the one we hoped we'd never see on the Hill." As they approached the fire, he began assessing the situation. He picked up the microphone and clicked the switch, "Dispatch, Engine 804."

"Go ahead, 804."

"Wind is blowing smoke and fire east away from the road. Southbound lane is clear. Traffic is stopped below the scene on the southbound lane. We're having some difficulty getting past some of the vehicles to the scene. Over." Johnston turned toward Janine and instructed her, "Bump a couple of these vehicles out of the way if you need to. We're gonna try to get up past the burning bowser so we can catch a hydrant and get a better idea of how to approach this beast."

The closer they got to the inferno, the fewer cars they encountered that had dared to go further, until finally there were none. As they drove past the blaze in the opposite lane, not fifty feet from the burning wreckage, Johnston could swear he felt the intense heat from the fire through the closed windows of the Rescue Engine. Ahead, Johnston could see flares and the wigwag lights of a deputy sheriff's patrol car. An officer stood on the road waving his flashlight.

Johnston could tell that Janine was flustered by the time she got to the accident scene because she almost ran into the deputy sheriff's squad car. He recognized the deputy and rolled down the window and shouted with bravado, "Who the hell are you? The parking valet?"

"I'm doin' a hell of a job, don't you think?" the deputy grinned as he shouted back at him.

Captain Johnston surveyed the wreckage and hopped down from the engine. "You're doin' great. Looks like you only banged up a couple so far. I'm gonna need a lot more parking spaces when my party arrives." He turned to look behind Engine 804. He could see the flashing lights from the next engine coming up through the snow. "I figured a few of us would go up the exit ramp and come back on the other side."

"How many are coming?" the deputy asked.

"Close to half the department's gonna show up plus reinforcements."

"We got most of the cars out of this lane." He pointed toward the overpass. "The two that are left are stuck. Your guys will have to push them off to the side of the road."

"Sounds like fun," Johnston answered. Their eyes met. The captain could tell they both knew there would be nothing fun about this rescue. "Can we get the freeway traffic bypassed at the last exit on both ends?"

"We've got it under control. We're getting it rerouted at Cody Street on the north end. We've got the overpass closed off, too, except for emergency vehicles. The State Patrol and Sheriff's Department have six more cruisers on the way. We'll bypass the northbound traffic to Highway 2. Traffic control will be a huge job until this mess is cleaned up."

"We may need to use Number 2 and Cody Street for the back route to get the ambulances into town." Johnston suggested, "See if you can route them another way until we get the freeway opened."

"You've got it," the deputy responded.

"Looks like the overpass is a good spot for a command center."

"Don't leave me, Captain," the deputy appealed, pointing at the vehicle crashed into the guardrail. "That car is starting to cook. Looks like there are two people in the front, but neither one responded to me, and I couldn't get the door open. Could be some kids in the back seat, too. They could really use some help. Do your own assessment, but I think that the five vehicles closest to the fire are all in imminent danger."

"Kids? Imminent danger? You just said the magic words." The captain turned to Janine, "We're staying here. I'll set up a temporary incident command center on the spot until the Chief gets here to take over. There are more vehicles here than we can handle, but by God, we'll get a good start and hope that reinforcements get here soon."

Johnston hopped up into the cab and told Janine to pull ahead a safe distance and make room for Engine 802 to set up behind them, pulling over as close as she could get to the center rail. As Janine set the brakes, Johnston called for his crew to change their radios to the fireground frequency. "Engine 804 to Engine 802," Johnston radioed as Janine jumped down, chocked the wheels, and prepared for action.

"Engine 802 here, Cap'n." Gramps maneuvered the FMC pumper engine with lights blazing to the center rail.

"I have a deputy sheriff with me. He says he's got people trapped and in danger in several vehicles immediately behind the fire, so I want you to set your engine up right where you are. We'll start with the sedan that's up against the guardrail. Looks like two criticals in front and possibly a couple children in the back. Next we'll work our way into the pile and rescue as many as possible."

"That's affirmative, Cap'n," Gramps responded. "We'll set up right behind you." The big 1981 FMC triple pumper engine braked to a stop behind the rescue unit. Gramps jumped almost effortlessly down from the cab and started chocking the tires.

Johnston continued giving orders, "Engine 801, go up the off ramp and catch a hydrant. I want you to lay a solid four-incher down the northbound ramp to Engine 802. Do you copy?" They carried a thousand-plus feet of the rigid pipe. With that line, Engine 801 could suck the water out of the hydrant without collapsing the hose. They could get enough water from the hydrant to supply a curtain of water, two hand lines, and a supply line to Engine 802. The four-incher would get them part way down the entrance ramp from the hydrant. There was one problem—all the hydrants were on the opposite side of the freeway. The crew would have to lay pipe across a road and block traffic. Johnston chose to block the southbound entrance ramp nearest the hydrant, then run the line across the bridge. After they got the piping to the other side of the bridge, they could run it under the bridge and through to the waiting engine.

"That's affirmative, Captain," the response came over the radio.

"As soon as you get hooked up, I want you to start a curtain of water between the burning vehicles and the cars immediately behind them. Then hook a two-and-a-half incher up to Engine 802. You'll have to pull a lot of hose, but I want you there to piggyback the water supply from your engine to 802. You got that?" he asked them.

"801 copies you, Captain. Over." The 1990 Ford LS9000 triple-combination fire engine growled and clanked its chains as it worked its way up the freeway exit ramp.

"All right, everyone, you know your jobs—get going. I'm gonna report in to the Chief. 804 is moving to the main channel. Clear on fireground frequency." Captain Johnston radioed a short report to his boss, the Duluth City Fire Chief, who was en route from headquarters with five more units. The chief would set up his command post on the overpass that overlooked the grisly scene when he arrived.

Johnston made contact with the Proctor Fire and Rescue team and gave them their instructions. One engine company would go up to the Skyline Parkway Rest Area, which was perched above the freeway. The second engine company would come down the off ramp and hook up with the team above them. Next, he called dispatch to alert the hospitals that they would soon be busy with emergency patients. Johnston switched the radio back to his crew in just over two minutes. "Eight-Zero-Four is back on fireground frequency."

Medic 803 pulled up ahead of Engine 804. Smitty and Sawbones secured their vehicle and began opening panel doors, pulling out their crashbags and other equipment.

Crew members began disgorging from their vehicles. Gramps had Engine 802's pumps up to operating pressure by the time Fearless donned his helmet and facemask and hoisted his airpack onto his back. Captain Johnston watched him as he gently rolled himself over the guardrail and carefully approached the subject vehicle.

Janine stepped to the back of the rescue truck to grab a prybar, tarps, and other tools she would need before proceeding to the dented center railing where the luxury sedan sat. Another firefighter, also in full turnout gear, was close behind with an armload of tools.

On Engine 802, firefighters peeled off the first fifty feet of hose from the back of the pumper and approached the car. They sprayed it and the road under it with a couple quick shots of "wet" water from the five-hundred gallon reservoir tank in the truck. Steam rose from the heated vehicle. Johnston expected the Engine 802 firefighter would remain ready with a fully charged hose until the rescue was completed. Gramps would stay at his work station, tending the truck and its panel of controls throughout the incident.

Two firefighters moved in to stabilize the vehicle by placing blocks under the tires and letting the air out of them. They checked for immediate hazards like fire, electrical sparks, undeployed airbags, and five-mile-per-hour safety bumpers that were waiting to pop back out. Any one of those potential hazards could severely injure both victims and firefighters.

Fearless called his fireman's identification code on his portable transmitter, "Eight-Twenty-One, Cap'n. I'm going in. I'll try to open a door. Get a floodlight on me."

"Copy, Fearless." A bright beam of light hit the car.

Johnston watched Fearless as he approached the steaming automobile. He pulled on the right rear door. No luck. He tried to open it with a prybar. No go—it was crimped shut. He tried the others, but none of them would work. "Captain, it looks like we're gonna have to tear the roof off."

"Janine, do you have the Jaws unpacked?" Johnston asked.

"Got it, Captain," she answered as she pulled the extrication tool from the rescue engine. She and another firefighter rolled over the guardrail and carried the bulky piece of equipment over to the vehicle. They would extricate the trapped victims by cutting off the roof, their second in three days.

Fearless tried to peer inside the vehicle's windows, thoroughly obscured by snow, ice, and steam. He called to the occupants, "Can you hear me in there?" There was no response. "I'm going to break the glass. If you can hear me, cover your face now." He heard nothing. He gave the bottom corner of the left rear window a sharp whack. The window shattered into a thousand pieces, showering glass on the little boy who sat quietly in his car seat. Though startled from the glass breaking and Fearless sticking his masked face in the window, the two children remained quiet.

"Oh, my God!" Fearless clicked his mike button, "Hey, everybody, there are two kids in the back seat! Get some help and some tarps over here, stat!"

XXVI

"'Tis our own eyes that are blind"
—Author, 1996

Jeff Arneson hovered in the blowing and melting snow over the hospital supply truck. He watched the pillar of fire as the flames rose above the burning tanker. The sights and sounds of the crash had so thoroughly distracted him that he couldn't remember getting out of the car. Somehow, he managed to move down to the southbound lane of the freeway across the guardrail from the burning truck. Two cars drove right through him before he decided to get out of the way. It didn't hurt—how strange! It was as though they didn't even know he was there. Hell's bells! Nobody even honked!

Jeff knew where he was—he just didn't know why he wasn't inside his own car. His car! Jeff had to find his car—and his family. He walked through the guardrail in front of the hospital supply truck, then moved between the two trucks. Nearby, the fire raged out of control as Jeff peered into the burning wreckage. Three others were moving around the fire, but none of them looked familiar. It was so weird! Here he was twenty feet from the fire, yet he felt no pain from the searing heat.

I must find my family, Jeff reminded himself. Turning away from the fire, Jeff moved around the hospital supply truck. There it was! My God, it was a mess! Jeff ran over to it, hoping....

He heard Danielle screaming inside the wreck, "Help! Somebody please help us!" she shrieked.

Jeff hollered to her, "Dani! I'm outside the car! I'll get you out." He tried to look inside, but the windows were obscured. "I can't open the doors!" Over and over he tried to grab the handles, but his hands slipped right through them.

Danielle kept screaming, "Somebody, please help!" Her plea rang inside Jeff's head.

"Dani, get out of the way," Jeff shouted. "I'm going to break the window." Jeff hoped a karate-type kick might work. He raised his foot and noticed he was barefoot. *The hell with it. Shoes or not, I've got to get inside.* He gave the window a hard kick. His foot passed through the glass, but the window didn't break! *What's going on?* Two cars had driven through him, he'd walked through the guardrail, and now this—Jeff finally realized he was out of his physical body! He had a thought—might as well give it a try.

Jeff thrust his head into the window. He was shocked when it passed right through the glass and metal. Relieved, he found himself face to face with Danielle. "Honey, don't cry. I'm here."

"I never should have left the house," she lamented. "Why didn't I listen to my father? I'm so scared, Jeffrey." Danielle grabbed his neck and pulled him further into the car. She sobbed, holding Jeff tightly.

Jeff put his arms around her and tried to comfort her. "It's okay, baby." He looked into her eyes. "I'm here for you." The children sat crying in the back seat. "How are Joey and Melissa?" he asked.

"They're scared. I don't think they're injured, but we could all burn up if we can't get out of here. Where did you go, Jeffrey? I was so scared."

"I was outside. I watched the whole thing from the air—it was terrible," he told her. "How are you?"

"I don't feel so good, Jeffrey. My body keeps kicking me out. I tried to go back in, but now I can't do anything. I'm stuck. Look at me. What can I do?"

Jeff was so intent on comforting Danielle that he'd barely noticed the two lifeless bodies in the front seat until now. A man was slumped over the steering wheel, face drenched in blood. Next to him was a woman's crumpled body, lying on the seat in a pool of blood that oozed from the right side of her head. Jeff choked up when he tried to touch her wounded head and his hand passed right through it. A ton of bricks was poised to hit him as he asked Danielle, "That's me in the driver's seat?"

"That's not you, Jeffrey. It's only your body."

Jeff stammered, "I am... you mean I'm...."

"Now, do you believe me? Look at us! This is horrible."

Danielle communicated as if she was thinking out loud rather than speaking. It didn't matter to Jeff how they communicated—it only mattered that they could.

"Calm down, Dani. There must be an explanation for all of this." As he strained to rationalize, Jeff looked down to where he should have seen his own torso, legs, and feet. Instead, what he saw was an ethereal bodily form—lighter, brighter, and almost transparent. The strange part was that it felt completely natural! Although this vision of himself seemed surrealistic, he still had control of his limbs and his thinking process, as much as they'd been under his control during the thirty-four years he'd been alive.

Jeffrey panicked as he realized their fate. "Oh, God! We must be dead! It's all my fault for following that truck so closely. I'm so sorry, honey," he apologized.

"We can't dwell on the accident. We can't let this happen to us, Jeffrey. We *must* get back inside our bodies so we can help the children!" Joey and Melissa continued crying, still buckled into their safety seats.

"I'll try to help them," Jeff said.

"I'm going to try lying very still in my body to see if I can get back inside," Danielle explained.

Jeff moved through the seatback to the children, hoping to pull them out of the car and away from the burning trucks. He couldn't get a grip on them. His hands passed right through their car seats, through the seat belts, through Joey and Melissa as though they were not there! Frustrated, he thought, *It's no good. What am I going to do?*

"Jeffrey! Jeffrey, where are you?" Danielle anxiously called to him from the front seat. He turned and looked. Danielle was sitting, connected at the hip to her motionless body that lay on the seat. She looked like a double exposure as she propped herself up on the seat with one arm.

"I'm right here, baby." Jeff leaned over the seatback as he answered, "I can't get the kids out."

Danielle sat crying in the front seat. She looked like Siamese twins joined together at the hips. "It's no good, Jeffrey. I can't get back inside." Jeff could still make out her features of arms, head, and torso, but she was clothed in a garment far different from the outfit she'd worn for work.

"Can't you help them?"

Jeff felt completely helpless. "I can get to them, but I can't do anything," he responded. "I can't even release the buckles."

"We need to get help," Danielle said.

Jeff remembered seeing others moving around the crash scene. Maybe they were in a similar condition and knew what to do. Jeff said, "Wait here. I'll be right back." He stepped out of the car through the door and looked around.

Next to the burning truck, three men circled around a teen-age boy. Jeff approached the group. He could hear them yelling. It must be the fuel transport driver and the others who were in the crash! They were busy relaying their anger to the young man who had caused the accident, telling him how they didn't have bodies to return to. They scolded him for trying to beat them onto the freeway from the entrance ramp and losing control of his car. They yelled at the boy, telling him he could go straight to hell for doing this to them. When Jeff interrupted them, they invited him to give the young man a piece of his mind. It was obvious to Jeff that they were in no mood to give any type of aid, so he decided to return to his own wrecked car and his family.

As Jeff turned back toward his car, the young man called out to him. "Wait, mister, please!" he begged. He came over to Jeff and communicated, "I'm very sorry, mister. I didn't mean to hurt anyone. Please forgive me."

Jeff didn't know what to think, so he just reached out to him and touched his hand. The others started moving toward them to continue their lectures.

The boy asked Jeff, "Do you think you can go back?"

"I don't know."

The boy reached out and placed something in Jeff's hand. "Please, mister, give this to my mom and tell her I love her." Jeff looked at the object in his hand. It was a small silver cross on a necklace.

Jeff returned to his car. He passed through the back door, intent on comforting his wife and children. Danielle sat in the front seat, still partially attached to her body. Tears rolled off her face as she sang to the children, "Hush, my little babies, don't you cry...."

"Looks like we have to wait for help," he told her.

Danielle put her index finger over her mouth, gesturing for Jeff to be quiet. Jeff listened as she sang her mournful lullaby. The children must have sensed her presence because they had stopped crying.

Suddenly, Jeff heard a whooshing sound and felt himself being sucked through a dark tunnel. The pain was excruciating! He moaned a couple times, let out a breath, and passed back out. It was like he'd been drawn into his body, then blown back out. Again he found himself outside the car, so he went back to his family.

"Where did you go?" Danielle asked in a soft voice.

"I think I went back into my body."

Danielle became excited. Her thoughts immediately were transmitted to Jeff, "If there's any chance at all, you must go back for the children."

"I don't appear to be in control of that," he responded. "Besides, I want to stay here with you."

A beam of light enveloped Danielle. She sparkled as she looked up, as if she could see through the roof of the car. Her voice cracked, "I think they're coming for me, Jeffrey."

"Don't go, Dani. Stay with us, please!" Jeff pleaded as Danielle ascended through the roof of the car. Then he was shocked as a side window exploded into a thousand pieces and flew around the interior of the car. Bright lights flooded the car's interior as a silhouette shoved its masked head into the open window. So many strange new things were happening at once, it was confusing.

XXVII

"...but the chaff he will burn with a fire unquenchable."
—*Bible* (KJV) *St. Luke* 3:17

Date: Wednesday, November 26, 1997
Time: 7:30 A.M.
Place: Interstate 35, Thompson Hill, Duluth, MN

Station 8 had more fires, wrecks, and rescues than they could possibly handle, but they would do their best until reinforcements arrived. Captain Johnston hoped their best would be enough. After hosing down the luxury sedan, the hose tender kept a spray over the other vehicles near the fire to cool them down.

The vehicle closest to the blaze was the hospital truck. They needed to check it out. Johnston clicked his shoulder mike, "Hose down the truck. Sawbones, check out the truck driver while the others block and stabilize that car."

A shower of water suppressed the fire that smoldered under the hood and helped cool the cab down. Under the captain's watchful eye, Sawbones reached for the driver's side door handle and pulled. The door opened. He climbed up into the cab to make an assessment of the driver, then jumped down. He pressed the microphone switch on his portable radio. "Captain, the driver is dead. There are no vital signs. He'll wait for extrication." There was no sense wasting time moving a corpse. "Wouldn't hurt to keep some water on the truck though. It'll help shield us from the big fire."

"That's affirmative, Sawbones." Johnston called to the FEO, "Gramps, how much water is left?"

Gramps answered him, "We're down to two hundred twenty-five gallons, Captain." Over half their water supply was already gone.

Johnston ordered, "You better save the water for the cars until we get hooked into the hydrant."

"I copy you, Captain," the firefighter tending the hose responded and shut the hose down.

They desperately needed more water. Johnston turned and looked for Engine 801. He saw it working its way across the overpass. Two firefighters were under the bridge preparing a section of line to attach to the four-incher when they got to the corner. The engine turned down the ramp where it would connect to the four-inch water line and begin running hoses to Engine 802. Johnston would have them set up a protective water curtain between the rescue scene and the fire that blazed ahead of them. It would still be a few minutes.

Sawbones joined the crew as they continued working on the luxury sedan. Two firefighters had already taken tools resembling can openers and pried the rubber seals, first around the laminated pieces of broken glass that used to be the windshield, and then around the unbroken rear window. Once the rubber seal was popped out, the windows were easily removed from the vehicle by two firefighters. Quickly, firefighters covered the victims inside with protective tarps and knocked out the rest of the side windows.

Bones and Smitty moved in and did a quick assessment of the occupants. "Smitty, something's wrong. These kids are too quiet. They should be scared and crying. I'm afraid they could have internal injuries. They must be in shock."

"We'll keep a close eye on them," Smitty said as she did her assessment on the little girl. "We sure don't want one of them to crash on the trip to the hospital."

Sawbones and Smitty worked on the two children as firefighters moved in with the Jaws of Life. Using the pneumatic tool, they cut off the hood hinges, pried the crumpled hood loose from the car, and moved it out of the way. Next, they cut the battery cables, eliminating ninety percent of the chances for an electrical short or fire. They began cutting the door posts and metal parts that held the roof to the car. Two others helped to lift as they cut the entire roof off so they could get at the two children who sat quietly underneath protective blankets.

Once the roof was off, Bones and Smitty unbuckled the infant seats and lifted the two children out, car seats and all, letting the seats serve as splints to keep them immobilized. The two paramedics handed the children to two firefighters, also trained EMT's, who carried them to the safety and warmth of the waiting ambulance.

Three firefighters remained with Sawbones and Smitty while the others moved the Jaws to the next vehicle and prepared to extricate more victims. Ahead of them, all the vehicles were engulfed in flames. There was no hope of anyone escaping that inferno. They'd surely been consumed by the fireball of burning gasoline, so the firefighters would focus their attention on the vehicles immediately behind the fire. Behind them lay a long trail of cars and trucks littering the road.

Bones and Smitty pulled the tarps off the parents in the front seat. Bones could see movement and labored breathing efforts in the driver. His face was bloody—probable broken nose, brain contusion, and neck injuries.

On the passenger's side, Smitty did her initial observation of the female, checking for heartbeat, pulse, and respirations. "Sawbones, I see severe trauma to the right side of the passenger's head with a possible skull fracture and broken neck." She peeked underneath the matted and bloodied hair. "I can see gray matter coming through a puncture wound at the source of the bleeding."

"What are her vitals?" Sawbones asked.

"There's no definite signs of life—no pulse and no respirations." She described what she saw to Bones. If they left her in the car, she could cook in the heat from the fire. If they took her, they might lose someone else who had a better chance of being saved.

Sawbones asked her, "Is your conclusion that she's sustained catastrophic damage?" Sawbones knew it was possible, given unlimited resources, to save such a patient to a life with brain damage and questionable quality.

"I really think so," Smitty told him. Under adverse circumstances such as these, their training told them to move on to the next patient. It was such a shame, a damned shame.

"We'll just take the driver. Cover her." Sawbones directed the work of the firefighters as they performed a rapid extrication on the male, working with them to stabilize the patient's back and neck on a longboard with straps and duct tape. There was no time for cervical collars or other fancy work. They had to minimize spine and head movement and get him out of the danger zone quickly. Two firefighters carried the longboard, or rigid stretcher, to the staging area, which currently was the back of Medic 803. Smitty and Bones moved on to the next vehicle where firefighters were busy removing another roof.

Just as the tanker fire seemed to be burning itself out, a bulkhead between storage sections of the trailer blew out. Burning fuel exploded into flames as it found spark and oxygen, sending a new fireball that engulfed the hospital supply truck not twenty feet from the luxury sedan. Too late to help, firefighters reacted by running away from the ball of fire. Johnston knew that if the flames had reached his crew, they would have been burnt toast. The hose tender stood his ground and opened the nozzle of his firehose, pathetically small for the situation, to meet the huge fire that threatened them. For a moment, fire and water existed together as he fought the flames with his few remaining gallons of water. Slowly, the fire receded back behind the shower of water to the hospital supply truck.

"Captain to crew, are you guys okay?"

"Fearless here, Cap'n. Whew! That was close, but we're all right... just about got the roof off the next one."

"You have one minute of water left. When it's gone, you fall back to a safer position and start extrication on cars twelve and thirteen. You hear me? If there's anyone left in those forward vehicles, you're to leave them 'til Engine 801 gets more water on line to us."

"But, Captain..."

"That's an order, Fearless!"

"Ten-Four, Captain." Fearless clicked off his radio.

Johnston knew they would run out of water before they were able to finish opening the second car. He knew he'd be right in ordering them to fall back, even though he, too, hated the idea of leaving any of the victims stranded. Johnston watched as Fearless and three other firefighters finished popping off the roof. Bones must have crawled in through the rear window, because he was now sitting in the back seat and working with the patients, doing what he could to make sure they came out quickly. "How are they, Bones?"

"Both victims have injuries, Captain," Sawbones reported on the fireground frequency. "They're conscious and very scared." They were sliding the boards in under the patients when Engine 802 lost water pressure.

"Captain to all ground units, time to fall back."

"Captain, we've just about got these two. Give us one more minute and we'll have them out."

"You grab them and go," Johnston affirmed, then called to the hose tender, "Back out with your hose. Do you read?"

"Affirmative, Captain," he answered back.

Captain Johnston watched as they retreated with two more patients on backboards. They moved back fifty feet and began blocking and prepping another car as they waited for water. Ahead of them, firefighters from Engine 801 finished pulling three hundred feet of line for the water curtain. They set it on the roadway ahead of the just-emptied vehicle, and one of them called on the fireground frequency to their FEO, "She's ready—let her go." The FEO opened the valve, charging the two-and-a-half-inch line. A spray of water shot into the air, creating a curtain of water over twenty feet high and forty feet wide between the burning wrecks and the victims still trapped in their vehicles.

Johnston gave a sigh of relief and watched as the Engine 801 crew charged a two-and-a-half incher to Engine 802, bringing a welcome water supply back to its hose. The firefighter resumed hosing around the next three vehicles. One was in the left lane behind the Arneson car and the other two were locked together in the right lane behind the roof they had just removed. They had only pumped hydrant water for thirty seconds when the next sets of lights came into view from the south.

XXVIII

"It was a place where time had no meaning."
—Common observation by near-death experience survivors

It may have been a second, a minute, or an hour since the accident. Jeff had lost his sense of time. He'd watched Danielle as she floated through the roof of the car and had waited anxiously as the firefighters cut off the roof and removed the children from the car. He was also a spectator as they began working on his and Danielle's bodies in the front seat.

"Jeffrey, I'm up here." He looked skyward. Danielle, wrapped in a white mist, floated thirty feet above the car. Jeff called to his wife. "I knew that help would be here. The kids'll be safe now." Danielle was silent as she watched her children being carried to the ambulance.

She beckoned to her husband with outstretched arms. "Jeffrey, they're coming for me. Come, say good-bye."

Not knowing how he did it, Jeff levitated to her and entered the mist that surrounded her. He felt no panic, only peace and calm. This was like nothing he'd ever experienced. It was more than any reality. It was like super-reality.

Jeff's eyes met hers—she was crying. He held her and tried to comfort her. Danielle seemed to have a sense about what was happening. She telegraphed her thoughts to Jeff, "You can't help me, but just stay close as long as they let you."

Jeff watched as three beings approached them. Danielle shrieked, "It's Papa!"

Jeffrey was shocked when he recognized Danielle's deceased father among the beings. *He must be here to help her*, Jeff thought.

"Oh, Papa! You must help the children!" she begged.

"It'll be all right, baby. Don't fear for their safety. Those nice people who took them from the car will take care of everything. They've done this before. They are very good humans," her father assured her.

Jeff could hardly believe what he was seeing. He'd just scolded his wife for having her dream, obviously a premonition, and now here was her father standing before him! His father-in-law looked much better than he had during his final days. After Papa's first heart attack, he languished in the ICU until the second one finished him off. It had been a difficult week, especially for Dani. She'd been very close to her father.

Papa seemed to know what Jeff was thinking. "I'm much better, don't you think?"

"Is it really you?"

"Yes, Jeffrey."

"How did you know we were here? I mean you're here—you're not dead!"

"Yes, son, it really is me. I should ask you the same question. I hoped neither one of you would be here. I tried to warn Dani, but now it's too late. *She* must go with us, but *you're* not supposed to be here."

"Well, I am," Jeffrey answered. "There doesn't seem to be much I can do about it. None of the others in the accident know what to do either."

"You spoke with the others?" Papa asked with concern, then relaxed. "I hope it didn't hurt anything, but I'm sure it didn't help. You shouldn't visit with them until your journey is completed. They are angry and confused. Their guides may do something different with them. They may not even go to the same place. If you try to communicate with them anymore, it may hinder your own transition."

"Okay," Jeff agreed, "but don't leave me here alone with them. Please, I just want to be with Dani, even if it's just for a little while."

Papa turned and consulted with the other beings. He turned back to Jeffrey, "I guess we need to do something with you. We'll take you with us."

"Who are the others?"

"They are Winnifred and Crusias. When you were a child, you called them angels. They are here to help and guide you. Don't be afraid; just do what they tell you."

Jeff had no clue how he could be flying or where they were going. It was like riding on a space shuttle, only much faster. The crash scene shrank, then disappeared. Their view of the entire earth diminished. Smaller... smaller... until it was gone. They all traveled together—Jeff and Danielle, Papa, Winnifred, and Crusias.

Jeff thought there was something different about the two beings. Their presence seemed so powerful that negative thoughts and worries just melted away. He turned to his father-in-law, "Where are their wings?"

Papa appeared amused by the question, "Son, look all around you. Do you see anything to stand on?"

Jeff looked around. They were surrounded by the universe.

"Do you have wings, Jeffrey? How can you fly without wings?" If there had been a way to fall, Jeff would surely have done it. Papa smiled, "Don't worry. You won't fall."

"Why are they here?"

"They're here to help," Papa's thoughts came to him. "Their kind has been helping us since the beginning of time."

Jeff watched them. They were particularly attentive to Danielle. He could not sense what they were doing or saying to her, but they appeared very businesslike in their "work". His only sense of movement now was a blur of lights. They could have been in night traffic, but Jeff sensed that it was more than that. It could be sunbeams or stars. Then came an intense light, much brighter than the others. Through the light, Jeff focused on a point that grew in size. Perhaps, he thought, it was a planet. As the group approached this place, Jeff thought it looked like pictures he'd seen of earth taken from space.

Jeff felt as though they were coming in for a landing, but the place may have been coming to them instead. There were hills and sky, clouds and a horizon, rivers and lakes, trees and flowers, and cities and villages, just like earth, only these were more beautiful, brighter, clearer, cleaner, newer. "What is this place?" Jeff queried.

The one Papa had called Crusias answered, "This place will be Danielle's new home."

"Am I going with her?"

"We don't know yet. That is why we've only spoken with her. We don't think your time has come."

"When will you know?"

"We'll know when you do. Until then, I'd say you are along for the ride." Crusias confided in Jeff, "This is very difficult for Danielle. Your being here with her gives her much comfort, but she is gravely concerned about your children. She will not be able to return, but she senses that you could. You may be given a choice between returning to them or staying here with her," Crusias told him. "I shall continue to be here with you. Winnifred will attend to Danielle."

When they landed, they were at the edge of the scene they'd just flown over. They were separated from the beautiful place by a great chasm with a river running through it. They "stood" before a great gateway that appeared to be the demarcation between them and the beautiful scene Jeff had just seen. They were still surrounded by structures and natural topography similar to the view from the "air," but there was less color, less intensity, less "life" to the scene on this side of the chasm.

Jeff sensed Danielle's thoughts as they were transmitted to him. "I am so confused. I want you to be with me, but I also feel that only you can go back to be with the children. Winnifred has told me that you may have a choice." Jeffrey could feel Danielle's pain and her love. He sensed they would not be together long.

Crusias invited Jeff and Danielle, "Come before the Master." The moment he said this, Jeff saw a bright light in a swirl of clouds. It looked like a ball of lightning filled with smoke and fire glowing from the area that the gateway had occupied. Jeff was reminded of a scripture reading, "All those who come to the Father, come by me."

The light was so very bright; bright enough to blind the human eye; bright enough to shine right through one's own body; bright enough to cast a light on every good or bad thought and deed. It was a penetrating light. Jeff felt the greatest sense of love he had ever felt. It was strong, accepting, and giving. As Jeff watched, he thought he caught a glimpse of the Master. He was not *in* the light—He *was* the Light. Jeff turned his "eyes" away, for the being was so bright that it hurt his newly found senses. He looked toward where the others had been. If they were still there, he could not see them. The Master addressed him, "Why are you here? Do you think your life is complete?"

In a microsecond, his thoughts were read and the Being of Light transmitted an answer back to Jeff at the same time as Jeff realized his questions. "You have been badly injured. If you go back, you will suffer much pain before you recover. Let us see if you are ready to come home."

Jeff's mind whirred with memories of his earthly life. They were his memories, but he sensed he was not in control. It was like seeing a movie. All the characters of his life were in it—his mother and father, his sister, all of his family, his teachers, his friends, and his enemies.

Jeff recalled times when he had done both good and bad. His darkest secrets were revealed. He saw himself playing and fighting with his brother; with his family during their work, their meals together, and their vacations; with people he loved and the ones he hated; with Danielle; with other girls before her. He saw the day he and Danielle were wed. With shame, he watched his affair with a co-worker while his wife was pregnant with their second child. He felt the effect of his absence on his family because of his drive to succeed in the firm.

Jeff saw the impact all of his actions had on others whose lives he had affected. His entire life was laid bare before his eyes by the Being of Light. He felt great shame for his sins and fulfillment from his accomplishments. He experienced the hurts, anxieties, and joys all over again. Yet, through it all, Jeffrey felt loved.

Jeffrey was aware he was being questioned about each situation, questions like: What did you learn from this? What would you do differently? Do you have any regrets about this? In a flash, it was over. He was alone in the Light. Jeffrey begged to understand why Danielle's life's work was finished, why the accident had happened to them, and why these beings didn't look like the pictures he'd seen of angels. Many questions were answered, but he was told that much would be forgotten, or blotted out, if he returned to his physical life.

The Light addressed him, "You have come to the time of decision. Danielle must come to me in Eternity. If you come to me, you will keep the answers to all of your questions and gain great wisdom. You will be with your wife and many other loved ones, but you may never return to your children. Once you cross over, you may never return to your earthly state. It is your choice."

Jeff turned to where Danielle had been. He could not see her but sensed her presence. Apparently, his life story had also been laid bare before her and the small group. He could hear her words. "I forgive you, Jeff. It hurts to see the whole truth, but I still love you. Thank you for sharing so much of your life with me. Please, you must go back to the children. Let them always know that I love them."

He felt the shame once again. He wished he could somehow...

"Jeff!" She commanded his full attention. "You will make it up to me by going back. Please! Say you'll go back to the children for me, for us!"

Jeff knew what his answer must be—he would return. The Light knew Jeffrey's decision.

Danielle approached him—he could see her in the glowing light. Danielle said, "Look at me. Hold me. You will not see me again for a long time."

Her essence embraced him. It was a closeness like nothing he'd ever felt with her before. They were complete, one with each other. Their souls merged in the Light of the Father.

"Good-bye, my love." Her words went to his very core. And then, it was over. Jeff tried to hold on to her, but he felt her slip away as she disappeared into the Light. It was time to go back.

The Light dimmed. Jeff could see Crusias offering his hand, so he took it. The great gateway grew dim. A voice called out to him, "Do not let your heart be troubled. She will be safe with Me." The scenes of the other world disappeared as Jeff sensed himself traveling through a passageway. Then he heard other voices, human voices, urgent voices. He felt something pulling on him like a giant vacuum cleaner sucking, tugging at him. There was a whoosh as waves of terrible pain led him to the blackness.

XXIX

"He knows not his own strength that hath not met adversity."
—Ben Johnson, "Explorata," *Timber* (1640) (p. 11)

Date: Wednesday, November 26, 1997
Time: 7:40 A.M.
Place: Interstate 35, Thompson Hill, Duluth, MN

With only two paramedics and one ambulance at the scene, Sawbones had to act as both medic and triage officer until reinforcements arrived. He established a triage station out the back door of Medic 8. He'd studied triage, the process of evaluating and treating the injured and deciding who received medical treatment first based upon who needed it most desperately and who had the best chances for survival. Sawbones knew the process well, but he disliked being the one to decide a patient's fate. He and Smitty had already left one woman with a catastrophic injury in her car, and he feared there would be more.

Returning from the wrecked car with their first set of patients, Sawbones examined the two children. Both children were crying now which was a good sign, and both had cuts from the broken glass. He cleared the glass from their seats as best he could, checked them for obvious injuries, and took their pulses and blood pressures. Their vital signs were good. Sawbones knew their child seats and seat belts had helped to save their lives. It was a calculated risk to delay sending them to the hospital, especially since they had been in the same car as the woman they'd just left for dead. They were short of assets so Sawbones decided he would have them brought in by squad car with Medic 803 riding behind them as soon as there was adequate staff at the scene. He gave them each a yellow tag which meant they needed to be transported soon, but had no life-threatening conditions.

Sawbones moved to the male driver. Under the lights behind the ambulance, Sawbones saw the extent of Jeff's injuries. His pulse was weak, and he had irregular and shallow respirations. He was gurgling blood and sputum that had collected in the back of his throat. He was unconscious and unresponsive. Bones suctioned out the patient's mouth and throat and checked for blockages in his airway. His broken nose and facial cuts meant that he could be inhaling blood into his lungs after it dripped into his windpipe.

The patient's head was taped to the longboard so Sawbones did a jaw thrust to open his airway, then intubated him to keep it open, using a curved plastic tube that reached from the mouth into the trachea. He could now ventilate the patient with pure oxygen, helping him to breathe by methodically pushing air into his lungs through the ET tube, then letting it out. *This one's got a chance*, he said to himself, *but he could be bleeding internally. We need to get him out of here*. He put a red tag on Jeff.

Smitty returned with three firefighters and two more patients on long boards. They set the stretchers down next to the red-tagged male. Sawbones said, "I need some help over here." A firefighter took over ventilating Jeff Arneson as Sawbones began the triage process on the next patients. More would be arriving soon.

"Fireground Command, this is MN DOT 2801. Please acknowledge." MN DOT designated Minnesota Department of Transportation.

Johnston keyed his portable radio, "MN DOT 2801, this is Fireground Commander Captain Johnston. Go ahead."

"Yeah, Captain, I have three state plow trucks standing by if you need us." The gang of three snowplow trucks that was moving south on the freeway had returned in the northbound lane.

"MN DOT, what's your Ten-Twenty?"

"We're waiting by the Spirit Mountain off ramp about four hundred yards behind you."

Johnston looked back. Through the falling snow and sore, strained eyes, he could see the blue strobe lights flashing from the large trucks. "Thanks for coming, guys," he said. "Two of you can plow and gravel up the ramp and across the overpass. One of you can open Boundary Avenue into Proctor, and the second can plow Highway 2 into the city for the emergency vehicles. The third truck can move forward with some tools so we can take down a couple of the center barricades. He can help clear a staging area and move some of the stranded cars. Over."

"That's affirmative, Captain. Plows are moving. Give your people a 'heads up' on our movement."

Johnston watched the three sets of blue flashing lights moving as per his orders when another set of lights appeared at the overpass.

A voice came across the fireground frequency, "Fireground Command, AIRNAT FOUR is on the scene at the overpass. Where do you want us?" It was the Air National Guard tanker engine with a roof-mounted articulated nozzle. The huge fire engine was designed to shoot out a layer of fire suppression foam on a runway or burning aircraft. They would use it to suppress the fuel fire.

"This is Fireground Command. You guys are a sight for sore eyes! AIRNAT FOUR, come down the off ramp and set up on the fuel bowser. Pull over as close as you can get to the center rail. Do you copy?"

"AIRNAT FOUR copies. Over." The huge truck backed up twenty feet, then made a wide left turn down the wrong way onto the off ramp.

The captain had a serious traffic problem. It was time for some quick decisions. He clicked his microphone. "All units coming up Thompson Hill, if you can see the fire, stop! I repeat, STOP." Slowly, AIRNAT FOUR drove past the captain and the Station 8 vehicles and parked near the center guardrail fifty feet from the burning wreckage. The crew, safely inside the cab, hit the pump control and aimed a stream of white foam directly at the burning truck and trailer. It would only take a few minutes before the inferno was under control.

As quickly as AIRNAT FOUR was in position, Johnston called back to the others, "All responding units coming up the hill, you may now proceed."

Ten vehicles slipped and slid as their chained wheels rolled up the snow-covered hill to the scene. They included the Duluth Fire Chief's command vehicle, four fire engines, three medic units, and two rescue vehicles.

"Fireground command, Double Oh-One. I have you in view," the Duluth Fire Chief called to his captain.

"Go ahead, sir." Johnston could see the chief's truck.

"Double Oh-One is prepared to transfer Incident Command."

"Affirmative, Zero-Zero-One. Recommend you set up your command on the edge of the overpass."

"Double Oh-One copies that." Johnston listened as the Chief began his orders.

"Stations 1 and 7, all rescue and medic units stay on the southbound lane and form a triage area just beyond the off ramp. All other engines, follow me up the ramp. Engine One-Oh-One, go back down the northbound ramp and set up next to Engine Eight-Oh-One. Next engine up will run a line to you from Hydrant 602S. We'll get another water curtain up and a feeder line out to AIRNAT FOUR." The Chief instructed the three remaining engines to stand by with their lines utilizing their on-board tanks. He dispatched the firefighters from those engines to help with rescue operations.

In all, Johnston figured they would lay over three thousand feet of hose and hooked lines through three hydrants and six sets of pumps to bring a steady supply of water to the scene. Laying the line was comparatively easy. Pulling it back up and drying the hoses after the fire was the tough job. There were going to be a lot of sore muscles tonight.

A van with large lettering that said KDMP TV had arrived at the scene. The local television station set up a camera crew on the overpass and began filming for the 12 o'clock news.

A Duluth Transit Authority bus had even shown up at the triage area as part of the rescue operation. It would hold the "walking wounded," giving them a safe, warm place to wait until they could be transported to one of the hospitals for evaluation and treatment. Johnston figured twenty or more drivers and their passengers were waiting, shivering from the cold, when it arrived.

Firefighters and paramedics were assigned to teams. The teams went to work, extricating and stabilizing the vehicles assigned to them. Everything got so busy at ground zero that the chief assigned one firefighter to traffic control for all the emergency vehicles.

The accident scene filled with headlights and flashing lights from more than twenty emergency vehicles. The morning's light was filtering though the winter storm clouds. The night blackness had turned to morning gray. The fire was reduced to steam clouds that blew away with the snow.

Rescue teams and engine companies went about their work quickly and efficiently. There was a minimum of chatter on the fireground channel. "Move this unit." "Spray that vehicle." "Get some help over here."

With three more medic units and a newly assigned triage officer from headquarters, Sawbones and Smitty were anxious to get their first "red tag" to the hospital. Smitty waved Fearless and another firefighter over where the guardrail used to be. "Time to go," she told him. Fearless took off his airpack and turnout coat and shoved it in the passenger's side of the ambulance. They put the children in the deputy sheriff's squad car and loaded Jeff Arneson into the ambulance.

Sawbones spoke into his portable radio, "Transportation officer, Medic 803 here."

"Go ahead, Medic 803."

"I have a red tag in this unit and two young children in the deputy sheriff's car. Request permission to transport to Mercy Hospital."

"Medic 803, permission granted." The transportation officer helped guide Fearless away from the triage area, away from the accident scene, away from the car with the woman left inside, up the exit ramp to the freshly plowed alternate route into town.

Sawbones reached for the radio inside the cab. He changed the channel, "Mercy Hospital, Medic 803, come in...."

XXX

"In thoughts from the visions of the night, when deep sleep falleth on men, Fear came upon me, and trembling, which made all my bones shake."
—*Bible* (KJV) *Job* 5:13-14

Date: Wednesday, November 26, 1997
Time: 7:55 A.M.
Place: Mercy Hospital, Duluth, MN

Ben heard a knock and a voice at the door, "Dr. Bradley?"

"Yes, what is it?" He sat up in bed, surrounded by darkness.

"I'm sorry to wake you. I know you were up late, but we just received a call from the 911 dispatcher. There's been a multiple vehicle crash on Interstate 35. They've activated disaster status. We should start seeing some victims coming into the STU in ten or fifteen minutes."

"No problem," he said. "I'll be right out." Ben got out of bed and stumbled over to the door. He called out to the voice in the hall, "What time is it?"

"It's five to eight."

In disbelief, Ben opened the door and poked his head through to the nurse on the other side, "What day is it?"

"It's Wednesday, Doctor."

"Thanks. I must have slept really hard." He closed the door, felt for the light switch, and flipped it up. The seventy-five watt ceiling light filled the room with a reassuring glow. The dream was still fresh in his mind. Before him was his drab reality—a bed, a desk and chair, a telephone, a sink and mirror, and four bare walls.

No family, no children, no dog, no loved ones, and no window. No window? He was drenched from head to toe. He thought to himself, *Sweat, right? Better wash up before I get dressed.* He walked around the room. He touched the walls, hoping to find some evidence, some hint, of a window. There was none. He moved over to the sink, turned on the faucet, and gazed into the mirror as he waited for the tapwater to warm.

The mirror! Lord Almighty! Could he have passed through the mirror? Ben reached up and gently placed his trembling hand on it. He pushed on it thinking somehow his hand should pass through the membrane of glass and silver, but it was solid. He looked at his reflection in the mirror. Or was he looking into the lake again? It was a dream, right? It couldn't be real. Reality was so fragile. Somehow, Ben felt pressured to decide.

XXXI

"And he that was dead sat up, and began to speak..."
—*Bible* (KJV) *Luke* 7:15

Date: Wednesday, November 26, 1997
Time: 8:10 A.M.
Place: Mercy Hospital Emergency Entrance, Duluth, MN

The ambulance and deputy sheriff's squad car struggled for traction the entire trip into the city. The two vehicles pulled into the emergency entrance at Mercy Hospital after a fifteen-minute ride, covered with a filthy layer of snow and ice. Fearless jumped down from Medic 803 and stepped quickly, opening the back door of the ambulance.

Dr. Bradley and several hospital staff members, most wearing blue surgical scrubs, moved in to help. Sister Celeste was one of few not in scrubs. *True to form*, Ben thought, *she is saying her prayers*. As they lifted the patient out of the ambulance, she tried to move in close enough to touch the patient.

Ben took control. "I've got it now, Sister. You need to move back so we can do our job. Thank you for your concern."

"May I just stay near him for a minute?" she appealed.

"No." His word was final. Ignoring Celeste, he turned his attention to the back of the ambulance where Sawbones was helping to unload the patient. "What are his vitals?" Ben asked. He would triage the patient again. Bones quickly gave him the information. His vital signs had remained viable during the long ride to the hospital. "Take him to Bay Two of the STU." They would test and treat this patient aggressively in the Shock/Trauma Unit. "Did you find any identification?"

"Name's Arneson, Jeffrey A. He's an attorney here in Duluth." They began a rundown on known data.

"Everyone..." Dr. Bradley started giving orders. They were merged with the assessments that were done automatically: BP, pulse, and respirations every five minutes.

"He's been exposed to the cold for nearly an hour," Sawbones told Ben.

"Get the Bair Hugger on him, stat, then do a temp, Glascow Coma Scale, and oxygen saturation." Ben watched Jenny as she checked his reflexes and began the process of rating his neurological responses. Ben continued giving orders, "We need a full blood draw for the lab and X rays of the head, chest, and abdomen. We need a full tox screen." They would check for toxins, alcohol, and drugs. "Do we have a blood type?"

"Yes, Doctor. He had a donor card in his wallet. He's Type O Positive," the recorder piped in.

"Good. Double check the blood type. Let's get a second line going and get two units of blood ready to hang. Put his fluids on preheat and get him on a respirator." According to Ben's instructions, they would warm the intravenous solutions to help raise Jeff's body temperature. The respirator would replace the manual bagging efforts. "I want a full set of monitors on him, including the EEFM."

"You got it, Doc," one of the team members responded.

Ben expected that the Bair Hugger, similar to an air mattress filled with warm air, would help reduce Jeffrey's exposure to shock. That was the good news. The bad news was that the patient's circulation at the surface of the skin and tissue would improve. Any broken and torn blood vessels would bleed much more quickly. Ben also needed to watch for acid build-up in the blood.

Dr. Bradley continued, "When you move him onto the table, you've got to keep his neck stabilized and totally immobilized. You got that?"

"They've got him stiff as a board." It was Jenny who answered this time. Everyone on the team knew the patient had to stay immobilized until he was neurologically stable and conscious, free from the effects of any numbing drugs. To prevent further nerve damage, they would not let his neck or back move. Ben knew he was belaboring the obvious.

"Just do it!" Ben ordered. "And pass the word that he's an attorney. I want people to act like we put an orange ID tag on his big toe. Attorney or not, we need to get this guy into the STU, stat!" Everything the medical staff did and said could be held against them in a court of law. The word "attorney" was often synonymous with the word "enemy," especially when it came to malpractice lawsuits against attending physicians, hospitals, and their staffs. The "orange tag status" would enhance Ben's apparent foul mood and make things tense in the emergency room.

Ben barked orders as the Shock/Trauma team moved out of sight. Sister Celeste stood back and watched as they wheeled the patient into the hospital. She felt insulted and discouraged by the rebuff. *Dr. Bradley must have gotten up on the wrong side of the bed*, she thought. Nevertheless, she knew that he was the undisputed captain of the ship; and she followed the captain's orders, even if he was having a bad day. Celeste felt a hand on her shoulder and turned to look.

Fearless motioned to Celeste and said, "I know somebody you can help." He led her to the deputy sheriff's car which was parked ahead of the ambulance. Two nurses stood by waiting to take over for Smitty and the deputy sheriff. They were much more willing to accept the kind of help Celeste could provide. The two children, though cut and bruised, sat quietly in the back seat of the squad car with Smitty in between them, talking and singing to them as she continued with their medical needs. Dr. Bradley would assess their conditions once they were inside the ER.

No human eyes noticed the two beings riding in on the gurney or the one that was waiting near the Emergency entrance. Crusias had returned with Jeffrey and was busy trying to insert his sleeping energy field back into his body. It was not going well. His EF was as compliant as clay in the hands of a potter, but it was the flesh that was giving Crusias problems. Jeff's body was rejecting his energy field, and Crusias was holding on for dear life. A rejection could result from any number of physical problems, starting with a deterioration of the DNA chains in the body. He called out to the being by the entrance, "Will you come and help? Or are you just going to stand around and watch?"

"What do you want me to do?"

"Try to keep his legs attached. I'll keep holding him down to his head and chest."

By the time Ben was ready to assess the children, the deputy, Sister Celeste, Smitty, and two nurses had them inside the ER receiving area. Smitty gave him their vitals. Ben examined them and ordered several tests and X rays.

"Where are the parents?" Ben asked Smitty.

"We believe the patient you just sent to the STU is the father. The children were in the car with him. We think it was the mother that we left behind in the car," she answered.

"Black tag?" he asked, not knowing what words the children might understand.

"Correct," she answered.

Ben turned to Celeste, "Well, Sister, you should get a social services case worker down here and start looking for the next of kin. The male isn't doing well either."

"I'll get right on it, Doctor."

Dr. Bradley turned to dismiss Smitty, saying, "Thanks for your help. Sounds like we should both get going."

"Yeah, it's a real mess up there on the Hill." Smitty gave Celeste's hand a squeeze and said, "Take good care of them. They're really scared and confused."

Ben answered, "I *always* take good care of my patients." He turned and walked away.

Smitty looked at the others and shrugged her shoulders. She turned and walked back to the garage with the deputy, muttering under her breath, "He can be such an ass."

"Kind of like a legend in his own mind?"

"Something like that. I guess he's so good that he takes himself seriously."

It was time to restock the ambulance with another long board, a fresh tank of oxygen, and a few things from the supply closet. As the large overhead door opened, Medic 803 and the deputy's car got under way with lights and sirens for their second trip to the top of Thompson Hill.

Crusias and his helper stayed with Crusias' charge, trying desperately to hold Jeffrey's EF in his body. If the medical staff would hurry up and get the body stabilized, perhaps they could get it to "take," or absorb, the EF. Medical staff kept moving around and through the two EF's as they performed their duties with the patient. One of the nurses commented that it felt like the room was "charged" with energy.

"What are *you* doing here?" Crusias asked the other being.

"I was visiting with Ben Bradley. He's an old friend," Jim answered. "Crusias, are you sure this patient is supposed to go back?"

"I have it from the Highest Source. He's to go back in his shell and return to his children. Nobody said Humpty Dumpty would be easy either. Help me with him, and I'll nominate you for sainthood," Crusias joked.

"Hmm. Saint James," Jim mused out loud. "It has a nice ring."

He transmitted another thought to Crusias. "What do you think about waking the patient?"

"I hate to. It can get so messy. Besides, he's been through a lot already."

"He might be able to help, especially if he's determined to get back inside."

"It's worth a try. We're not getting very far this way."

Ben ordered a full workup on Jeff Arneson. There were superficial examinations for bruising and cuts; X rays to check the head and neck for injuries and to see that the ET tube was installed properly; CT scans and X rays to check the chest for injuries and see if the lungs were expanding properly; blood tests, catheterization, and urine specimens. They inserted a nasogastric tube to let the air out of his stomach to relieve pressure on his heart and lungs that had resulted from being ventilated for over thirty minutes. They also pumped fluids out of his stomach, checking further for internal bleeding. The small amount of blood they found had probably just been swallowed.

Under Ben's watchful eye, team members turned the patient over to check for injuries to his backside. They checked him for anal wink and stool specimens, looking for lack of tone in the rectum and bloody stools, sure signs of spinal damage and internal bleeding into the colon.

They checked out the seat belt bruises, facial cuts, and any other possible signs of external and internal injuries. The diagnostic capacities were significant but time-consuming. The patient was still unconscious, still unresponsive. Time was wasting.

"Jeffrey! Jeffrey, wake up!" the voice startled him.

"What?" he responded. "What do you want?"

"Jeffrey! Open your eyes. You must wake up."

"Where am I?" Jeffrey asked. He felt as if someone was shaking him by the shoulders.

"We're back in Duluth at Mercy Hospital." Crusias continued his effort to awaken him. "We're trying to get you back inside your body. We need your help."

Out of the darkness of sleep, Jeff visualized Crusias' face directly over him.

"Look at me, Jeffrey," Crusias implored. "You must wake up and help us. The medical staff is working to stabilize your body. We're having trouble getting you back inside." Jeff sat up and looked around. Sure enough, he was in some kind of medical setting. He was surrounded by people wearing surgical masks, caps, and gowns. They all seemed preoccupied with something very close by. He could see two faces, but only recognized Crusias. Jeff looked down where the other unmasked worker was holding his legs down on the table. There was another set of legs... he followed them up to the torso, then to the head and shoulders located directly under him. He recognized his own body.

"I expect you'll be able to maintain your in-body condition once we get you inside and stabilized. Right now, it's not going well."

Jeff questioned him, "Am I dreaming? Should I be afraid? Am I dead?"

Crusias answered him, "It's all true. What happened was a memory, not a dream. Jeffrey, this isn't going to be pretty, but you must trust the Master. He's given you a second chance, but it looks like we can't do it all for you. You're going to have to work to get back inside to your earthly life." Jeff looked confused. Crusias continued, "We'll help the best we can. Look around you at all the people who are working to save you. Even with all of us doing our best, we might fail if you don't help us."

"What must I do, Crusias?"

Jeffrey listened as Crusias instructed him in the art of returning to his physical body. The instructions were brief and concise. "Above all, you must not be afraid, because fear will defeat you. Do not let yourself be distracted by the humans and their work. Do not let your heart be troubled. You will feel many strange sensations—the worst part will be the feeling of being twisted around and turning inside out. When that is complete, you will be inside. You will black out when you get back inside because your body and brain are unconscious, but once you are inside, you should recover. We have much to do. Let's begin." He placed his hands on Jeffrey's head and began pushing him down toward the body. "Try to relax. There, that's better."

Jeffrey cried out, "Ouch! That hurts, Crusias."

"I can't help it." Crusias cautioned him, "You must stay focused and relaxed, Jeffrey. Imagine the most peaceful place you have ever been, but keep your focus." Jeff watched as Crusias looked upward and said, "Not my will, O Master, but Thy will be done."

Jeff tried to relax. He tried to focus on the keyway, the portal Crusias told him to find. It was so strange to be looking inside his own head. Each time Crusias pushed him inside, he could feel the pain as his essence connected with parts of his injured body. Crusias let up on the pressure. Jeffrey popped back out.

"Can you find the portal, Jeffrey?" Crusias asked.

"I can see it, but it seems to be blocked."

Ben watched as the radiology technician put the X ray films and CT scan slides up on the viewer. Examining the pictures, he said, "I think I see the main problem." Ben pointed to the slow bleed inside the brain. "He has a subdural hematoma. He's building up some pressure against the brain. We could be conservative and wait to see if it goes down by itself, but I want a second opinion. Recorder, go find out when we can get the neurosurgeon down here."

"Yes, Doctor, right away." She picked up the telephone and began calling.

"I want another view of this section while we examine our options." He pointed at the problem area. "Before you take him, give him .25 milligrams per kilogram of Versette. Inject it slowly over two minutes."

"Yes, Doctor." Per Ben's instructions, the nurse anesthetist estimated the patient's body weight in metric to calculate the total dosage. Versette was a sedative/hypnotic drug commonly used as a general anesthetic. It often caused amnesia in the patient, helping to block out memories of painful surgical procedures.

176

"Crusias, we can't let him do that," Jimmie told him.

"Do what?" Crusias asked.

"Jeffrey can't have Versette—he's not fully inside his body. If he gets the medication before he's back inside, all his memory will be blocked out. He won't remember a single thing about this experience or anything else in his life."

"Are you sure?"

"I've seen similar cases. If the essence is not inside when they administer the drug, it works as a blocker on that part of the brain. The doctors call it retrograde amnesia. His memory will be like a blank sheet of paper. I must stop him."

"Well, you better do something fast," Crusias told him. "The nurse is ready to start the injection."

"I'll try, but Ben is not in a good frame of mind. He still thinks these communications are just a dream." Jim focused as well as he knew how.... "Ben, no Versette!" He repeated the sentence over and over.

"Who said that?" Ben was clearly upset.

"Nobody said anything, Doctor," Jenny answered.

"Somebody countered my order," he pursued the matter. "Who's upstairs? Parkhurst!" He barked at the speakerphone, "Are you up there?"

"Yes, Ben, I'm here." David's voice came over the loudspeaker. "I didn't say or hear anything."

"Nurse! Hold it with that injection."

"I've already drawn it. I'll have to throw out this dose." The nurse/anesthetist's surgical mask did not conceal her frustration.

"Dammit, don't look at me like that! Just wait a minute," he scolded.

"Ben, no Versette!" Jim continued to project to his friend.

"There!" Ben exclaimed. "You heard it that time, didn't you?" He looked anxiously around the room. There was nothing but blank stares. "Come on, you guys. This isn't one bit funny." The blank stares continued.

"Ben! Check out the monitors on the EEFM," Parkhurst called from upstairs. "There were so many people in the room, I almost lost track of the patient."

"I'm a little busy down here right now, David," Ben answered.

Jim's message continued to register in the middle of Ben's consciousness. "Ben, no Versette!"

Parkhurst continued, ignoring Ben. "I had to eliminate the signal frequencies of the staff people. When I painted them all out, I could see that the patient's EF was only partially in his body. And the way I see it, Ben, there's two extra EF's standing with you at the table. They're doing something to the patient!"

"Who's saying that!" Ben looked around the room.

"I just said it, Ben. Look at the monitor!"

"Dammit, Parkhurst, I didn't mean you."

Ben's conscious mind was filled with the voice, "Jim. Jim. Jim."

"Not now, Jim," Ben spoke out loud.

"Doctor, I'm still waiting," the CRNA reminded him.

"I said to wait a minute!"

"Look. Look. Look," Jim projected.

Ben's eyes moved around the room, then settled on the monitor screen of the EEFM imager. There they were! Three EF images remained on the screen. One hovered over the patient's body. The other two stood directly opposite from where Ben stood.

"Is that you, Jim?" Ben spoke to the monitor.

"Thank heavens you got his attention," Crusias told Jim. "Can you wave at him or something?"

Jim raised his left arm and waved at the EEFM sensor. He projected his thoughts to his friend, "Come play with me, Ben. You'll see. Everything will be fine." The electromagnetic image on the monitor appeared to wave back at Ben. "Oh dear," Jim said. "Jeffrey's leg is rising back out. I'll try to get it back down."

Ben didn't catch himself before he said, "I can't play, Jim." He was dumbfounded by what he saw. Parkhurst and Jenny watched the figure wave at the same time.

Jenny gasped, "It's trying to communicate with you!"

Parkhurst said, "Looks like we know which one is the patient."

"Goddammit, David." Ben took great pride in his self-control. Control was a sign of a good trauma surgeon, and now he'd lost it. "If this is some kind of joke, you've gone way too far. This isn't funny. Not one damned bit funny."

"I swear to you, Ben. I'm not doing anything but recording and monitoring these bogeys."

"Oh, come on, David, you know better. All your scientific and medical training tells you there's no such thing as ghosts, or whatever you call these images."

"And all of our training did nothing to prepare us for this. The fact is the bogeys are there in the room with you. Besides, you're the one talking to them."

"If I shut the damned machine off, we can get back to work." Sweat dripped from Ben's forehead. Jenny wiped his brow with a cloth towel.

"I don't think that's a good idea, Ben. If this can help us save a patient, we'd best try."

"What do *you* think I should do?"

"I don't know, Ben. I've never done this before—why not try to communicate with them?"

"I already am," Ben's eyes were fixed on the waving EF.

"Don't they know we're not here to play games?" Crusias was disgusted. "We have a job to do."

Jim replied, "They need to know we're real, Crusias."

"If they know the truth, things will never be the same."

"Perhaps that is the plan." Jim turned and waved at his old friend Ben, chanting, "No Versette. No Versette!"

Parkhurst called out, "Ben, who are you talking to?"

"Jim," Ben answered.

"Who?"

"Dammit! I think the image that's waving at me… I think it's Jim." Ben collected his thoughts with difficulty. Where to start? He spoke to the images on the screen. "Whatever you call yourselves, I want you to leave, and let me do my work."

"NO!"

The voice resounded in the middle of Ben's head. Ben physically felt the shock wave from the answer. Someone must have heard that! He looked around the STU. Nobody else reacted. He called out, "Parkhurst! They seem to be intent on interfering with my patient."

Parkhurst came back, "Ben, based upon what we're observing, maybe 'interfacing' would be a better word choice—they seem to be intent on interfacing with… with us."

"Trying to speak across the dimensions is hard work," Jim declared. "It's easier when they're asleep."

"Save your strength for Jeffrey," Crusias ordered. "Your friend can be most disagreeable. If he were evil, I'd know how to deal with him."

Jim responded, "He's just proud and stubborn, Crusias. He doesn't understand."

"He doesn't want to understand," Crusias told him.

Jim continued, "None of them really understands; that's the problem. None of them understands until they are forced to face their own mortality."

Crusias grumbled, "You know, I resent their interfering with my work. They can be so uncooperative. The few who even try to understand think we have nothing else to do but sit around with harps and sing songs. It's a good thing I enjoy my work."

"Ben's a good man, Crusias. I've known him since we were kids. In the human's ways, he has saved many lives. True, he concentrates on the body more than the actual being, but it's all he knows. It's all he could see until now. You can help him, Crusias; you can help him understand."

Crusias responded, "What makes him so proud? He can't create life. Only the Master can do that. These humans cannot breathe life into a single flower or a blade of grass. They see no wisdom or love in all of this. Until this strange little machine, they could not even see their own life force. It's preposterous to even imagine that the universe is a random accident." Crusias understood all that, but the humans were still learning.

The nurse/anesthetist asked, "Doctor, what shall I do with the Versette?"

"I'm changing the order. Do *not* give him the Versette." The nurse/anesthetist grumbled as she set the syringe down.

"Are you sure that's what you want, Doctor?" Jenny asked.

"Call it a hunch, a gut feeling. I just don't think this patient will tolerate the normal meds." He turned and asked the EEFM monitor screen, "Is that all right with you?"

Again the arm raised and waved one time, then moved to hold the patient's EF in the body on the table. By now, everyone who could see the screen was watching.

Ben addressed the images on the EEFM monitor, "Do we need to take the pressure off his brain?" The arm waved again. Ben walked over to the slides and X rays hanging on the wall. He pointed to the site of the bleed. "Is this where we need to go?" The arm waved, then moved back to hold Jeffrey's essence in his body. "Will he remember this?" Ben asked the screen. Once again, the arm waved at him. Ben wasn't sure he really wanted his patient to remember the pain, but if he did remember, it would be an interesting story.

Ben spoke to the image on the screen, "Jim, this will be on your shoulders." He thought through the irony and said, "I guess it will be on my shoulders." He asked the recorder, "Is the neurosurgeon available?"

"She's finishing in surgery. She says she can be ready to go in about thirty minutes."

"Thirty minutes!" Once again, Ben faced the screen, "Can we wait that long?" There was no response, no sign of movement on the monitor. "I said, 'Can we wait that long?' Wave once for yes and twice for no." Ben waited.

"I'm waiting for an answer." Once again, Ben wondered if he wasn't being played for a fool. This was a cruel joke. Whoever was playing was betting this patient's life.

Crusias looked at Jim. "Jeffrey is losing his strength. If we wait for the neurosurgeon, it will be too late."

Jim glanced at Crusias, "How do I explain that by waving my arm?"

"Maybe we don't have time to answer," Crusias told him. "Something's happening. The rejection feels stronger."

"Doctor, the patient's pulse is dropping and his blood pressure is rising." It was the respiratory therapist.

Jenny called out, "Doctor, he's posturing."

Ben turned back toward the patient. As the pressure from the cerebral edema increased, Jeff's hands started curling up and his arms were drawing toward his chest. Even his toes were curling. "Okay, folks, we need to stabilize him until we can get him in to see the neurosurgeon. Let's get his blood pressure down and slow down that bleed." He turned to the respiratory therapist, "Raise his respirations to thirty per minute. I want him hyperventilated."

Ben instructed Jenny and the others, "Take the preheat off all the IV fluids and drop your inputs to half." Those actions would help to lower his blood pressure. With the blood pressure reduced, Ben hoped they could slow the bleeding and prevent him from having a full-blown seizure. "Give him ten milligrams of dexamethasone sodium phosphate and fifty milligrams of phenytoin sodium intravenously, stat."

Jim broke into a smile, "See, Crusias? I told you he was pretty good. That might be the break we need."

Crusias looked at Jeff, "How are you doing?"

"I feel like I'm having convulsions, like my body is trying to buck me off. It hurts a lot, Crusias."

"Do you still want to go back inside?"

"I promised Danielle. I must go back to my children." His determination was growing.

"Then stay focused. We'll keep trying."

Ben watched as the trauma team finished with his instructions. "That's about all that's humanly possible for us to do, short of finding an off-duty neurosurgeon in a snowstorm in Duluth." He feebly tried to be a bit lighthearted, "Unless you can find a holy man, about all we can do is monitor his condition."

Jim spoke to Crusias, "It seems to be helping. The convulsions are not as strong. Can we get him back in?"

"The body is resisting less, but we're not making any progress. I think we're getting tired at a critical time."

The three computers powering the EEFM began clicking as they searched for the new frequency that had just entered the room. "You don't have him inside his body yet? This is serious."

"Thank heavens you're here, Winnifred," Crusias said. "You're right, it's not going well. We're getting tired. Come. Bring us your energy." Winnifred approached them and laid her hands on Jeffrey's midsection. "I can feel your energy, Winnifred. Let's hope it's enough."

In the Trauma Monitoring Room, Parkhurst was the only one on the team who wasn't too busy to watch the monitors. His eyes practically bugged out when the third bogey entered the room and moved in to help the patient. Reinforcements! The bogeys were bringing in the reserves! What was that crack that Ben just made? *Unless you can find a holy man*! He hit his forehead. "Shit!" Parkhurst jumped to his feet and ran out the door toward the elevator. The monitors would have to work on autopilot.

XXXII

*"Do not be too timid and squeamish about your actions.
All life is an experiment."* —Emerson, *Journals,* 1842 (p. 642)

Date: Wednesday, November 26, 1997
Time: 8:25 A.M.
Place: Mercy Hospital, Emergency Treatment Room, Duluth, MN

Sister Celeste stood outside the door of the treatment room and watched as a young emergency physician and a small staff of nurses and technicians surrounded the two children, attending to their medical needs. The social worker was in the room, commanding the telephone, busying herself with the details of trying to find comfort and protection for the children. Even *she* had shooed Celeste out of the room saying something like, "It's all right, Sister. I'll take care of everything now." The only time they seemed to need her was when the patient was gone. What help was that? What possible good could she do?

Dejected, she turned and walked to the elevator. Then she stopped, leaned against the wall, and started to cry. Ashamed of herself, she ducked through the fire escape door and walked down two flights of stairs to the basement level and the sanctuary of her small office and the chapel. *No one should see the Assistant Chaplain crying*, she thought to herself.

Celeste walked into the unlit chapel and genuflected. She crossed herself and knelt before the altar. Other than the red light from the votive candle, the gray morning struggled to peer through the single stained glass window over her. The words and tears flowed as one. "Lord, I am a useless old woman. Is it time for me to end this charade—time for me to grow old and wither away? O, Lord, You know I've tried. I've been Your servant for over forty years. I no longer understand these people and their modern ways. If You cannot give me understanding, then give me the strength to stop trying to help them...." She sat in the darkened chapel until her thoughts and prayers were interrupted by the sound of a door opening and footsteps on the tile floor.

"Sister Celeste?" the voice called into the office area.

No. Not now, she thought. Maybe whoever it was would go away. The chapel door squeaked as it opened.

"Sister Celeste, it's me, David Parkhurst. Are you in here?"

"I'm here." She tried wiping her eyes without being seen.

"Thank God, I've found you. They need our help in the STU."

"You must be joking, Doctor."

"I couldn't be more serious. Come on! We haven't a moment to lose."

XXXIII

"Goosebumps don't lie."
—Brenda Gallagher, October, 1997

Date: Wednesday, November 26, 1997
Time: 8:44 A.M.
Place: Mercy Hospital, Shock/Trauma Unit, Duluth, MN

"Respirations are being assisted at thirty and his blood pressure is coming down nicely. Pulse is up to eighty," Jenny said.

"Good. Let's hope it does the trick." They needed to buy time. "How much longer until the neurosurgeon is ready?"

"Fifteen minutes."

Ben turned back and faced the EEFM monitor screen. Now there were three bogey images hovering over the patient's EF and the body. Something was wrong—their colors were all changing. It didn't take a rocket scientist to figure out that the fourth image, lying on the table, must be the patient's. *Watch closely*, he told himself. *Watch what they do.* It was all so strange.

"Jeffrey! Do you see the keyway?" Crusias asked.

"Yes, it's right in front of me." He strained and pushed, trying to get any part of his essence through it. "There's too much pressure. I can't get inside."

Winnifred asked, "What do you think it is?"

"The humans are reducing the pressure. There should be less resistance than this. I think it's the host body. It must be rejecting him."

"I'm tired," Jim said. "Maybe we should rest for a minute."

"The longer we wait, the more his proteins will break down. The body is a barely compatible host. We need more energy in the body, a positive charge to attract his essence."

"That's it! Crusias," Jim said, "you're a genius."

Parkhurst briefed Celeste as they came up in the elevator and moved to the scrub room in the Emergency Department. He handed Celeste a set of surgical scrubs. "Here. Put these on." In seconds, he had his mask, cap, and gown on. "Hurry, Sister."

"How about gloves? I forgot my latex gloves."

"You won't need them," he told her. David took her hand and led her to the glass-panelled door of the STU. As they stepped in front of the infrared sensor, the door slid open. They entered the STU, and the door closed behind them.

"Who are you?" Ben tested the two masked arrivals.

"It's me, Ben. David Parkhurst."

"I thought you were supposed to be upstairs."

"I needed to bring Sister Celeste in here."

Ben reeled around and faced them directly. "You what?"

"I think I figured out what the EF's are trying to do, and I believe Sister Celeste can help us." The Assistant Chaplain stood behind Parkhurst, out of the line of fire.

"And I think you'd better get her out of the room. She's contaminating the sterile field."

"You don't have to be mean. Besides, it was your idea."

"My idea? What are you talking about?"

"You said, 'Unless we can find a holy man.'"

"It was just a figure of speech, David. I didn't mean...."

"Well, if you're looking for a Buddhist priest or a Lutheran with a beard, I can't help you, but I did find this nice Catholic lady."

"You're not being funny, Parkhurst."

"Don't you understand? The bogeys are trying to get the patient's EF inside his body."

"I figured they were trying to do something to it."

"No shit, Sherlock." He turned to Celeste, "Pardon me, Sister." He returned his fire to Dr. Bradley. "I watched the patient's EF. It doesn't conform with the lines of the physical body. It keeps moving around." He pointed to the screen. "It's not inside. They're just holding it in place, waiting for it to assimilate back into the body. They're hanging on for dear life while we're wasting time arguing."

"Medically speaking, we've done everything we can. We've got him stabilized until he goes to neurosurgery."

"If we don't get the EF back inside the body, you won't need the neurosurgeon," Parkhurst pushed his hand down over Jeff's body.

"What do you propose to do?" Ben watched Parkhurst's gesture.

"Lay hands on him."

"You must be kidding."

"You heard me, Ben. I want Sister Celeste to help us lay hands on the body." He pointed to the images on the monitor. "Just like they are."

"What earthly good can that do?"

"I don't really know." He waved his hands in the air with impatience. "Call it intuition or whatever you want, but for God's sake just try it."

Ben looked at the images on the monitor. "Jim, if that really is you..." He searched for the question, "Did you hear what Dr. Parkhurst is suggesting?" Ben watched the EF image wave one time. All eyes were glued to the screen. "Will it help to lay hands on the patient?"

Jim looked at Crusias, "What do you think?"

Crusias gave an affirmative nod, then said, "Maybe this won't be so bad after all."

Jim waved his hand once. Gasps surrounded the patient. The room buzzed with speculation over what they'd seen.

"Let's have some quiet in here!" Ben turned and walked toward the doorway, then turned and made a bowing gesture, "He's all yours, Sister," he said curtly. "Just don't bump anything." Ben walked to the door and waited for it to slide open. "Parkhurst, just because you feel compelled to do this, doesn't mean I have to watch." He stormed out of the room. Stunned, the STU team stood and watched the door close behind him.

Jenny was the first to regain her composure. "Dr. Parkhurst, you know what you need to do. I'll try and talk with him." She went out after Ben.

Parkhurst was the next to speak, "Okay, Sister, I want you to show us how to do this." A very timid Sister Celeste approached the patient. Parkhurst asked, "What should we do?"

Celeste pointed at three points on the EEFM screen, "I can only guess that we should touch the body in the same places where the images are holding the patient."

"Sure," Parkhurst said, "our energy fields might be combined with theirs to help draw the patient back in." He looked around the room. "If there's three of them, there should be three of us. I need a volunteer. Who wants to help?"

"I'll do it." It was the nurse/anesthetist.

"You can hold his legs. I'll put my hands over his abdomen, and Sister Celeste can touch his head. Let's do it." Gently, they took hold of the patient.

Parkhurst said it first, "I feel some sort of energy, like a mild electrical shock."

"It's wonderful!" the nurse/anesthetist exclaimed. "My hair is standing on end."

Celeste looked heavenward as she prayed, "Lord, this man is *Your* child. He needs the power of *Your* healing touch so that he might return to his body; so that he might return to his children; so that he might fulfill his life's purpose as *You* have planned for him. If it is *Your* will, make us instruments of *Your* strength and power...."

As Celeste prayed, Jeff looked up at Crusias. "I can feel the warmth of their hands. Do you think it will help?"

"I hope so, child. Let's try this one more time." Once again, he pressed the EF into the head of the physical body. "Jeffrey, do you see the portal?"

"Yes, Crusias."

"You must try to get inside."

Together they pressed down until ethereal hands met earthly hands. Spiritual and physical worked together to help bring a young father back to his children.

"I feel such warmth, so much love. I feel like it... like it's drawing me back...." Then Jeffrey was gone, back into his unconscious body.

Jim continued holding Jeff's legs down as he asked, "Crusias, how ever did they figure that out?"

Crusias smiled, "Never underestimate the power of the Spirit."

All stood in communion with each other, not knowing how long they needed to hold, not wanting it to end.

Jenny found Ben in the scrub room, sitting on a stainless steel stool, leaning back against the wall. He had removed his gloves and mask and sat with his arms folded, letting one foot swing in a pendulum fashion.

Jenny initiated the conversation, "Do you want to talk?"

"I don't know where to begin." He stared at the floor.

"How about, 'You kind of lost it in there'?"

"I guess I deserve that. I just don't know where to go from here. If I can't control the STU, what good am I?"

"You should save the self-pity for someone else."

Ben's eyes narrowed as she challenged him. She was bold to tell him off. He looked into her beautiful brown eyes and softened, "Does it show?"

"Ben, you're making history in that room. That machine has connected us to dimensions mankind has only dreamed of contacting. For all I know, you may have connected us to eternity. It's fantastic! You just need to be humble enough to learn from this experience."

"I'm not supposed to be humble—I'm a trauma surgeon."

"So, you're not a god. You're still a damned good doctor, and I'm proud to work for you. Now, are you going back in there and finish the job? Or will you let your bruised ego keep you pouting like a schoolchild in the hall? Come on! You've still got work to do."

Ben stood up and silently walked back into the STU with Jenny at his side. Parkhurst looked up at them. "I think it worked! The patient's signal strength is improving on the EEFM. What are his vital signs?" Team members started reading out the slowly improving numbers. "We need to know if the EF will stay inside. The only way we'll know is to let go."

"Go ahead. Give it a try," Ben encouraged him.

Parkhurst looked nervous as he lifted his hands away from Jeffrey's abdomen.

"Will he stay?" Winnifred asked her cohorts.

Crusias answered her, "The only way we'll know is to try. Winnie, you go first." One by one they raised their hands and "unplugged" themselves from the patient.

All eyes were glued to the monitor as the bogeys moved away from the patient. "He's back inside, isn't he?" Parkhurst asked. The image waved back. "I'll take that as a yes. Ben, it looks like we have our patient back. How much time 'til the neurosurgeon is ready?"

"Five minutes."

Celeste stood motionless, her hands still gently touching the patient's head. Dr. Parkhurst put his hands over hers, "Thank you, Sister. We need to prep him and move him up to neurosurgery. Ben, I hope you're still in charge here. What's next?"

"I'm not so sure." Ben turned to the monitor. "Does the patient still need to go to neurosurgery?" Jim waved once for yes. "Should Sister Celeste stay with him?" Again, Jim waved one time.

Ben turned to Sister Celeste, "Sister, I'm sorry I've treated you poorly. I hope that I can make it up to you. Maybe we can talk sometime soon. For now, this patient apparently needs you more than he needs me. Would you please help take him upstairs?"

"I would be honored," she beamed.

It took less than two minutes for the team to get organized. Celeste's hands remained on the patient as seven STU staff people moved in unison to wheel the patient and equipment carts down the hall to the surgical elevator. Two bogeys left the room with the team. Somehow, Ben felt the patient would recover. He'd need more surgeries to repair his facial damage and his other injuries, but he would survive.

A single bogey image remained on the monitor screen. Parkhurst and Jenny watched as Ben called out to it, "Is that really you, Jim?" Jim waved once for yes. "Will I ever see you again?" He waved once, and then he was gone.

Ben, Parkhurst, and Jenny stood in silence, watching the screen until Ben reached to the controls and shut it off.

Ben broke the silence, "I suppose the textbooks will call this case a mass hallucination."

"No, Ben," Parkhurst answered. "We've got it all on tape. I hope we have the wisdom to know what to do with it."

"You know, this will profoundly change the way we doctors treat our patients around the world."

"And how we treat spiritual helpers," Parkhurst added.

"We have much to learn. This is a whole new reality."

"Maybe it's how we view it that's new," Parkhurst conjectured.

"A new look at an old reality." Ben let the words settle on himself. The electric door slid softly as Parkhurst walked out.

Ben watched Jenny in silence as she moved around the STU picking up soiled supplies and instruments. He knew there would be more patients on the way. They'd need the STU again this morning. She looked up at Ben, "How did you know his name?"

"It's a long story, Jenny. I hardly know where to start." He thought to himself, *She deserves the long answer. After all, what am I afraid of? I'll tell her the whole story.* Ben felt awkward as Jenny smiled, waiting for his answer. "When we're finished in here... if it's okay with you... er, well... how about I tell it to you over lunch?"

XXXIV

"If we live only to be obliterated by death, what's the purpose?"
—Author, 1995

Date: Saturday, November 29, 1997
Time: 11:30 A.M.
Place: Duluth, MN

The funeral was well attended. Four hundred family and friends had been there to pay their last respects to the deceased. Midwestern towns are like that, and Duluth was no exception. It always seemed that everyone knew everyone else and their business.

Jarod Martin had been a friend, a brother, a neighbor, or a hardware advisor to nearly everyone in attendance. Some people accumulate a lot of friends in forty years. Jarod had worked hard at it. Now, at age fifty-three, Jarod Martin's body had come to his church one last time and had made its final departure to the Trollwood Cemetery.

The weather was cold, windy, and clear. The storm was over. Except where the plows had been, over eighteen inches of snow lay on the ground, explaining why most of the mourners had either stayed at the church for coffee and lunch or had already gone home.

Jarod watched in silence with Crusias and Winnifred as less than one hundred, including the family and closest friends, made the three-mile procession behind the hearse to the cemetery. Crusias had told Jarod that funerals were also to let the deceased know that he had actually died. They arrived at the final resting place for Jarod's body and the nine thousand souls who'd been interred before him at Trollwood.

As Jarod looked on, the funeral home director and his assistant stepped out of the gray Cadillac hearse and instructed the eight pallbearers in the proper procedure for removing the coffin from the back door of the hearse.

A motley group of uniformed honor guard members gathered fifty yards beyond the hearse, stamping out their cigarette butts and preparing their guns and the colors. Several of them were straightening out their ill-fitting uniforms, a common problem for most of the older Veterans of Foreign Wars local post members. The bugler blew air through his horn to warm it since he'd left it in the car during the funeral service at the church. They shivered from the cold damp wind that penetrated their old wool dress uniforms as they mustered for the march to the gravesite to afford proper military honors to another comrade-in-arms.

Jarod had not been an active club member of the local post, but he appreciated the show of respect. He knew it was customary for the honor guard to retreat to the post and tip one or two in remembrance of the deceased after the ceremony. *Today*, Jarod thought, *they'll look forward to warming their insides.*

The widow, Betty Martin, watched the assemblage around the gravesite from the back window of the black limousine, which was provided by the funeral home as part of the eight thousand dollar burial package she vaguely remembered talking about with the funeral director. Betty always prided herself in being a strong-willed, no-nonsense wife and mother. Since Jarod's death, she'd felt so helpless, which added to her distress. *At least the kids are with me,* she thought. She sat with Julie and Michael in the large leather back seat.

Thoughts about the children were little more than a fleeting distraction as Betty intently watched the pallbearers carry the box with the remains of her best friend, her partner, her lover, and her husband of twenty-eight years. She desperately hoped for this day to be very different; for Jarod to come back to life; for the box to open; for him to come back home where he belonged. Today, in the depths of her despair, she knew that those things would not happen. Jarod would not come home tonight. The kids would soon return to school, and the empty nest would turn into a tomb for the living. Tears welled up in her eyes.

The limousine driver stepped out from behind the steering wheel and opened the graveside door for Betty and her two children. Michael squeezed his mother's hand to comfort them both. "We have to do this, Mom," he said. "Let me help you step out."

"Just let me wipe my eyes for a second." She raised a crumpled tissue to her eyes and wiped tears and mascara from her face. Julie did the same. Michael stepped out and reached back to help his mother, then his sister. Together, they walked to the gravesite, arm in arm, holding on to each other more for moral support than balance.

The other mourners stood shivering around the gravesite. Reverend Matthew Lockner spoke, "We are gathered here today to say good-bye to our dear friend, brother, father, and husband, Jarod Martin. Lord, look down upon us with a kind heart and give us comfort as we mourn Jarod's death and our loss. Fill us with the true and certain knowledge that he is in your loving arms. In the book of John, chapter eleven, verses twenty-five and twenty-six, Jesus said, 'I am the Resurrection and the Life; he who believes in me, though he die, yet shall he live, and whosoever lives and believes in me shall never die.'" He followed with a short prayer.

Reverend Lockner signaled to the burial platoon commander that it was time for military honors. The platoon stood in formation to the side of the burial plot. The commander wore a dark blazer, tie, military cap, and white gloves. A distinguished service cross, two purple hearts, and a small array of other medals hung on his chest. He stood as straight and proud as any overweight seventy-six-year-old veteran might.

"Platoon, hhh-right face! Form a line." The words came as a remnant from their pasts. Two of the veterans looked behind themselves as they formed a straight line. "Prepare to honor the dead... Present haharms!... Ready!... Aim!... Fire!" The nine-man platoon included seven riflemen, who fired their first shot of blank cartridges from their well-oiled M-1 carbines. The first volley split the silence of the graveyard. "Reload!" the commander ordered. They refired twice more, totaling a twenty-one gun salute.

They stood at attention and saluted as the bugler played "Taps." Several attendees were also veterans. They, too, saluted while others held their hands over their hearts. After a short silence, the commander and the bugler proceeded to opposite ends of the coffin. They picked up the four corners of the flag that was draped over the coffin and folded it into its required triangular package. The commander carried it to the widow and presented it to her with his white-gloved hands.

"On behalf of the President of the United States of America and the United States Army, I hereby present you with this flag as a token of our appreciation for your husband's honorable military service to his country. Our country, its government, and all the veterans of Post 1287 also wish to extend our sincere condolences to you and your family." He stood at attention and saluted her.

As she placed the flag on her lap, Betty Martin responded so softly that only the commander and her two children could hear her, "Thank you, Bernie."

Bernie stepped back two steps, made an about face and saluted. "About face!" They turned. "For'rd hhharch!... Left, right, left, right...." His voice faded quickly as they approached their cars, where they would respectfully wait until the end of the service.

Reverend Lockner said another short prayer, then led the group in one verse of "Amazing Grace," one of Jarod's favorite hymns. Many tried to avoid staring into the faces of their own inevitable fates, preferring to think they were there purely to share in the loss of a friend. Yet the realization, the certain knowledge, that their own bodies, just like Jarod's, would all end up in holes in the ground was difficult to avoid. To some, it brought an extra shiver in the cold and damp wind. Funerals were like that.

Reverend Lockner continued, "Blessed be God the Father, God the Son, and God the Holy Spirit." He made the sign of the cross over the head of the casket facing the burial party. "Lord of grace, You have given Your blessed assurance through the promise of Your Son, Jesus Christ; that You will remember us in our time of need. Look with favor upon Your servant, Jarod Martin. Take him into Your arms and give him comfort in his new life. In Your great compassion, give consolation to those who mourn...."

The three EF's stood nearby as they watched the service. Jarod was glad to be in between Crusias and Winnifred. They held onto him and comforted him. He, too, mourned being separated from his family and friends. They would bury his body before the frost went into the ground. His physical life was done. Watching the funeral made it very clear that Jarod could not go back.

"He sure gives a nice talk," Winnifred spoke.

Crusias hushed her. "We should let Jarod listen."

Jarod spoke, "It's all right. I understand."

Winnifred continued, "So many humans at the service. Jarod, you certainly have a lot of friends."

Jarod looked at her, "Don't you mean 'had'?"

"Not at all. Soon enough, you'll see. They'll all come home. Don't worry, you have eternity on your side."

Reverend Lockner continued, "Jarod's spirit has left his earthly body. The Lord's plan for his time on earth is complete. He has completed his course in faith and now may rest from his labors. He is freed from suffering and pain."

"Are you serious?" Jarod asked. "I'll really see them again?"

"Sure, if you want to see them," Winnifred answered him. "You may even see some of them before they come over. It happens all the time."

Reverend Lockner stopped to hold the page of his manual down in the wind. He pulled a small vial from his pocket.

"Shhh!" Crusias interrupted the two. "Jarod really should hear this part. Let's just watch for another minute and then we can go somewhere and talk."

"We commit Jarod's earthly body to the ground from which it came. Almighty God, by the death and resurrection of Your Son, Jesus Christ, You have destroyed death and conquered the powers and principalities of darkness. 'For I know that my Redeemer lives, and at last, He will stand upon the earth; and after my skin has been thus destroyed, then from my flesh shall I see God.' Job, chapter nineteen, verses twenty-five and twenty-six.

"In this sure and certain hope of the resurrection and the life everlasting, we commend the spirit of our brother, Jarod Martin, unto You, O Lord, and we commit his body to the ground. Earth to earth, ashes to ashes, and dust to dust." He reached forward over the head of the casket and poured the sand out of the vial, forming a small cross on the polished mahogany. Then he raised his right hand and made another sign of the cross. His eyes were red. His voice cracked. "And now, my dear friend, may the Lord bless you and keep you. May He make His face shine on you...."

"I miss you, too, Matthew. I miss you all." Jarod did not wait for them to finish the service. He looked at Crusias. "May we go now? This is too hard to watch."

"It will be all right. You'll see," Crusias told him. The trio rose into the sky above the crowd and began the trip home.

XXXV

"And the glory of the Lord shall be revealed..."
—*Bible* (KJV) *Isaiah* 40:5

Date: Saturday, November 29, 1997
Time: 10:00 P.M.
Place: Gary New Duluth, Martin Home

Betty Martin had sat quietly in her living room, politely waiting for her visitors to leave. Tonight she was feeling like the events surrounding Jarod's funeral seemed to take forever. When she had to say good-bye at the interment service, however, it was over in a second. It was a lot like life. Forced to face her fears of death and loneliness, time passed ever so slowly. When she'd said good-bye to Jarod, time passed like the flash of an airport beacon against a small woods on a black night. It was nine-thirty when the last of them had said good night and then it was just Betty, Michael, and Julie. The children busied themselves straightening up the kitchen and covering and refrigerating the leftovers. Once the domestic chores were finished, the children came and sat with her.

"It's so quiet with everyone gone," Betty told the children. "I wonder why everyone left so early."

"Everybody said such nice things about Dad," Julie told her mother. "I hope it was comforting for you to have them all around here, Mom. I'm sure you'll be getting company and calls for a long time."

"I wasn't a very good hostess. It feels so strange to have company without your dad being here." Betty felt awkward; she didn't know how to mourn and still be open and friendly to the people who were reaching out to her. How could she have known it was a time of such strong and mixed emotions?

"I can't get over how many friends Dad had. The church was packed. I recognized a lot of faces, but there were a lot of people I didn't know," Michael volunteered.

"Many of them were customers from the store," Betty told him. "I've met most of them over the years, but I couldn't keep all the names straight —not like your father. He was really good at asking and remembering their names. He made it a point to visit with them."

"Nobody was a stranger for long," Michael said.

"Mom, would you like to look at some of the cards?" Julie asked. "There must be five hundred here. We've got a lot to go through."

"Sure, we can try, honey." They sat together and tried to read through some of the cards from relatives and friends. That didn't last long. It was too emotional.

"Let's talk about the future." Betty tried to visit with the kids, telling them what their father's hopes were for them.

"I can quit school and come back home to work in the store," Michael offered.

"Michael, you shouldn't even think about doing that."

"Don't you think you need help?"

"I'd rather sell the store than make you quit school. We've got good help. I'm sure I can make it work," she told him. Even if she did have to sell, she'd never let Michael quit school.

Michael advised her to not do anything rash and Julie agreed. It was too early to make any major decisions. They needed a little time. They could all talk more about it at Christmas. A little before eleven, there was a lull in the conversation.

"I'm going to go to bed. I'm not fit company. Maybe I'll feel more like talking in the morning." Betty excused herself and retired to her bedroom for another lonely night, the sixth in a row. She felt relieved not to have to make any big decisions or commitments. She pulled the drapes, undressed and put her pajamas on, washed her face, and brushed her teeth in the little master bathroom she had so enjoyed through the years. Jarod had built it. Everywhere she looked, there were reminders of him.

Betty remembered back to their first day in their "new" house. She and Jarod were so excited. It really had been a big old "fixer upper," but it had seemed brand new to them. Jarod had surprised her with a candlelight dinner and hired a violinist to serenade them as he served her champagne and caviar amidst the moving boxes.

Together, they had dreamed of their pre-retirement years, their "kick-back-and-relax" years. Jarod was young by modern American standards. Now those dreams were gone.

Betty climbed into bed and tried reading for about twenty minutes. That didn't work any better than trying to visit—nothing worked. It was so quiet. She loved Jarod, and now she missed him. She was sure that nothing would replace the void his death had created in her life. She put the book down on the night stand and turned out the light.

Betty was wound up tightly. She could feel the tension in her body. She was clenching her teeth. Her hands were formed into fists. *Why God, why? It's not fair! We were so happy, and now he's gone.*

Sometimes prayer helped. She had to try something. Betty forced herself to concentrate. She prayed for Jarod. She prayed for the children. She thanked God for all their wonderful friends who had reached out to them today. She asked God to comfort her and help her understand the irony of

Jarod leaving her and prayed that God would help keep her from becoming bitter. She thanked Him for the wonderful years they had enjoyed together, and even prayed that she would see him again.

It was tough to stop crying and impossible to get comfortable. She sat up in the bed, thinking she'd go downstairs for a soothing cup of herbal tea when she noticed a small cloud at the foot of the bed. Betty thought it strange at first. Perhaps it was a reflection from the street light, but she had closed the drapes! She became alarmed as it glowed brighter, concerned that it may be smoke or the start of a fire. She felt paralyzed. She could neither move nor call out for help.

Betty peered into the cloud. She thought she could see Jarod's face. *Oh my goodness!* she thought. *Now I'm seeing things.* The image cleared. The vision was smiling at her. She could see Jarod reaching out to her from the cloud!

"Jarod?" she called out softly to the image.

He stood at the foot of the bed smiling at her. "Hi, Boops. How're ya doin'?" The familiarity shocked her. Jarod had called her by that nickname for years after a disastrous trip to the beauty parlor. She'd come home with a set of very dark and tight curls. He said she reminded him of a different Betty, the cartoon character. The curls disappeared years ago, but the name stuck. It was a term of endearment used only by Jarod, but widely known by family and friends. It must be him! It must be her husband.

"I must be dreaming." Betty rubbed her eyes and took a second look. The image remained. "Oh, Jarod, I feel so awful. We didn't even have a chance to say good-bye. I came to the hospital, but you were gone."

His face turned to a frown, "Don't cry, honey. I'm fine. Really." His smile returned. "I saw you driving to the hospital. Didn't you see us fly by?" His face looked youthful. He had regained some of his boyhood charm.

"What are you talking about?" She'd seen nothing.

"I saw you driving to the hospital. It was really neat! Crusias helped me out of my body and took me to the Master."

"How can that be? I saw you lying dead in the Emergency Room at the hospital." She paused then asked, "Who's Crusias?"

"He's a new friend. He helped me get out of my body."

"Jarod, I prayed that you would come back to life, that you would come home where you belong. But you didn't come back. We buried you today!" It was a good time to get hysterical.

"I know, I was there. Pastor Lockner did a beautiful job, didn't he?"

Tears welled up in Betty's eyes. "Jarod, how can you be so casual about it? I buried you. You're dead!"

"Come on, Boops. You need to calm down. I'm sorry I left you—I couldn't help it. It wasn't my choice, but it *was* my time. I can't go back to my body, but see? I'm here. It's true! It's really me. We don't die; we just get out of our bodies. It's so *amazing!*" Jarod wasn't sure his words were having the desired effect.

"How do I know you're real?" she asked.

"Maybe you won't know for sure until you die. Oh, I'm sorry. That's such a terrible word for something so wonderful. Maybe you won't really know until you 'come across.' There! That's a better way to say it, don't you think?"

"Oh, Jarod, please come back. I miss you so much."

"I can't, Boops. I just came back to say good-bye, to reassure you, and to let you know I still love you." He paused for a moment. "You know the old fellow, the one who crashed into me? He says he's really sorry. He'd already 'come across' when his car came over the centerline at me. He's a nice old guy, and he knows he shouldn't have been driving. I was pretty upset with him for a while, but there's so much love around here, it's impossible to stay angry. We're going to get together and do something. I just feel bad because we had such grand plans now that the children are grown up, but everything happened so quickly."

They visited about the important things like messages for the children, plans for the future, Betty's hopes and fears of the future. Betty was just getting comfortable talking with an ethereal being, when Jarod said, "I must leave. My time here is ending."

"Please don't leave me. I can't do this alone."

"You've prepared all your life for this time. You're very capable of completing your work. Don't feel insecure. You'll do fine. Remember, if you really need me, you can call. I want you to know that I am in a place that is full of beauty and love. Even in my wildest dreams, I didn't imagine a place like it. Don't be afraid. When it's your time, we'll be together again."

Betty held her arms out to him, pleading, "Please, Jarod, hold me. I'm still afraid."

The cloud and Jarod rose above the bed. As it moved toward Betty, she could feel a tingling sensation as she lay down on the bed. She felt him wrap himself around her. She gazed into his eyes. "I love you, Jarod."

Jarod replied softly, "I love you more." He gave himself completely to her. She surrendered to him. Betty had the incredible sensation that he was penetrating her! She could feel Jarod inside her! She felt him enter her in every conceivable place. Every pore of skin was filled with his essence. She breathed him in. She could feel him in her ears, her mouth, and her nose. All her senses recognized his presence. Betty could feel him swirling inside the core of her body. She moaned and trembled from the sensation. It was a closeness that was more complete than she'd ever experienced when they made love. It had to be real! Only Jarod could possibly share the gift of this kind of intimacy. And then he was gone.

Betty lay on the bed in the darkened room... waiting... wondering...

until she heard a knock at the door.

"Mom! Mom! What's wrong?" Julie was at the door.

"Come in, honey. The door is open." The light from the hallway pierced the darkness and illuminated the bedding as Julie opened the door.

"Are you all right, Mom?"

"I'm fine, dear."

"I was worried about you. I thought I heard voices."

"I was having a dream about your father. It was so beautiful. He wanted us to know he's doing fine, and he wanted me to tell you that he loves you. He loves us all."

"Wow! That must have been some dream! You were groaning and moaning. I couldn't hear what you were saying, but you sure scared me."

It would take time for Betty to be comfortable talking about her experience. Someday, she promised herself, she would tell Julie the whole story. "What time is it?"

Julie responded, "It must be after two."

"I guess time really does fly when you're having fun." Julie looked quizzically at her mother. Betty smiled, "It's okay, baby. I'll be fine." She knew it really was true. "You can go back to bed. Really, I'm fine."

"Okay. Good-night, Mom. I love you." She bent over and gave Betty a hug, then turned to leave.

"Julie?"

Julie stopped and turned toward her, "Yes, Mom?"

"How are *you*?" she asked.

"I can't sleep."

Betty reached over and turned on the lamp on the nightstand. "Come here, honey. Let me comb your hair. We can talk." She looked at the alarm clock. It was 2:55 A.M.

XXXVI

*"How strange are the tricks of memory, which, often hazy
as a dream about the most important events of a man's
life, religiously preserve the merest trifles."*
—Sir Richard Burton, *Sind Revisited* (1851), v.1(p. 395)

Date: Sunday, November 30, 1997
Time: 1:35 P.M.
Place: Mercy Hospital, Duluth, MN

The reunion of Jeff Arneson and his children was filled with joy and sadness. Jeff was tired after two hours of visiting and lunch. It was time for him to rest and for the children to go back to the house. Even if Jeff couldn't sleep, Joey and Melissa needed their naps. Thanks to their child car safety seats, the children had only suffered minor bruises and cuts. The social worker had located Jeff's brother, Don, and his wife, Frances. The kids had been released within twenty-four hours into their custody. As they finished their visit, Frances began bundling them up.

Time for one last hug before they went back home with Uncle Don and Auntie Fran, who were also Joey's godparents. Joey and Melissa clambered up onto the bed in their jackets and boots. The good-bye hugs were as exuberant and intense as the hellos had been a couple hours before. Don and Frances said they worried they might somehow injure their father. Jeff didn't seem to mind, even though he grimaced when they accidentally squeezed and hugged his bruised flesh.

"Daddy?" It was Melissa.

Jeff helped her with her mittens. "Yes, honey."

"Are you sure Mommy can't come back and live with us?"

"I'm sure of it, honey," he told his daughter. They had talked about this several times. Repetition did not make the child more secure.

"Daddy?"

"Yes, honey."

"Can't she come back and visit us?" she persisted.

Jeff tenderly held her head and looked into her face. "I don't think so, honey."

Melissa's eyes moved up into their thinking position. There was a short pause. "Daddy?"

"Yes, honey."

"Will we ever see Mommy again?"

"Yes, honey, we will all see Mommy again. I promise."

"When we die, right? That's what you said."

Jeff cradled Melissa's tiny hands in his own, "Yes, honey. We'll see her again when we leave this world." Melissa's questions were so innocent, but so straightforward. He tried his best to answer them.

"Daddy?"

"What, honey?" Jeff's eighth response was a little abrupt.

Melissa lunged at her father and hugged him, "I love you." Those three little words could melt stone.

"I love you, too," Jeff said as he stroked her hair. "I love you both very much." Jeff wondered why he ever wanted to fill his life with more than their love.

Joey bounced on the bed while Jeff hugged and kissed his daughter good-bye. Somehow they had all managed to survive. Too soon, the room was quiet. As Jeff lay on the bed, he heard a knock at the door. "Come on in," he called.

Dr. Bradley stuck his head into the room. "How was the visit?"

"Wonderful," Jeff answered.

Ben stepped into the room and stood next to the bed. Perfunctorily, he put a stethoscope to his patient's chest and listened. "Can you cough for me?" Jeff obliged him three or four times as Ben listened to his lungs. "Well," Ben inquired, "how does it feel to be back among the living?"

Jeff looked at Ben. "I'm so glad to be back with my children, you'll never know. It won't be easy for me to raise them by myself, but I know it will be tougher for them than me."

"They are fortunate to have either one of you back."

Jeff continued, "Danielle's funeral will be on Tuesday."

"Yes, I heard. I'm sorry." Ben was solicitous.

"They delayed it until I could be there. I'm supposed to get released tomorrow. That's correct, isn't it?"

"You're right," Ben confirmed. "You're doing very well, but you'll still need some more corrective surgery."

"I understand, Doc," Jeff said. "The hardest part will be really getting to know the children better. I was so busy working on my career, I didn't give them much of myself. That's going to change. It won't be easy trying to do more around the house and spending more time with them, but I made a promise." He paused as he looked into Ben's eyes. "Could we talk?"

"That's fine, if you're not too tired." Ben pulled up a chair, sat next to the bed, and examined Jeff's dressings.

"You can correct me, but I believe that most of us don't get a second chance like I just got."

"You were very lucky, Mr. Arneson." Ben looked into Jeff's swollen and bandaged face. What he could see was still black and blue. It was only Jeff's second day out of intensive care, but he was healing quickly.

"It wasn't luck, Doc. And, please, don't call me Mr. Arneson. Call me Jeff. You all treat me so politely. It's like you put a big orange tag on me that says, 'Caution, Handle with Care.' What's everyone so afraid of? It's like you think I'm going to sue the hospital or something."

"Well, everyone is aware that you're an attorney."

"Heavens," Jeff chuckled. "Is that what all this 'walking on eggshells' is about? I have no intention of suing the hospital or the staff. You helped save my life, even if you did walk out of the room right in the middle of my crisis."

"Who told you that?" Instantly, Ben was on the defensive. "There's no way you could remember that. You were unconscious."

"I remember up until I went back into my body."

Ben pushed the chair back and moved to stand up. "Perhaps it would be better if we didn't continue this discussion."

"Relax, Doc. I'm not thinking about a lawsuit. Just because I'm an attorney doesn't mean I have to act like one. Hey, I'm just thankful you didn't give me the Versette. I could have come back as a vegetable."

Ben was incredulous, "Somebody told you that part, too, right? You couldn't possibly remember that."

"Well, Jimmie had to practically hit you over the head with the prescription."

"His name is *Jim...* You saw Jim? No way!"

"It's true, Doc. He stayed and helped. He was already here when Crusias brought me to the hospital. Anyway, I want you to know that I appreciate everything you and your staff did to help me get a fresh start on my life. None of what I need to do includes filing a lawsuit against you or the hospital." Jeff thought Ben looked tense. "Really, Doc. I mean it. If anyone is to blame, it's the kid who drove in front of the trucks who should be held responsible. He wasn't having a very good day when I talked with him. Anyway, I don't think the mother could even afford insurance. The boy probably shouldn't have been driving."

Ben was inquisitive. "You knew the young man?"

"Never met him until the accident. I got the impression that he'd been raised by his mother. He gave me a necklace with a cross on it and asked me to give it to her and tell her he loved her."

Jeff picked up a small tablet and pen from the bedside table and scratched out a note. When he was finished, he handed it to Ben. "Here, this is a sign of my good will."

Ben read the signed and dated note. It said, "For one dollar and other valuable consideration, I, Jeffrey A. Arneson, being of sound mind and body, do hereby commit one hundred hours of my personal legal services to Mercy

Hospital and its staff members. I hereby waive any rights to recourse against said hospital and personnel for their actions from November...."

Jeff said, "It's a legal document and a bonafide offer. You can sign as witness."

"That's very generous of you, Mr... I mean, Jeff."

"You understand what it means?"

"I'm not sure," he replied honestly.

"It means that the hospital and staff are my clients. It means I can't sue you, and it means our conversations are confidential client/attorney communications."

Ben still looked confused. Jeff reinforced the statement on the piece of paper. "Doc, you can say anything you want. I can't hurt you." Ben just sat there with the paper in his hand. "Really, Dr. Bradley, you can relax."

"If I'm going to call you Jeff, then you should call me Ben. All right?"

"Deal." Jeff pretended to spit on his right hand, then offered his handshake on the arrangement. Jeff took Ben's trembling hand. "What's the matter now?"

"I'm sorry. You just jerked me back into another time in my life."

"I think a handshake tells a lot about a man." Jeff firmed his grip before he let go. "Now, where were we?"

Ben reminded Jeff, "We were talking about you meeting the boy at the accident scene."

"You have to promise not to laugh."

"Really,... Jeff, I am very interested."

"I was afraid you wouldn't want to hear—that you'd tell me I forgot to take my medicine."

Jeff was animated as he told Ben about his encounter with the boy and the others who died in the accident. Ben listened as Jeff told him about how helpless he and Danielle had felt as they waited for somebody to rescue the children, about the beings and his father-in-law, about his fantastic trip, and about how he made a choice to come back to the kids and finish his life's work. Jeff cried as he told Ben the whole story.

When Jeff was finished, he said, "Thanks, Ben, I needed to tell someone." He stopped, closed his eyes, and tilted his head back as he tried to visualize it all. After a short pause, Jeff began, "You know, I'll never be afraid of dying. If I'm afraid of anything it's that someone will try to take this experience away from me."

Ben had listened intently, leaning closer and closer to Jeff. "Why do you think it wasn't luck that you returned?"

"It wasn't, Doc. I got a second chance. I came back to finish my life's work, or maybe I came back to start my spiritual journey. I don't have very many answers, but I do know that I'm not afraid of dying. I know that Joey and Melissa are part of my purpose in returning, and I believe that sharing my experience with you is part of my purpose, too. You can say I'm crazy, but I think you know people who want to hear about the other side and what the images on your machine really mean."

"Well... ah, Jeff," Ben backed away. He didn't know what to say. The man had spilled out information like a computer doing a file dump. How could Jeff know about the EEFM?

"Doc, I know you didn't want anyone to touch me, to lay hands on me, to help me get back inside my body. You said something about a sterile field before you walked out. You didn't want to try. You said you'd done everything you could for me, medically speaking. You didn't have much to work with because I was gone. I was gone a long time. I remember being out of my body from the time the deputy sheriff found our children. My body didn't want me back inside. That's why the beings were there, to help me get back inside."

"Do you actually think it was real?" Ben questioned. "It could have been a dream?"

"It's not like that. I don't need to think or believe. I *know* where I was. Even that isn't the right way to say it. It was more real than anything else I've ever been through. It wasn't like a physical place, like earth or Duluth."

"Would you call it Heaven?" Ben asked.

"I suppose you could. I don't feel compelled to give it a name. Once you've been there, it's... it's like... a name just doesn't seem so important. It's not Catholic or Protestant, Buddhist, or Islam. It just is. It's ageless, timeless, and not a part of this dimension. Yet, it's right here, in front of our noses. Human words can't do it justice. I mean, they're so inadequate. That's saying a lot for a guy who makes a living with words," Jeff chuckled. "The words I want to use are words of appreciation. Thank you for all you've done for me. I want to thank everyone who helped to bring me back."

After a long silence, Jeff asked, "When I came to the hospital, did I have a necklace with a cross on it?"

"If you did," Ben answered, "it would be with your personal belongings."

"I went through the things they said I had before I sent them home with my brother yesterday. I didn't find it." Jeff's face showed his disappointment.

"Do you want me to ask the paramedics?" Ben asked. "You could file a lost and missing report."

"No, that's all right. I..." Jeff stopped.

"What?"

"I was hoping someone found it. I was looking for hard evidence — something that would stand up in a court of law."

"What do you mean, Jeff? You're making me nervous again."

"Since there are no witnesses to corroborate my story, I had hoped that I would have a tangible artifact as proof. The cross that the boy gave me for his mother would have been proof."

Somehow, Ben knew he should trust this man. He was so open and sincere. He sure could use the help getting things sorted out. Ben pretended to spit on his hand and offered it to Jeff. "Well, Jeff, if you're willing to help, I'm willing to work with you." Ben told him, "You may not have the necklace, but we've still got the tape recording of everything in the STU." The handshake was solid.

XXXVII

"There is one body and one spirit."
—*Bible* (KJV) *Ephesians* 4:4

Date: Monday, December 1, 1997
Time: 9:30 P.M.
Place: Duluth Skyline

The storm had finally passed. Truckload by truckload, the snow was removed from the city as Duluth dug its way out of the snow left by the Thanksgiving blizzard of 1997. Mercy Hospital staff members returned from their Thanksgiving holidays, and hospital operations returned to normal as the Christmas season approached.

The blizzard in Ben Bradley's mind began to settle as well. There was time to sleep, to think, to relax, and to renew. Ben sat in his den with a cup of mocha java, writing in his journal about the extraordinary events of the past week...

> *In the past few stormy days, I've learned much that shall forever change how I view and treat my patients. Our research team has observed the energy field which is contained in the host body of every living thing.*
>
> *Parkhurst was right! It's more than some remnant of chemical and biological reactions in the body. It's an essence which exists beyond the physical death of the host body. It has a consciousness and will of its own, and it survives without the support of the host body. It interacts with other energy forms as easily as humans or animals interact with each other. The ancient term for it is 'soul.'*
>
> *As an informed, scientific society, we must pursue our understanding of these energy fields, especially since we now know we can communicate with them.*
>
> *Instead of distancing myself from my patients' near-death experiences, I've learned that I should embrace them and recognize their potential for*

linking mankind to another dimension. As I do this, I'll also learn more about what it means to be human.

If I do nothing, I won't need to answer questions about the origin of visions, essences, and other-worldly beings. But why should I wait until it's my turn to be confronted by them? Then, I'll discover that it's too late for me, just as it's been too late for each of my patients who have died.

If my science and medicine are not there for my patients, how can I hope for help when it's my turn to face the darkness alone? If forty percent of all patients who are resuscitated have recollections of their near-death experiences, I have at least that same probability of facing the same experiences. Must I then heal myself? There must be a better way.

I know how strange and uncomfortable these experiences are. I've been confronted. I have resisted, trying to erase them from my consciousness, but my recollections have not tarnished with the years. They have affected my life and continue to do so. I haven't feared death since my own encounter. Why should I fear eternity?

I've observed that precious part of us that lives on. I'm also learning about being connected. I know that I am linked with every living thing.

I am more than a body.
I am more than carbon and water.
I am more than a cosmic accident.
I am a part of the spectrum of all energy.
I am energy. I am eternal.
I am indestructible.
I can neither be created nor destroyed...
...I can only be changed.

XXXVIII

"Hard is the heart that loveth nought in May."
—Chaucer, *the Romaunt of the Rose,* (circa 1370) (p. 566)

Date: May 9, 1998
Time: 7:00 A.M.
Place: Duluth Skyline, Duluth, MN

After being reset by banging the snooze bar, the clock/radio played for the second time. The sheets rustled as the occupant sat up, stretched, and walked into the bathroom.

"For all you sleepy heads just joining us, it's 7:00 A.M., time for the morning news this Friday, May 9, 1998." It was the Marty and Jones Morning Show. Marty mouthed the noises as if he were a teletype machine. "Dit, daa, daa, daa, dit, di...dit. This bulletin just in..."

The news stories carried into the bathroom until the shower started running and the glass shower door closed.

Ben Bradley listened to the national and local news as he read through his notes.

Jones continued, "On the lighter side, police are on the lookout for two men who streaked through an English Literature class at Santa Scholastics University dressed only in ski masks and tennis shoes. Apparently, these two had been there before because plainclothes police were on the scene waiting to apprehend the two men when they 'showed' themselves in the building. The streakers evaded capture after a brief footchase into a nearby woods. The school psychiatrist was trying to get an accurate count of the students who would be going through critical incident stress debriefing after being exposed to such depravity. The literature instructor, Dr. Prunella Bixby, told reporters it was much ado about nothing."

"Ahh, yes, Mr. Jones," Marty interjected, "spring is in the air."

"You must have something more to add than that, Marty."

"Yeah, I do. We were in such a rush to get out of there, I think I got the wrong underwear." Marty yukked it up. "And furthermore, where does this Miss Prune-something come off talking about us like that. Why, I oughta...."

Ben Bradley thought, *Some things never change. These two sure get a lot of mileage out of reworking old jokes.*

"Back to the news," Jones interrupted. "Two more ships will depart today from the port city of Duluth. They are the tanker *Clifton Wales* and the freighter *Seawinds.* In fact, as I look out the lakeside windows of the studio,

I can see the first ship of the day approaching the aerial lift bridge. It looks like the freighter *Seawinds*. Well, bon voyage to all of you who are leaving our fair city. May good fortune and fair winds follow you, wherever you go."

The water stopped running. Jenny stepped out of the shower, towelled herself dry, then wrapped herself in a large brown terry cloth robe.

"This public service announcement just in. Dit, dah, di, dah. As a special tribute to mothers all over the state, Governor Archie Nielson has declared today through Sunday, May 11, as Mother's Weekend to properly recognize the efforts of all you little mothers out there in Mosquitoland."

"Aw, c'mon, Marty. You're kidding, right? There's no such thing as Mother's Weekend."

"Sure is," Marty replied. "We're here to remind all you listeners out there: if you have a mother, remember her with a thoughtful gift or dinner this weekend."

Jones added, "How about mothers-in-law?"

"I've got mixed emotions about that."

"What do you mean, Marty?"

"Mixed emotions. I've had them ever since I saw my mother-in-law drive over a cliff in my new Cadillac." Marty started laughing.

Jones was ready for him, "I understand your pain, man. I've seen your mother-in-law." Jones chuckled.

Jenny giggled as she walked out of the bedroom into the living area. Ben stood in his bathrobe, staring out the sliding glass balcony door toward the lake. She walked up behind him and put her arms around him. "How long have you been up?"

"About an hour. I made some coffee. I'll pour you a cup."

"I can get some in a minute. Right now, I want to hold onto you. It's like I'm in a dream. If I let go, I'll wake up and you'll be gone."

Ben turned toward her, "You won't get rid of me that easily." They hugged and kissed.

Jenny asked, "Were you writing?"

"Yes, I was jotting down some ideas about changes I envision for medical care practices that result from what we've learned about interfacing with the non-physical dimension."

"May I read it?"

"Any time you want."

"How did you sleep?" she asked.

"Like a baby."

"No nightmares?"

"None. I only dreamed of you." Ben kissed her on the forehead. "At least that I remember. It helps to accept Jim as being real."

"He doesn't come to you as often, does he?" She leaned her head against Ben's chest.

"No, but he still comes when I call him. He says our work isn't done, but he doesn't want to interfere with our relationship. He's still my friend—that's forever, you know." Ben turned back toward the lake, keeping one arm over Jenny's shoulder.

Staying in touch with Jim through methods other than dreaming also helped. Ben was experimenting with several methods far more intentional than dreaming. So far, he'd tried altered states of consciousness through self-hypnosis and meditation to open his own mind. All provided inconsistent results. The EEFM still provided the most consistent results, but the images and communications remained poor.

"Do you plan to see him soon?" she asked.

"Actually, I have an appointment with him this afternoon." He remained uncomfortable talking with fellow humans about such strange, but fascinating, encounters. Ben had opened up to Jenny, Parkhurst, and his new friend, Jeff Arneson. Letting more people inside Ben's head would take time. For now, he wanted to change the subject. "You see that ship going through the aerial lift bridge?" He tapped his fingertip on the glass door.

Jenny gazed at the ship. "Yes. Is that the one they were talking about on the radio?"

Ben answered her, "Yes. I think it's called the *Seaward,* or the *Seawinds.* Yes, that's it."

"I think it's neat how they mention the ships that put into harbor here." Duluth was small enough to notice each ship that passes through. "It's sure a gorgeous view from here." She snuggled in closer to Ben.

"You know, Jen, somehow I feel drawn to that ship. It's like a part of me is going out to sea with it."

"Didn't one of our patients work on a ship?"

"Of course!" Ben suddenly recalled. "His name was... Paul. He was one of the first patients with the EEFM."

"The hypothermia case?"

"Right! I talked with him during his recovery. He had a particularly bad experience. He told me the whole thing. He was afraid he'd never be able to get back on a ship again. At first, I told him he should try to forget it, that it was probably just a bad dream, but Jim convinced me to try something different. That's when I realized that it didn't make any difference if the patients could prove their near-death experiences were real. What was most important was that it was the patient's own experience. Paul's experience was real to him just as mine was real to me. I sent him to the psychiatrist for some therapy to get over his fears. Remember? That's when we started counseling our patients to embrace their experiences."

"That's when you embraced your own experience, after all those years," Jenny observed.

"I've learned a lot since then." Ben was pensive.

"I wonder if Paul is on that ship."

"Maybe that's why I feel connected. I wonder where it's headed."

"Maybe it's headed for adventure," Jenny suggested.

"That's a nice way to think about it." Gently, he placed his hand on the window glass and said a silent farewell. He turned to Jenny, "C'mon. Let's get you that cup of coffee. Then we need to get ready for work. We've got three more EEFM units going into the hospital this week. David's got some enhancements hooked up to the Energy Field Imager that may help clarify the images on the monitor."

Jenny pulled playfully on Ben's robe. "I have a better idea. How about breakfast in bed?"

"Jen! We really need to get going. Besides, there are no drapes and it's light outside. The whole town can see us." Ben covered his mouth to hide his feigned shock.

"They cannot, you silly." Jenny stuck her hand inside Ben's bathrobe. "Oooh, Dr. Bradley! You're not wearing pajamas!"

"Jen, look at the time," he half-heartedly protested.

"Oh, come on, Ben. Where's *your* sense of adventure? Let's skip breakfast and go back to the waterbed and slosh around for a few minutes. I'll try to make you seasick."

"God, Jen, you're hopeless. You should be on the radio with Marty and Jones. They'd get a kick out of you." Seductively, Jenny dragged Ben back into the bedroom as the radio program continued.

"The weather is beautiful out there today. The forecast is for temperatures in the seventies, blue sky, and severe clear."

Marty interjected, "After the winter that hell froze over, it's nice to stick our heads out of the igloos without getting frostbite."

Jones continued, "It's going to be so clear today, you could almost see forever...."

The broadcast ended abruptly as a lazy hand bumped the snooze bar one more time.

XXXIX

"The things we remember best are those better forgotten."
—Baltasar Gracián, *The Art of Worldly Wisdom,* (1647),
262, translated by Joseph Jacobs (p. 395)

Date: Friday, May 8, 1998
Time: 8:30 P.M.
Place: Lake Superior

The freighter *Seawinds* churned its way to the northeast at a cruising speed of fifteen knots. By the end of the day, it had passed Copper Harbor on Keweenaw Point. The northernmost point of the Upper Peninsula of Michigan was behind them. A light tailwind, now dying, assured that they would reach Sault Ste. Marie and the Soo Locks early the next morning. The ship would soon turn to the southeast and ride a nearly straight line to Whitefish Point and Whitefish Bay.

Where the ship would turn to the southeast was the approximate point that Third Mate Paul Sanderson guessed to be the whereabouts of the remains of the ship that had foundered and sunk more than sixty years ago. Sixty years ago was when the ship and crew of Paul's worst nightmare had been forgotten after an embarrassing episode in the shipping company's history; when hungry steel mills cared not a whit when the winter storms began; when ships and men were but a conduit to great wealth for greedy owners; when safety and weather conditions were impediments to profits; when iron ore was cheap and plentiful; when sacrifices had to be made to secure and maintain a major shipping contract.

It was true. The day Paul had nearly died in the Great Lake was the sixtieth anniversary of the death of twenty-eight good men. It took Paul a long time to find any information on the shipwreck. The *Lord Perry,* loaded to the gunwales, sank with a load of iron ore in a wild nor'easter on a stormy November night. All hands were lost as the ship disappeared in the dark of night. No survivors or bodies were ever found. Any traces of debris floated undetected into the Michigan shoreline.

There had been a very quiet memorial service for the ship's crew. Few kinfolk or friends attended the service. The ship's crew had signed on from all corners of the globe. Only the captain and the first and second mates were U.S. citizens. Although the shipping company was local, the ship itself was of foreign registry. There were so few mourners at the service that the Duluth newspapers called it the "wreck of the ship that never was."

The ship's name and roster of its crew were not even listed with those of lost crews and ships on a plaque under a statue in the old town square. Paul knew the crew had been forgotten. He wanted to change that.

Physically, Paul had recovered from his accident in thirty days. The mental stress of his near-death experience was another matter. Learning about the *Lord Perry* had scared the hell out of him. He'd told his story to Dr. Bradley who referred him to a psychologist who had worked with Paul over several counseling sessions to help him get over his fear of the lake and the monster that Paul believed lurked deep within. For the rest of the winter, he'd avoided the lake. He'd even given the title and the GPS coordinates the Coast Guard had given him for his sunken four-wheeler to a salvage operator, who had successfully retrieved it through an eight-foot hole chopped through the late-winter ice. Paul didn't care about the machine. Material possessions offered little comfort as he tried to cope with his traumatic memories of his brush with death.

Paul was convinced. If the *Lord Perry* was real, that meant that everything else must have been. His psychiatrist told him all about the strange things that hallucinations do to a person. Paul had heard about tricks that one's mind and memory play, especially after a major stress the likes of which he'd been through. When he showed his psychiatrist the yellowed newspaper articles and information he'd gathered on the shipwreck, the man suggested that Paul might have felt compelled to fabricate a story to fit the news clippings. Paul found the most help in the comforting words of Sister Celeste, where he gained a sense of "being claimed." A true knowledge that he was loved, that his sins were forgiven, and that he would maintain this status into the next life gave Paul a level of comfort he could not find elsewhere.

Paul wasn't sure that his experience was Catholic, though Sister Celeste was willing to give his experience a name. "Purgatory" she called it. Paul was more than willing to accept it. He urgently needed to believe and found safe harbor, cradled in the loving arms of a Catholic Jesus Christ, even though he suspected that a Protestant, Jewish, Buddhist, or Islamic claim ticket may have worked.

Paul never found any solid scriptural foundations for the name of this evil spirit which had nearly claimed him. The closest he came was in chapters one and two of the book of Revelation. Celeste followed up with some research in an ancient text. It implied that during the time of the apostles, there was a satanic presence that falsely claimed to be Jewish. That evil presence was called the Schurke, not the spelling that Paul expected, but the story of the Schurke offered chilling similarities. In the story, the angel of the church of Smyrna defeated the Schurke in a great battle, then banished it to the depths of the oceans where it would circle distressed ships and scavenge the sea bottom, subsisting on the souls of drowned sailors until the time of the Second Coming. Paul believed he'd come as close as any human to knowing the truth about what had awaited him.

Over the months of winter, with its short days and its long dark nights, Paul had worked to change the rest of his life. He quit smoking, began exercising, and lost twenty-two pounds. He looked and felt better. He enjoyed time with his children and his wife. He took special pains to help his son, Douglas, begin his own search for his manhood. Paul credited his near-death experience as the moving force in changing his life. Whether it was real or if it only existed in his mind, Paul Sanderson committed himself *never* to return to the place of no hope.

Being claimed helped Paul restore his courage to go back to work on the lake. After working on ships all his life, Paul didn't know how to do anything else. He had to get over his fear of the Smoane. Being claimed as well as being committed to keeping his promise to the ghostly crew helped. Paul did the best he could.

Tonight, Paul had requested and received break time from his duties. The weather was clear, and the ship was running well. He'd take the midnight watch. He had tried, unsuccessfully, to sleep for a couple of hours; he had something on his mind... something he needed to do.

In the privacy of his cabin, Paul fished through his yet unpacked duffle bag, placing his personal belongings in his locker until he found what he was looking for. He pulled out a small package wrapped in plain brown paper. He stuffed it under his windbreaker and made his way out from the crew's quarters, up the steel stairway, to the main deck of the ship. He walked briskly along the starboard gunwale toward the stern of the ship. When he reached the stern rail, he stopped, rested his arms on the railing, and absorbed the view.

Paul could feel the continuous vibration of the huge diesel engines that powered the drive shafts and propellers some thirty feet below him. It had been a long time since he'd last enjoyed the smells of diesel smoke and the lake. Lake Superior was dead calm, except for the propwash boiling in the large wake of the ship that was longer than a football field. The wake was illuminated by the gleaming light from the setting sun as it neared the horizon. Several seagulls flew behind the ship, perhaps examining the behemoth that interrupted their evening feeding activities—perhaps waiting for someone to throw scraps of food to them.

Paul looked to the starboard, then to the port side of the stern deck for shipmates before he began his private memorial service. This was the best advice he'd gotten from all of the therapy sessions he'd had. Paul knew his therapist thought he was overreacting to take his experience so seriously. He was very polite and understanding as he listened to him, but Paul still saw the disbelief in his eyes when he talked about it.

Sister Celeste had seen the beings on the EEFM. Now a trusted member of Dr. Bradley's team, she'd told Paul she understood the urgent nature of Paul's mission. She had even made a modest contribution to the cause.

The last thing Paul needed was for his shipmates to think he was crazy. They would hear his story, but Paul would tell it to them as if it were a tale of the sea.

Paul felt compelled to offer a memorial to fulfill the final request of a long-dead sailor, whose brave act had helped Paul to have a second chance at life.

Satisfied that he was alone, he pulled the package out from under his jacket and unwrapped it. He raised the object over his head. Looking to the heavens, he shouted out loud, "I AM CLAIMED!" as bravely as any mortal dared. "Do you hear me, Smoane? I AM CLAIMED. You are powerless over me. I have been saved. And I REMEMBER!" He stretched out his arms as if he were gesturing to an audience of thousands. "I thank God and all His legions of angels and guardians for saving me from a terrible and frightening fate, a fate worse than death, the fate of a thousand deaths. I thank the doctors, nurses, and especially the people who risked their own lives to save me. Thank you, rescuers! Thank you, paramedics! Thank you, Crusias! Thank you, First Mate Thorson, for your bravery against hopelessness and fear! Thank you, Sister Celeste, for giving me your strength. I even thank you, old Smoane. Without you, I would not know how truly precious my life is."

Paul watched the wake turn as the ship gradually turned to the starboard. It was perfect timing. *Seawinds* was moving directly away from the setting sun. Sunlight reflected off the wake of the ship and glistened up toward the lone man standing at the stern rail. The light was so bright that Paul could see the red blood and flesh of his raised hands as if he were shining a flashlight into his outstretched palms.

"All you trapped souls, the crew and prisoners in the *Lord Perry,* hear me! You asked me to remember. I make you this vow. I shall do all in my power to help men and women remember you until you are freed from your bondage or until my life is over. As a sign of my pledge, I offer this." Paul held a small bronze plaque in his hand. "This plaque is a replica of the one I have commissioned to be placed in your memory."

Paul knew that Peggy had thought he'd lost his mind when he told her how much it would cost. They would have to give another mortgage on the house if he couldn't solicit enough contributions from his fellow sailors or the shipping companies. She had told Paul it was worth it if it would help him find closure to his brush with death. She'd also told him her scalp still tingled every time she recalled when she "knew" that Paul was back.

Paul kissed the plaque to seal it with his promise. He wound up and threw it as high and as far as he could, then watched it sparkle as it spun in the air. A seagull dipped from the sky, trying to catch it in the air, but missed.

It hit the boiling water in the ship's wake. Paul thought for a second that the splash from the bar sparkled a green phosphorous foam. It sent a chill up his spine. This memorial service was a brave act of defiance for a not-so-brave man. It was time to end the speech. After all, he was a sailor, not an orator. It was time for the company of other humans. Paul said a short prayer and made a sign of a cross over the scene, giving it his final blessing.

He turned and walked up the port side of the ship 'til he got to the galley hatch. He opened the half-door. The smell of coffee and the still-warm leftovers of a carved turkey sitting on the counter invited him even before the steward called out to him, "Hey, Paul! Good to see you! Are you hungry?"

"You betcha, Cookie," he answered the ship's steward as he pulled the door closed behind him. "Smells like I'm gonna gain weight on this trip."

"That'll be all right with me. I heard you had a rough go of things this winter."

"Do you want to hear a sea story, Cookie?" Paul asked.

"I'm always ready for a good story."

"Well, this one's a real corker...."

Winnifred and Crusias remained on the stern deck of the ship and watched as the sun settled beneath the horizon. "That was a nice memorial service, wouldn't you say, Crusias?"

"It's gratifying to see the progress this young man has made since we rescued him from the Smoane's lair. I'm not nearly as concerned about him as I once was."

"If he only knew what a ruckus he caused when we came to rescue him. The warrior was not pleased that he had to fight the old Smoane in her own territory. The fight against evil is such treacherous work."

"I'm very thankful she didn't catch me and suck my spirit dry before you arrived," Crusias added.

"Well, Crusias, we can all be thankful. You, me, our young charge, and all those poor unfortunate souls we found in the hold of that old ship after the Smoane was vanquished. I wish our Mr. Sanderson could know the rest of the story."

"He will know in his own time, Winnifred. For now, it is enough for him to appreciate his renewed life. The humans will learn much from his experience on the dark side. He's one of the first ones they saw on their new machine at Mercy Hospital. Perhaps they will better understand their own lives, how they are born and live, and how they come over."

"Oh, Crusias, I truly hope it works out for the best."

"I still wonder if it wouldn't be better for the Master to send down a lightning bolt and destroy that picture machine," he told her. "I fear now that they've seen us, there will be no faith, no mystery, no fear of death. If they do not fear death, how sacred will life be?"

"It's not for us to control, dear Crusias. We are but interfacers," Winnifred said. "The Master has decided that an incredulous and unbelieving world needs hope. For all the tumult it shall cause, the humans will find hope."

Eleven hundred feet below them, the bronze plaque hit cold steel. In the darkness, the deck of the old sunken ship glowed dimly with shades of faded green serpentine. It had not been painted for months. The Smoane, the ship's crew, and the captive souls were gone. Only twelve thousand tons of iron ore and the rusting hulk of the old ship remained.